RESTLESS SOULS

Dan Sheehan received his MFA from University College Dublin. His writing has appeared in the *Irish Times*, the *Los Angeles Review of Books*, *Guernica*, *TriQuarterly*, *Words Without Borders*, *BOMB*, and *Electric Literature*, among others. He currently works as an editor at Literary Hub and lives in New York with his wife. *Restless Souls* is his first novel.

@danpjsheehan

RESTLESS SOULS

DAN SHEEHAN

WEIDENFELD & NICOLSON

First published in Great Britain in 2018
by Weidenfeld & Nicolson
an imprint of the Orion Publishing Group Ltd
Carmelite House, 50 Victoria Embankment
London EC4Y 0DZ

An Hachette UK Company

1 3 5 7 9 10 8 6 4 2

A CIP catalogue record for this book is
available from the British Library.

ISBN (Hardback) 978 1 4746 0585 4
ISBN (Export Trade Paperback) 978 1 4746 0586 1
ISBN (eBook) 978 1 4746 0588 5

Typeset at The Spartan Press Ltd,
Lymington, Hants

Printed in Great Britain by Clays Ltd,
St Ives plc

www.orionbooks.co.uk

for Téa

Is there a time for keeping a distance
A time to turn your eyes away
Is there a time for keeping your head down
For getting on with your day

Miss Sarajevo

Give me the waters of Lethe that numb the heart,
if they exist, I will still not have the power to forget you.

Ovid, *The Poems of Exile*

DUBLIN

Chapter 1

I haven't seen Tom in three and a half years. He came home for a month or so in December of '92 – the day after Christmas – because his father was on the way out, bisected by a bad stroke and pining for the whole family to be around him at the send off. That winter Tom was shaken, a little darker no question, but still more or less the same lad he had been when he was eighteen, and sixteen, and twelve: sombre, intense, obsessed with the notion of bearing witness to the kind of shit we couldn't bring ourselves to watch on TV. The sort of fella who'd list off body counts from Central American combat zones like they were football scores, whose bucket list of travel destinations looked like the index page from a particularly bleak foreign policy dossier. That's why he disappeared out there in the first place, barely a week after they declared a state of emergency. Just after the city went into total lockdown. Even after *The Times* told him point blank that they couldn't afford to pay another foreign correspondent, especially a trainee who had yet to clock a single hour on the ground in

3

an actual foreign country. Even after his GP told him Sarajevo was the last place on earth a person with cardiomyopathy should be holed up. Even after he promised us all he'd turn back at the border, once the photos were taken and the locals quizzed. It took him six days, two planes, a boat, and three trains to get into the city, while the rest of us sat at home trying to find the place on a sun-bleached primary school atlas. God only knows how he managed to sneak himself back in the second time.

'They're getting cut down in the streets over there, Karl, blown apart in their homes,' he slurred to me over a flat pint of Guinness at a lock-in in Doyle's the night before New Year's Eve, 'and it's only going to get worse, if that's even possible.'

One of the barmen I didn't recognise was singing 'Carrick-fergus' with his head bowed and his eyes closed tight like a man battling the daybreak.

'Then why go back?' I asked him, because I didn't understand. I still don't really understand.

*

At the arrivals gate in Dublin airport we stand around with our sweating hands buried in our pockets. In the line next to me I can hear Baz crack his knuckles through the cloth, his thumb pressing them downward one by one like he did before any exam we ever took together. During the forty-minute car ride over, he chain-smoked five Marlboro Reds, a brand I have not seen him buy since that week Sarah Dalton thought she was pregnant. His predictions for this trip we're about to take have already been somewhat less than optimistic.

'This is gonna be a disaster.'

'So you've said.'

'Listen, why do we have to go to America to do it? I fucking hate America.'

'You can't hate America, Baz. You've never been to America.'

'Well, I hate Americans.'

'You only hate Americans because that Brandy girl called you a hick.'

'I'm from Dublin! How can I be a hick if I'm from fucking Dublin?'

'Well, if anyone can find a way.'

'What's the point of flying halfway across the world if I'm just gonna strike out with all the birds there?'

'You strike out with all the birds here.'

'But at least that only costs me the price of a taxi home.'

'This may come as a shock to you, Barry, but pulling birds is not the primary objective of this trip.'

Makeshift cereal-box placards bounce up and down around us. In a rainbow of Crayola colours they read 'Welcome Home, Charlie', 'Corporal Brian Clarke', 'DADDY!!!' Every few seconds someone else catches a teary pair of eyes and the same broad smile spreads across another weary face. A stocky soldier in crumpled fatigues takes a knee and catches his daughter in his arms. She's dropped a naked Barbie doll on the floor by the conveyor belt where the last beat-up duffel bag – Tom's, I suppose – is resigning itself to another slow rotation. I want to take a picture of her, vice-gripped to her parents' legs as they embrace, but Baz scoops up the doll and holds it out to her before I can get the lens cap off my camera. For a second it seems like the girl doesn't understand what this tan piece of plastic, its bleached blonde hair pig-tailed with human-sized scrunchies, is. Baz holds Barbie by the tips of her feet – for the sake of decency, I imagine – and seems unsure of what else he can do to clarify. He coughs, and turns the doll rightways up, as if positioning is where the confusion lies. Then the girl's huge brown eyes light up wide and she grabs the doll with both hands.

'What do you say, darlin'?' Her father's voice is hoarse and soft.

'Thankyouthankyouthankyouthankyou.'

And then they're gone. Out through the stuttering automatic doors and into the street. What comes next? They'll drive back slowly to a small starter home that's cleaner tonight than it's ever been. The little girl will want to tell her daddy everything that's happened to her over the past week, because that's all she'll remember, and her father will listen and do everything he can to keep his eyelids from drooping shut. When she finally falls asleep this man in the crumpled fatigues and his wife will want to strip down and press so close into one another that they can't breathe, but they won't. Not tonight. Tonight they'll collapse on top of the covers with only their shoes removed, with the lights still on, and sleep forehead to forehead. They'll both sleep longer than they have in months, until the vibrations of tiny feet jumping up and down on the bed rise them. And then they'll all start living again.

Still no sign of Tom. Five minutes have passed since the last passenger emerged from the tunnel. I'm taking deep, slow breaths through my nose, trying to calm myself. I can picture him foetal on the floor of the airplane bathroom, his long limbs curled around the cistern, refusing to leave.

'Why do they always take the clothes off, do you think?' Baz asks, his head jerking toward the automatic doors.

'What?'

'Off of the Barbies. Why do the girls always take the clothes off? We never stripped down the Action Men and dragged them round by the hair, did we?'

'Action Men don't have hair.'

'You know what I mean. What's the point in spending the extra money on Coke-Addled Divorcee Barbie, or whatever the fuck, if you're just gonna throw away all the special gear anyway?'

'Christ, I don't know, Baz. She's a kid. Why do kids do anything?'

'I'm just saying it's a waste of money. They should sell the things naked and save themselves the hassle.'

'Maybe suggest that to the managers at Toys 'R' Us, so. Go up to the desk and say you'd feel more comfortable if they stripped the dresses off all the Barbies.'

'As a cash-saving measure.'

'Right.'

'You holding up all right?'

'Yep.'

'It's fine. He'll be out when he's out.'

Tom rounds the corner as a charcoal-grey ghost. He's gaunt in a way I never thought possible for a man his size. Heavy bags sag down to the tops of his high cheekbones, like dog tongues of hollowed-out bogland. Three years under siege and six months in a padded room will do that to you I suppose. Baz and I tense up, like cadets awaiting inspection. His lank mane of dark hair, now slashed from the roots with silver, drags like a shadow across his left eye socket, emptied for over a year now. A patch made of thin black felt covers what I imagine to be the tunnel to a very private room, the part of his brain that stores the worst bits of it: the shelling; the snipers; the toes and fingertips and tufts of hair poking out from mounds of fresh rubble like spring saplings, and who the fuck knows what else. Tom stares at us for a full five seconds before he realises who we are. I left a message with the clinic's receptionist to say we'd be there to drive him to his mam's, but maybe he never got it. Or maybe we've changed more than I think. Inching his way through the not-quite-a crowd, grimacing, as if there's a steady wind blowing against him.

'Oh, sweet Christ, will you look at the state of him!'

'Quiet, Baz, for fuck's sake,' I hiss.

'He's gonna kill himself. This is actually going to happen on our watch. Again.'

'Stop. I'm serious. No more of that talk.' He must really be panicking to even brush up against this subject.

'Sorry, I didn't mean to . . . but I'm telling you, this is a mistake.'

'This is not a mistake.'

'Karl. Look at the lad. We won't be a night into this trip before he opens up his wrists in a hotel bathtub somewhere.' He taps his head twice with his knuckles and blesses himself.

'Have you developed Tourette's in the last few minutes?'

'He looks like a Bond villain. You're not concerned?'

'Of course I'm fucking concerned,' I hiss through a grin, because he's almost within earshot now, 'but you need to calm down.'

8

'I *need* to not have his mam cursing me out in the middle of his funeral, is what I need. You know what that aul wagon will say: "He was *fine* when he was in Bosnia. It wasn't till he got home to that *gurrier* Barry Connolly that he got down on himself".'

'*Shush.*'

Tom moves in measured steps. It's taken him an age to walk the few paces across the green linoleum floor to where we're standing, a distance every other passenger has covered in something approaching a run. We don't hug because that's not really how we are, and because even in his current state he must know how estranged we've become. Still, I put my hand on his shoulder as we shake and try to stare through whatever fog he lives under now. His hand is limp and calloused and dwarfs mine. Baz basically mugs him for his bags and tells him that it's been way too long, way too long, way too long. We are now the last three people standing under the florescent lights of the baggage claim. Their surgical glow exposes about a dozen tiny white slashes that cluster around Tom's right cheek and run to the curve of his jawline. He smiles weakly at us, and it's genuine, I think, but he still hasn't said anything. Why hasn't he said anything? Another horrendous silence descends. Baz's eyes are screaming at me. This, just this simple social awkwardness, is his nightmare. I've seen him all but pass out in similar circumstances. Tom brushes a strand of hair away from his face.

'How are you, lads?' Whispered, but it's him all the same.

'All right, man, yeah. You?'

'I'm OK.' If ever a man did not look OK.

'Are you hungry? Will we grab a bite to eat here before we head on?'

'No, I'm fine. Just a bit tired. I haven't been sleeping so well.'

'I'm not surprised, sure you're coming from a fucking war zone, aren't you!'

Baz actually grabs his mouth after he says this. I think I see a tiny smile departing Tom's face as I swivel back around but I can't be sure. I look at Baz to see if he caught more of it but he's busy examining his feet so I just let it hang for a few seconds before gesturing toward the exit.

'We'd better get going, all right, don't want to have your mam waiting up all night for us.'

'No rush. I don't think she sleeps that much either.'

Tom stops walking then, drops slowly onto his haunches, and unties the fat rope knot at the top of his bag. For a second I think he's going to produce a gift, until I realise just how ridiculous that would be. *A plastic bag full of bloodied rubble and an extra-dull butter knife from the nut house canteen? Tom, you really shouldn't have!* No, he's checking on something, turning it over in his hands to make sure it didn't break in transit. A battered metal box, tinted with rust, about the size of a small toaster. When he's satisfied that all is well, he pushes it deep into the centre of the bag, ties up the opening, and rises without explanation.

Chapter 2

Tom and his mam have never been particularly close. Ostensibly they both want the same thing: for the world to become a better place than the chaotic shitshow we all know it is. They both view the world as broken into jigsaw pieces, not shards, and they both think that one person, well intentioned and pure of heart, can help to put it back together again. Make sense of it all. Or at least they did, once upon a time. What they fell out over some twelve years ago, and during every significant discussion since, was how best to do this. His mother favours prayer. Tom prefers action. His mother hears choirs of angels. Tom hears helicopter blades and the cracking open of aid crates. His mother sees a vast, crowded furnace of eternal damnation. Tom sees nothing. That's just the way it's always been.

She got worse after his dad died, lost her tether. By the end of the first week, while we were all still too maudlin drunk to know which way was up, she'd turned the house into a pristine bunker of manic, muttered rosaries and psychological self-flagellation. Myself and Baz used to haunt the place back when we were all teenagers and his dad kept things on a relatively even keel. He worked in the Guinness storehouse down by the quays but never really drank much of the stuff because it wreaked havoc on his digestion and there was never much of a flush on their toilet.

I remember humid summer evenings playing three-and-in on the makeshift goalposts we'd built in the front garden in Ringsend. One side half a foot taller than the other because Tom had just come off the back of a massive growth spurt. The smell of hops would round the corner before his dad did and we'd all pause and sniff it in, as if we were our aul lads, sitting around the kitchen table at Christmastime, popping the caps off dusty bottles and pouring the thick black liquid into pint glasses like it was nothing at all. I'd approach them one by one with shitty pound-shop crackers that barely made a snap when you pulled them, just to get that waft of stout and plain soap and John Player cigarette smoke. It was, to me, the greatest mixture of scents anyone could concoct and it made me drowsy, and forgetful, and happy. There are pubs in the city I still visit just for that smell. The nostalgic alchemy of it.

We drive out past paunchy taxi men slow smoking on the bonnets of their cars. Tom in the front, knees touching the glove compartment. Baz in the back, tapping epileptically on the loose window pane. He's had a jittery vibe to him for the past few weeks and I can't tell if there's something other than Tom's return on his mind. I flick off the radio just before the hour turns so that we miss the news. Tom probably isn't even listening, but if Baz hears the word 'Bosnia' he'll throw a shit fit that might put me off the road. The sky opens as we drive through the city, sloppy drops of rain bouncing off the deserted footpaths. The dirty Liffey water swells and churns like it's trying to digest the thousand mangled shopping trolleys that carpet the riverbed. Two sullen junkies huddle together on the boardwalk, cursing through their shivers and tweaks. We had a friend called Alan Cullen when we were kids. He was a wild, reckless little headcase who would do absolutely anything that popped into his mind, provided of course that no one else had the balls for it. Otherwise what would be the point?

He lived in a mouldy flat in the inner city with a mother who never spoke and three older brothers he never saw. His father was in prison for driving the getaway car in a botched bank robbery back in the late seventies when bank robberies were all the rage. A nice lad on his good days, but lost – hopelessly, cartoonishly lost. I once saw him beat two grown men into hysterics over a stray elbow in a McDonalds queue. When it was over, the two of them bloodied and groaning on the sticky brown floor, he looked at his pulped knuckles like he'd forgotten to put the safety on, and burst into tears. Then, when we were about sixteen, some toothless freak who lived in the flat next door got him mixed up in heroin and that was pretty much it for Alan. I watched him ghost away from us for a while, float around the edges of house parties or the dimmest corners of the pool hall. I say 'watched' because that's all it was. I never remember trying to intervene. Probably should have at least once I suppose, just so I could tell myself I'd done something. He turned up on my doorstep six months later, looking like the fucking Phantom of the Opera under a mask of purple bruises, and asked me for ten pounds. I gave him a fiver and a cup of tea but he was gone before it got cold. That was the last any of us saw of him. Now, whenever I pass the flocks of feral skeletons that congregate on Middle Abbey Street or down by the quays, I look for him. When Baz has had a few, he talks about Alan like he never really existed at all. Like he was some imaginary sidekick we willed into being and then outgrew.

I drive an arseways route to the house because I want to look out at Sandymount strand as the last of the light leaves the sky. I do this most days. The tide is lolling back and forth, edging closer and closer to the piles of polished black rocks that coat the base of the harbour wall. In the distance the lights on the power station chimneys flicker into life. Their red glow the centrepiece of what passes for a skyline in this city. I've slowed the car right down to a crawl. Baz knows I do this. Ash drops from his cigarette while he's staring out into the ocean. He almost drowned out there once. The night we got our Leaving Cert results and celebrated by drinking warm cans of cheap cider and two thick green bottles of sparkling wine, the labels long since peeled away – left to die at the back of someone's parents' liquor cabinet. Sitting around the world's smallest bonfire, roaring laughing over school stories we all knew by heart and earnestly predicting futures that would never materialise. The night Clara Hennessy and me had sex for the first time on a blanket at the far end of the beach, fumbling and giggling and grasping at each other until we fell asleep pressed tight together, rolled up in that brown, sand-wrecked blanket like a giant, boozy cigar. The night Tom told me he'd made up his mind. He was going to train to become a war correspondent.

'Where?' I asked.

'Wherever they'll have me. Wherever there's a war.'

'I don't know if you've heard, but there's been one dragging on for the last twenty years a hundred miles north of here. You could always head up to Belfast for a stretch if you're that keen?'

'It's not the same.'

'Jesus. Are you really serious about this?'

'It's what I'm meant to be doing.'

'I'm not sure it's what anyone's meant to be doing, Tom.' He just nodded and looked out into the water.

'When can I expect to see you strapped into a flak jacket on the nine o'clock news, then?' I asked.

'I mean, it'll take a while. The training. The apprenticeship. You have to pay your dues. They don't just sign you up and ship you out.'

'No offence, man, but I sort of hope it takes forever. Or at least until you lose interest in the notion or they declare world peace, whichever comes first.'

'You and my mam both. I'm not going to lose interest in this though, Karl.'

'I know you're not, you big serious bastard. Why can't you be happy just being a useless sack of shite like the rest of us? It's not a bad life.'

If Tom hadn't wandered off on his own that night no one would have heard Baz's last hopeless yelp as the waves we never took all that seriously pulled his lumbering frame – still dressed in an army jacket, blue jeans, and Caterpillar boots – below the surface of the water.

None of them could remember how long they sat in silence on the edge of the seafront wall after Tom and Gabriel dragged him back up on to the sand. Enough time for me to drop Clara home and stroll back down the beach thinking about how fucking fantastic life was, even if I did fail my maths paper quite spectacularly. There was a piece of slick black seaweed hanging from Baz's ear. Beads of saltwater were still dripping from his curly hair and onto the toes of his sodden boots. The night had turned cold and a razor wind had kicked up around us. I remember the moon was a fat, full orb.

'You all right there, Baz?'

'. . . Yeah.'

I looked over at Gabriel and he nodded and smiled and softly clapped the back of Baz's neck. I took out my last four cigarettes and we smoked them quietly and listened to the splash of the breaking waves until Baz started to shiver and curse with a familiar mixture of discomfort and disbelief. By the time we reached Tom's front door we were laughing. All four of us.

Chapter 3

I haven't been inside Tom's old gaf since the week of his father's funeral. Technically this isn't my fault, though I still feel pretty shitty about it. We said we'd drop in on his mam from time to time just to make sure everything was all right while he was away. Make sure she hadn't relocated to the basement to build an ark or perform an exorcism or anything. According to Baz, these were very real possibilities. Of course, Baz's antics were part of the reason we couldn't get past the doorway in the first place. With Tom gone his mam stopped grudgingly letting Baz over the threshold and took on a new, unabashedly sour gatekeeper role. She would stand, arms knotted, in the shelter of the conservatory while we attempted small talk from the lowly dock of the stoop. I still get bone chills thinking about those grimy winter evenings bellowing awkward questions through the rain at her while Baz pulled his hood up over his head and roared 'For fuck's sake' behind my back. In fairness to her, she didn't budge. Not once. Not Christmas Eve. Not that month Baz had his leg in a cast – almost immediately defaced by scrawled initials and penis graffiti – from trying to drop and roll out of a bedroom window. Not any of the times we had to shake loose their neighbour's psychotic bulldog pup, Muncher, from the already frayed ends of our jeans. Never. Baz is convinced it's because she can't stand the notion of him wandering around her house, touching her icons, breaking her toilet, and he has a point, but truth be told I think it's more than that. I think she's as keen to keep me out as she is him. I've exchanged awkward phone calls with her over the past few months, a couple of letters about Tom's lack of progress at the clinic in England, but that's as far as it goes. I don't blame her. What Gabriel did, her generation still sees it as a mortal sin. It's sad really, because she always had a soft spot for Gabriel – how could you not – but she can't talk about him any more. Her house is a refuge now, a reminder of better days, days she hasn't seen in a while. The second we park ourselves down at her table to talk about her son, or Gabriel, we drag the real world in like shit on the heel of a shoe.

Tom already had the ticket booked and the bag packed when his mam asked me to have a heart-to-heart with him, to see if I couldn't talk him out of it at the eleventh hour. I did, best I could. It didn't work. Not that I thought it would. He left, and lost an eye, and a girl we never met, and a good chunk of his sanity from what we could tell through those increasingly fucked-up phone calls he made in the dying days of the siege. So the woman had a son and a husband taken from her in the same rough stretch. Like Alan and his smack, like Gabriel, I don't know how much of this is my fault.

*

'I wonder if that little shithound Muncher is dead yet?'

'I doubt it,' I say, 'unless someone took it upon themselves to poison him.'

'Would that work?'

'Would what work?'

We're standing in the middle of the driveway looking up at the single lighted window in Tom's mam's house. His house. Behind the net curtains I can see her silhouette moving back and forth.

'Poisoning the dog, would we have gotten away with it?'

'We? When were *we* planning on poisoning Muncher, Baz?'

'Well, Christ, if I'd known it was an option I would have suggested it years ago. I always thought there'd be an autopsy or something, and that we'd get stung that way. On the forensic end. That's why I never brought it up.'

'Wait, so you've been sitting on this scheme to poison a dog to death for how long exactly?'

'About five years, on and off.'

'On and off?'

'Well yeah I mean I haven't been sitting there daydreaming about it in the pub or on Christmas Day or while I'm throwing the lips on a girl, but y'know, pretty much any time I see a dog.'

'Any dog?'

'Yep. Well, except sheep dogs or guide dogs. I've got no issue with them. Functional dogs get a pass.'

'What about guard dogs?'

'Hmmm, a bit of a grey area there, but based solely on my own experiences, I'll have to say no. They can get fucked too.'

'Right, just so I have this straight in my head. You've been thinking about killing Muncher – and toying with the notion of committing genocide against the canine species in general – for about five years, and what's held you back has been the fear of what they'll discover on the dog autopsy table.'

'More or less.'

'You know Ireland has only one State Pathologist, right?'

'For dogs?'

'For humans.'

'Really?' He gives this a long stretch of thought. Then he says, 'So who swabs and slices open and runs DNA tests on the dead dogs?'

'Psychopaths, Baz. Psychopaths slice open dead dogs.'

'Should we maybe think about knocking on the door, lads?'

Tom is smiling now. Just a tiny upturn at the corners, but it's definitely a smile. I count back how many words he just uttered in succession. Ten. A near record high for the evening. Even in the near darkness, from the other end of the driveway, I can make out the flaking forest green paint on the front door. I feel ashamed at how damn useless the two of us have been in his absence, gatekeeper or no gatekeeper. There's things we could have done with the outside at least, maybe fixed up the shed or cleaned out the gutters or whatever messing people do with their back gardens to keep them from looking like the kinds of places you'd dump your broken washing machine. Tom doesn't make a move so I rap my knuckles hard against the door in the hope that she'll hear it from her room but at some point during our dog-poisoning discussion she must have snuck downstairs because my hand isn't back in my pocket before the door swings open and there she is, that hard little woman in a floral blouse staring out at us standing there like beggars, like children.

'Well,' she says, 'ye had better come in out of the cold.'

*

'Relax, Baz, it's only incense. It's supposed to be smoking like that.'

'How do you know?'

'I just know.'

'Fuck off. How?'

'I bought some once.'

'You did not.'

'I did. Clara used to be into it for a while. Artsy type, you know yourself.'

'Yeah, but she's a girl. You're a lad.'

'So?'

'So, is it not a bit, I dunno, *gay* or something to be sitting there in your room burning lavender smoke all over the place.'

The smell of sandalwood snakes down the hall alongside us as we follow Tom's mam into the kitchen. If Tom feels any more at home here than we do tonight, he doesn't show it. The pads of his fingers touch the bubbled cream wallpaper absentmindedly. We take our cues from him and do the same as we pass. The red bulb underneath the picture of the Sacred Heart seems just as bright as it did when we were teenagers. Aside from the incense there's nothing new out here to indicate that this is now a place of fevered mourning, or a cocoon of ritual-heavy Catholicism, or anything else other than what it is: a modest family home gone slightly to seed.

'I burnt it once or twice with Clara. How is that gay?'

'Well, let me put it to you this way. What do you think our aul lads, or our granddads, would say if they saw us at that?'

'We had sex afterwards, if that's any good to you.'

'Still gay.'

'*How* is that gay?'

Tom's mam gives me a stare that'd freeze your heart.

Clara was always a country mile beyond me, sophistication-wise. She was into art galleries and scented candles and not holding her knife and fork like the steering wheel of a race car at mealtimes. She just had class – *has* class – in a way that was entirely alien to the rest of us. Not that she ever gave a damn about the differences. Clara is maybe the least judgemental person I have ever encountered when it comes to that kind of thing, which is doubly impressive given her parents. I could never figure out if it was my background or the lads I hung around with or just my general way of navigating the world – most likely a combination of all three – but whatever it was, Mammy and Daddy Hennessy did not approve. Her father, *Vincent*, is some West Brit dickhead solicitor who, when he deigned to speak to me at all, would lower his paper, look over his half-glasses and ask me shit like, 'So, Karl, given any thought to college yet, hmmm?' Her mother is slightly more diplomatic, but an elitist bitch to her marrow. If her husband treated me like an irritating, over-sexed latchkey kid, helping myself to his food and sniffing around his little girl, Clara's mam saw me as more of stray dog. A pitiable nuisance that was liable to piss all over the carpet if not properly trained and monitored. She had this toxic fucking air freshener spray which, as far as I could tell, was used exclusively on the inside of my boots as they stood on their own special square of mat just inside the door. Clara's little sister, Saoirse, liked me well enough, I think, but by the time I became a fixture in the house she was deep into a monk-like rebellion of silence against the parents and impressive as that was to witness, it wasn't much of a help to me.

I don't think I've ever heard cutlery scraping plates as loudly as it did on those occasions when Clara forced us to have dinner together. It was so excruciating, it was almost funny. Almost. I'd be sitting there, sweating, putting every ounce of my energy into being as quiet and unobtrusive in my movements as possible. Meanwhile she'd be running her big toe up the inside of my leg or needling her parents with fun facts about me they couldn't give a shite about. I was so damn smitten back then though, I would have suffered through a thousand of those meals if she'd asked me to. Mercifully, she did not. 'This is pointless, they're never going to change,' she said one night as we stood on her porch passing a cigarette back and forth in the wake of a particularly muted pasta dinner. 'They're just not worth the effort, are they?' She was right of course, they were a pair of dyed-in-the-wool cunts, but I made my face a mask of solemnity anyway because I assumed that's what the moment called for. Turns out that was the wrong move. Clara doesn't fail at things, and she certainly doesn't quit anything she has decided to invest substantial time and energy in. To be honest, it's probably why we stayed together as long as we did. My expression that night introduced her to a concept she had very little first-hand experience of: defeat. Not knowing how to deal with it, she laughed the whole thing off like their approval had never been that important in the first place; but I knew it had wounded her, that final, long-overdue realisation.

Tom's mam has chocolate digestive biscuits and a pot of tea waiting on the kitchen table. Sure enough, it's still coated by that slick plastic cover – bluebells on canary yellow – that you'd have to peel your elbows from on warm days. It soaks up nothing, this tablecloth. Spill half a cup of tea and you're down on your hands and knees wiping it off the floor with the chewed up corner of your sleeve.

'Did you get in all right, Thomas?'

'I did, Mam, it was fine.'

She stares at the patch that makes her only child look like a slightly spectral pirate, but says nothing. Her tough little hands rub together at her chest. She turns her back to us, pottering over something non-existent in the sink, so I can't tell if she's started to cry or not.

'I . . . you're home now.'

'I am, Mam.'

'It's so . . . you weren't waiting long?'

'No. The lads picked me up soon as I got through the gate.'

'Well, that's good.' I can't get a proper read on her yet. 'Thank you, boys, for that.'

'No trouble, Missus Dempsey. We were only dying to see him.'

Baz pours us all tea and shoves an entire biscuit in his mouth at once so that he won't be obliged to say anything. It's too dry too swallow and I watch as he tries to force it down with a heavy slug of tea. I don't know if it's the heat of the thing or his own nerves having to sit here and make small talk like a civilised human being but either way his face is reddening and I know he's trying to clear his mouth before a coughing fit erupts. As a group, we stare at him and silently pray for his success.

Tom's mam is still shooting Baz daggers as he cleans the last of the regurgitated mess from the side of the kitchen cabinet.

'I'm sorry again about that, Missus Dempsey.'

'It's fine, Barry, just sit down and stop fidgeting, will you? You'll only end up breaking something, hopping around the place like a bloody child.'

I feel for her, having to put up with the sheer awkwardness of the pair of us when all she wants to do is sit down next to her son and hold his battered head in her hands like she did when he was a kid. Back when he'd get himself all worked up over another day of bloodshed in the north, or a flash of some unpronounceable war zone he'd seen on the news – horrified and fascinated in equal measure by places as alien to us, as removed from our reality, as *Star Wars*' deserts of Tatooine or Scaramanga's exploding Island from *The Man with the Golden Gun*. And it was always the news that sent him racing soundlessly into her arms, never anything normal like *The Omen* or a clap of thunder or the shadows that run across the kitchen floor on windy nights. She would hold him tight then, I still remember his father telling me once toward the end, till you'd need a crowbar to force them apart. She couldn't do it now though, not if they had an eternity alone together, and the cruelty of that loss leaves me silent.

The clock over the fridge has lost time but still ticks loudly, a metronomic knock against the wall of our mute stillness. It's an hour fast and I wonder if this has been done intentionally. If it's possible that she, all sixty-three years of her, has climbed up on top of one of these rickety kitchen chairs and turned the hands forward herself, so that even separated by a valley of pockmarked buildings, and a military blockade, and a continent, and the widening chasm of obsession that has made these two people so painfully unknowable to each other, even with all that choking smog, they might still share something. Or maybe it's just a dying clock, half fucked from years of neglect like most of the other furnishings in the house. I don't wear a watch so it's hard to tell for sure. I do not consider asking. When the hour turns, Tom's mam tells us where we'll be sleeping. Somewhere along the line it's been decided that Baz and I will be staying here, for tonight at least. It's Wednesday. Our plane leaves at seven on Saturday morning. Dublin to LAX. As we walk, single file, down the hall and up the stairs, I keep craning my neck to see if Tom and his mother have touched. If he has given her shoulder a squeeze as if to say *I'm still in here somewhere, Mam, I swear.* If she has brought her hand, the skin of which looks more like crinkled rolling paper than ever, to his lightly scarred cheek or brushed a strand of hair across his forehead. I am consumed with the thought of these things happening, of the necessity of their happening. But of course, they don't. We all close our doors softly, with single, sedated clicks, and feign sleep.

Sarajevo, 30 April, 1992

I got in. Two hours ago now. Un-fucking-believable. My heart is still beating like the clappers. A fat chunk of yellow plaster exploded above our heads as we were scuttling low toward the emergency entrance at the back of the hotel. The Holiday Inn – what a name. Nobody said a word from the moment we left the UNPROFOR terminal at the airport. Everyone trying to breathe steady. Every so often, scrawled across walls and buildings and cardboard signs on the stretch of road that runs through the modern part of the city, I saw the words *Pazi – Snajper!* A warning that required no explanation. They dropped us off at the pavement's edge and told us to run. Mac cursing in my ear the whole time. Hailstones of brick as big as your fist. Tracer fire lighting up the sky. I looked through the dark at the building's bullet-riddled brown and yellow skin and wondered how many shell blows it could take before collapsing.

The waiters inside all wore ironed jackets, white shirts, bow ties. I don't know what I was expecting. Fatigues? Kevlar? It's hard to believe I'm actually here. This must be how fidgety little kids feel when they're finally let off the leash at Disneyland. Over-stimulated. They told us where we should and should *not* stand, which buildings in the area housed sniper nests, where food would be served, how the radio system worked. As the concierge spoke, bullets ate through the air outside. I could hear them tearing through the dented metal husks of cars. These boxy little Yugos abandoned on the road. Fighting is heavy in the Grbavica quarter, he told us, stay away if you value your life. People laughed. I didn't. There's a babble of accents around every corner in here. Gung-ho war correspondents from around the world getting harder with every thunderclap of heavy artillery from the hills around the city. I suppose I'm one of them now. Or a groupie at the very least. A few were sat at the main bar drinking whiskey and smoking in frantic pulls. On each floor plastic curtains separate news teams replaying and editing today's footage on huge blinking monitors, stacked high and dripping with fat wires. People bark into satellite phones over the din. It's two in the morning and I can still hear them in the hallways and through the walls. Twice tonight the hotel has been rocked by mortar fire. There are mattresses pushed up against the windows in every room. Long, dank corridors lit by a single bulb. It'd be nonsense to say that I don't feel afraid. Not quite shit-myself afraid, though not a million miles away from it either. But there's a buzz to it all too. Something hyper-real about every small action. I keep thinking 'what if it were Dublin?' What hotel would my Bosnian equivalent be holed up in? What neighbourhood would fall first? What buildings would they target? How would it feel to watch it all crumble and burn?

Mac says it's useful to get everything out of your head at the end of each day though, journalist or not. 'Diary entries, letters, Post-It-note haikus – whatever floats your boat.' He says that otherwise all the twisted shit you see gets tangled up in itself until you can't pick it apart. He tells me there'd be a hell of a lot fewer people with shell shock, rocking back and forth in loony bins or drinking themselves to death in dive bars at the ends of the earth, if they'd written it all down. I don't know if this is true or if he's just trying to spook me. He seems sure. I suppose I believe him; or, at the very least, I believe that he believes it. His own diary is a yellow legal pad, covered in chicken scratch handwriting, peeling beer labels, spikey drawings of charred buildings and scowling soldiers, phone numbers, and grubby smudges that could be mud or food or blood. It is, he tells me, the sixth volume in what will eventually be a wartime memoir.

'Which war?' I asked.

'All of them,' he said. 'Any I can get near. There's always a war.'

I met Mac at a bar in Split. I'd been in the city for twenty-four hours and spoken only four words. When I got off the train one of a dozen older women in headscarves caught my eye and motioned for me to follow her up the hill to where her house was. It was getting dark and I was knackered, so I followed. It seemed like the done thing. We walked slowly up a springy, blue-carpeted staircase, through a pitch-black landing, and into a room that could have been my own. Sparse, save for an acoustic guitar, a dresser with a row of books and a couple of glass aftershave bottles, and two small, A4-sized posters on either side of the window. One of U2's *Rattle and Hum* cover, the other of a Yugoslavian football player I didn't recognise.

'Your son?'

'Fighting,' she said, and I nodded.

I guess I was hoping she'd sit herself down on the edge of the bed and tell me a bit more about him then. What I wanted more than anything was detail. Where he was posted. Whether he'd been injured yet. Why he joined up in the first place. How she felt about him being in the line of fire like that. But that was all she had for me. It made me think a little of Mam. How on her bad days there were all these fears whirring around behind her eyes and you'd wait and wait in the silence for some trace of emotion to leak out and you'd see the effort it was taking to keep it all inside. And then nothing.

'Thank you,' I said, handing her over a wad of Deutsche Marks. She smiled at me and put the money in her apron without counting it. 'Sleep,' she murmured, and closed the door before I could reply. I went through his drawers for badges, pamphlets, photos – anything that might tell me a bit more about who he was. But there was nothing. I shook off my boots and coat and lay on my back on her son's bed, trying to figure out my next move. I slept for ten hours straight on that lumpy mattress, until the sound of neighbours laughing and beating rugs with brooms outside the window woke me. I took a bus into town and spent the afternoon walking from bar to bar, trying to eavesdrop on the conversations of reporters clumped in corner snugs, and retreating to the bathroom whenever I accidently caught someone's eye. I just wanted to hear a little more, first hand, before I left.

At eight o'clock I sat down at the bar of a café near the water. Mac was on the only other occupied stool, four down from mine, guiding the bartender's finger along a shiny burn mark that runs the length of his forearm. She was tall and slender, with piercings in her nose and eyebrow and this thin streak of green running through her black hair. They both turned to me as the stool squeaked under my weight. Mac is probably still in his thirties but the greyed beard makes him look a decade older. The corners of his eyes crinkle when he grins. I opened my mouth and closed it again, twice, like a particularly stupid fish. 'Eh . . . beer?' I stammered. 'Beer,' she confirmed and knelt low to open the fridge underneath the counter. By the time she reached me, sweating bottle of Osjecko (not bad stuff) in hand, Mac and I were already nose to nose, his stare fixed unblinking like he was trying to place me from somewhere. Five or ten seconds passed this way till I was good and uncomfortable.

'Irish?'

'What gave me away?'

'Boom! Fuckin' A right you are. Masha, Masha, you hear that, honey? One word, "beer", that's all I needed. Didn't I just tell you I could read people? And you called it a line!'

'Yes, yes, very impressive.' She rolled her eyes and gave me a look that said he's all yours now.

'Fuck, I should have bet her a drink. Or maybe just bought her a drink . . . something like that. Meh. I'm Joe McCarthy, like the politician only redder. Friends call me Mac.'

'Tom.'

'The fuck you doing in Split, Tom? Don't you know there's a war on? You micks get the news back home?'

'We do, but only by telegraph and the machine at city hall is broken. Is the Cold War still going strong?'

'I like you, Tom.'

'Thanks, Joe.'

'Mac.'

'Mac. I'm trying to talk to someone about Sarajevo. Someone who's been inside.'

'That makes two of us. Five, actually, if you count the two Brits and my ornery fuck of a cameraman over there.' He nodded toward a back room where through the crack in the door I could just make out a group of men playing pool through the slow-rising smoke. 'Bit early for that though, chief. They're not running day trips in and out of the valley. Unless you came to interrogate spaced-out refugees en route to their in-laws', anyone who's been inside since it kicked off is probably still in there. You a journalist?'

'Sort of. Freelance I suppose. I was hoping to cover the city for the summer, but the job fell apart at the last minute. Or it may never have existed in the first place. I don't have a lot of on-the-ground experience.'

'But you figured, "fuck it, I already bought the guide book—"'

'I just, I need to get in there. It's important. None of the aid agencies I called would let me go right away.' I snapped this out, cutting him off. I don't know why I put it like that. When he turned back to face the bar, silent for a few beats, I assumed that I'd killed the conversation.

'Well,' he said, scratching the stubble over his Adam's apple, 'if it's important, you'd better come with us I suppose. Couple more days and you might not be able.'

'Seriously?' I said, rising to my feet, knocking my drained bottle on its side, 'How?'

'We're hitching a ride on one of those little four-engine Hercules models. The kind that'll rattle you sober. Plane leaves at eleven, flies straight in. From there we scramble our way to the Holiday Inn, fifth floor, and then the real fun begins.'

'But I don't, I mean, I don't exactly have the right credentials at the moment.'

'I figured as much. Mac has got you covered on that front too, my friend. Buddy of mine from Reuters had to bail this morning, brother got sick in DC and he's flying back there as we speak.'

'So . . .'

'So, you use his press card to get a seat on the plane. Put his helmet and flak jacket to good use. Once you're in, I'll call some people at Reuters and talk you up. Maybe they'll let you keep the gig.'

'Wait, slow down for a second, why would that work?'

'I mean, you're a journalist, you're here, what more do they want? Can you write unbiased copy?'

'I think so.'

'Superb. Those fuckers hate personality. Make it as unemotional as possible and they'll lap it up. And if not, who cares, you'll be in by then. Go find a gonzo team or the Red Cross if you like, tell 'em you're not leaving till they give you a T-shirt and put you to work.'

From the back room came a roar of 'bollocks' followed by the sounds of boots screeching and men straining to load bags onto their backs. 'C'mon, Jimmy, you fat fuck, if we miss this one I'm going home.'

'Well –' Mac downed the last of his beer and rubbed his hands together '– that's our version of a bugle horn. You coming, Tom?'

And that was it.

Chapter 4

After trying for a solid two hours to drift off – two hours of mattresses squeaking and pipes rattling and warped wood creaking – I'm woken by a double-thump. Two muffled blows in quick succession that can only be a giant's heels hitting the carpet after an unsteady leap out of bed. Baz has slept through his alarm clock enough times for me to be very familiar with what this particular action sounds like through a thin adjoining wall. I'm lying here, double checking in my mind that yes, the room to the right of me is Tom's and no, the noise couldn't have passed through his from Baz's, across the landing and to the left (though his fucking orca whale snoring has no difficulty making that trek). For maybe twenty seconds there's no more movement, but I'm sure I can hear murmuring. Faint, inaudible, maybe not even English, but it's there. Go back to bed, Tom. Just lie down and breathe. Calm yourself. Please don't freak out on me, not already, not tonight. I'm exhausted and I'm going to be exhausted for the foreseeable future, so please, just keep it together in there.

There are footsteps now, pacing back and forth and back and forth and back and forth, inches from where this limp pillow is wrapped around my head. I'm not getting up, I'm just not doing it. He'll tire himself out eventually and drop and that'll be that. He might even be sleepwalking, in which case there's nothing I can do but let it play out. Waking someone in that zombie state can cause an aneurism or a psychotic break or amnesia or something. I think. I'm almost certain I heard that from a reputable source. The murmuring is getting louder, angrier, the volume and cadence spiking as his footfalls become stomps. Each one shudders the floor and causes poor benevolent Jesus to hop out from the wall in his frame and settle back at a cockeyed angle. He'll wake himself up doing this. Any second now. He'll wake up.

But of course he doesn't, and within a few minutes, it's impossible to ignore.

*

'Easy, Tom, easy. It's only me.'

He turns his head to look at me for the first time, that lone bloodshot eye widening huge. Backlit by a shaft of moonlight, his frame looms skeletal over our corner of the room. I take a half step toward him. The long, crooked shadow of his arm separates me from the others. Tom is standing at the end of the bed, sweating, muttering something I can't hear. His mam is frozen in the doorway, one hand clamped against her mouth. There's silence for a few more seconds before Tom puts a palm to his temple, scrunches his eye closed and bellows, 'Just shut the fuck up, everyone, please! Just shut up and let me do this.'

'Do what, Tom?' I ask, inching closer. 'Tell me what you're trying to do.'

He doesn't register the question. It's like I'm not even there now. He breathes through his nose, steadying himself, and then notices the slow crawl of my silhouette across the carpet. He jolts backward and unleashes a battery of incomprehensible words.

'He's soaked,' I hear Tom's mam whisper behind me. 'Karl,' she says. 'Karl, his heart.'

'OK,' I say, 'all right, man, relax, I don't know what's going on but, but you're confused. Something happened and . . . it's me. Karl, remember? Can we just sit and talk about what's wrong? Just for a minute? Please?'

*

We're standing on the landing, his mam in an old-fashioned pastel dressing gown held close around her neck; me in tracksuit bottoms and an inside-out T-shirt from some long-forgotten charity 5K; Baz shivering in football shorts and a frayed Liverpool jersey from the mid-eighties. We're all staring silently at the door handle waiting for the whimpering to stop, knowing that it won't. Wondering if it's all over for the night. I suggest waking him up – in case we're only in the eye of whatever storm this bout of half-sleep has in store for him – and take their silence as consent, but I don't move and neither do they. We just stand here, shivering, waiting. Occasionally she looks up into my face, pleading for an idea.

'It's not doing any good, standing out here wringing our hands,' she says eventually, more to herself than us.

We mumble our assent and glance back towards the spare room, almost far enough away to escape the noise. It's nearly four in the morning. We haven't moved for the guts of an hour. Baz is trying to rub out the goose bumps that run down the length of both arms. Tom's mam purses her lips and nods, like she's made up her mind about something.

'I'd like to hear more about where you're taking him, Karl.'

'Now?'

'Yes, now, when else, for Pete's sake? Put some warmer clothes on that fella and I'll put the kettle on downstairs.'

She looks almost regal as she strides past us and down the scratchy carpeted stairs to the kitchen, the train of her dressing gown swishing back and forth with each downward step like the robe of a monarch gone to seed.

'I'm fucking dying, Karl,' says Baz.

'You'll be all right.'

'I can barely see straight right now let alone hold a conversation with that bleedin' harpy.'

'She just wants to know more about the place is all, how it's gonna help him.'

'Great. When you're done telling her maybe you can explain it to me.'

I exaggerate a sigh. 'How many times do I—'

'The coast. That's all I've got so far. We're headed out to see a quack somewhere on the California coast who'll do what, exactly? Hypnotise him? Electro shock the crazy out of his head? Dope him up on peyote till he forgets his own name? Tell me why we're dragging him halfway around the world when he should be in a fucking hospital. Tell me how we're going to fix *this*.'

Baz leaves his finger hanging in mid-air for a beat, long enough for us to tune back in to the rising and falling moans soundtracking Tom's nightmares.

'You want to commit him? That's your solution? You want to drive him up to the door of the nut house and leave him there, tell them he's become a danger to himself?'

Baz says nothing.

'Hospital, my bollocks. Fat lot of good the last hospital did him.' I mutter this at the daddy longlegs buzzing about on the ceiling. There's no more heat left in the argument.

'I just want to know more about it,' he sighs, deflated.

'I know you do, and that's why we're having tea at four in the morning.'

'C'mon so,' he says, 'let's go down if we're going.'

'Baz?'

'Wha?'

'Maybe throw on a pair of jeans? Unless you want to give her the full show down there.'

'Right. Best not to get her too excited. She's sweet enough on me as it is.'

Tom's mam has left her glasses upstairs which I've decided will ultimately be for the best, if I can read it with enough gravitas; this thin, less-than-inspiring pamphlet I waited on nervously for three weeks. It arrived in a carefully handwritten envelope with three crooked stamps peeling from the top right-hand corner. The cover image is that of a Californian coastal land-scape at sunset. A smattering of faraway seabirds, frozen in flight, sit underneath a vast and soothing skyscape. Soft pinks and purples against the last of the day's blue. In silver cursive across the top of the page the words *Restless Souls: Where the Wounded Come to Heal* glint up at me reassuringly. I show her the cover and try to read her face as she squints to follow the message across the page. I worry that the use of the word 'souls' might offend her pious sensibilities, but she betrays no emotion either way. Baz leans in and stares down at it with what I think is interest but which might also be a default look of near-total exhaustion.

'There's a map and a price list and all that on the back but I'll just read the important bits, right?' In a rare moment of unity for the pair, they grunt their approval.

'Right. OK, here we go. This is me reading it as is, OK, so it'll be straight from the page just the way they have it printed.'

'Just read the shagging thing, will you! Sorry, Missus Dempsey.'

'You're all right, Barry. While we're young, Karl.'

'OK. Ahem:

'Man has spent millennia learning to heal the physical wounds of war. We put our faith in the wonders of modern medicine to set broken bones, bandage wounds, amputate the limbs made useless by bullets and bombs. At the close of each new conflict, when the dead have been buried and the cities rebuilt, we find ourselves better equipped than ever before to piece back together our damaged soldiers, and the civilians they couldn't protect. We know what has to be done to fix the body. But what of the mind? What of the spirit? What of the soul?'

I can *feel* Baz's eyes rolling.

'How do we heal the wounds that cannot be seen? The wounds that perhaps cannot even be described?

'Doctor Arnold Saunders is a Vietnam War veteran who in 1972 was awarded a Silver Star for valour in the line of duty. During the spring of 1970, in the midst of a cowardly surprise attack by enemy forces, and despite suffering from an undiagnosed bout of Dengue fever, Commander Saunders stepped directly into the line of fire to drag three of his fallen comrades to safety, sustaining two near-fatal bullet wounds and killing six Viet Cong guerrillas in the process. Before he lost consciousness from blood loss, Commander Saunders managed to radio both a distress call and a timely napalm air strike of the entire area.

'For years Doctor Saunders struggled with Post Traumatic Stress Disorder (PTSD), as well as night terrors, alcoholism, drug abuse, agoraphobia, and the constant ache of loneliness that befalls so many returning veterans.

' "For years I lived a sort of half-life," writes Doctor Saunders in his 1990 memoir, *Rebuilding the Machine: One Soldier's Journey from Despair to Deliverance*, "wandering alone, half-starved, through the back woods of West Virginia while the world turned on without me. By day I would eat what little the forest could supply. When small game eluded me, I would gorge on sprigs of barely edible berries and scrape the bark from the trees, gnawing like an animal at the soft under-belly for nourishment. At night I would raid the makeshift moonshine distilleries the locals left unlocked. In my poisoned stupor, the tangled jungles of North Vietnam would come back to me, dense and terrible. Narrowed eyes red with fire would glow from the rustling thickets. Vine tendrils would coil themselves around my neck and from the earth the smell of burning flesh would rise and suffocate me. The desperate screams of my men would ring in my ears and the scars left by my bullet wounds would burn anew. Soon I had become more beast than man, unable even to contemplate suicide. Such was the depth of my mental anguish. As a child growing up on a farm in rural Ohio, I was taught to trust in the Lord, for he will provide. In my more lucid moments, it became clear to me that I was a lost lamb, separated from the flock, stranded in a forgotten field that even the Almighty's far-reaching gaze could not encompass.

' "But then, in the summer of 1980, I found a way back. On a lonely cliffside on the Californian coast, the sapphire Pacific stretching out in front of me like a beckoning lover, I had an epiphany. I realised that I had become a slave to the dark recesses of my own mind. That my trauma had muzzled the better angels that live inside me. That I was broken but, crucially, unbowed. I have seen the spirit of man grow huge and powerful on the field of battle. I have felt this spirit grow within my own person. If I could do this once, I thought, I can do it again. It was there, under the warm July sun of the Golden State that I began to heal . . ."

'Over the next five years Doctor Saunders developed many of his now-famous Conflict and Trauma PTSD recovery techniques including: Ocean meditation; Isolation Tank Therapy; Selective Memory Dampening (SMD); Hypno Self-Sedation; Celestial Spirit Recovery.

'Located on a secluded cliffside resort, only minutes from where Doctor Saunders experienced his epiphany, Restless Souls is a sanctuary where your loved one can find a way back from the darkness that has consumed them, and reclaim the precious former self that you remember.'

I let that last word 'remember' float around the room for a few seconds and try to gauge their reactions. It's embarrassing how nervous I am about this. I can feel my left knee bobbling up and down underneath the table. This fucking inscrutable silence is terrifying. Say something, anything. Get them started. At least then you'll know.

'Well?'

'Celestial Spirit Recovery?'

How did I know that this would be the one he'd pick up on.

'It's just one of the techniques, Baz. You know the Yanks, they love their buzzwords. It's probably something very straightforward. One of these new holistic healing techniques.'

'Right. Next question: what the fuck is a holistic healing technique?'

'Barry, please!'

'Shite, sorry, Missus Dempsey. Sorry sorry sorry.'

'Karl, I really don't know what to make of all this. Thomas wasn't, well, he's not a *soldier*.'

'But he might as well have been, Missus Dempsey. I mean, he was in a war zone for three years. He was injured. He lost people. All that stuff comes back to him. You know what the doctors at Wastwater said. This could be our last shot.' I look up to the ceiling trying, like an ass, to cue up a particularly loud scream. Something well-timed. Something to emphasise what I've just said; but what fills the silence is more of a whimpering. It's nearly dawn and Tom is all but worn out. Soon he'll be awake.

'I'm with Tom's mam on this, Karl. We just don't know

enough about the place. If it'll end up helping him at all. We're going all-in on a piece of paper drawn up by a fella who's probably more nuts than Tom.' Tom's mam is nodding, sadly, like it pains her to agree with the phrasing of the lug across the table, but she just can't dispute the sense he's making all the same.

'Maybe if he just stayed put here for a while, Karl,' she says, eyes trying to find mine. The pair of them, ganging up on me, leaning heavy on my name in that soft, soothing way I leaned on Tom's not two hours ago. Like I'm out of my mind for even suggesting this. 'Let Thomas settle back into normal life again.'

'This is what I've been telling him for weeks, Missus Dempsey, but he just won't listen.'

'This is some fucking time to be dumping cold water on the plan, Baz. You're supposed to be backing me up. That's what we agreed.'

'We didn't agree on anything. I said I'd support you because you had a plan and because you seemed so sure about it, but you know, well, I've had my doubts about taking him abroad from the start. And now, I mean, after hearing the details . . .' That's it, he just trails off and wanders over to the sink to pick at the edge of a wooden chopping board. Tom's mam stares down into her teacup, caressing the dulled wedding ring on her bone-pale finger.

'He's been away for so long, Karl. So many years.'

'So this is it, then,' I say, dialling up the self-righteousness as high as I can. 'This is as far as we go with him? Forget the flights, the planning, the fucking demonic possession we just witnessed.' On my feet now, raising my voice to a scared old

43

woman trying to hold on to the last bit of family she has left. This is definitely helping.

'Please, Karl. There's no need for that,' she whispers. Baz has swung back around as if me losing the run of myself somehow validates his backstabbing.

'Don't give me that look, you treacherous bollocks, like I'm the crazy one, like there's some eleventh-hour miracle you've been waiting to spring. "I know! Let's do nothing and hope for the best," as per fucking usual.'

He puffs out that barrel chest of his and squares up to me, black hairs dancing inside his flared nostrils. I step a half foot closer, till I can smell the stale fug of his morning breath. So far this carefully envisioned presentation is not going according to plan.

'You wanted our opinion and you've gotten it,' he snarls, 'so get out of my face before I knock you the fuck out.' He could too, probably without breaking a sweat, but I can't let him know that.

'C'mon then, big man, gimme your best shot.'

'That's enough! You two should be ashamed of yourselves. In the name and honour of God have we not had enough of violence to last us a lifetime?'

Jesus, she's livid. I'm actually scared. Baz seems to have shrunk about a foot. We slink back to our seats, muttering apologies over and over like decades of the rosary till she calms herself and drops noiselessly into her own chair. Then silence once again. Minutes tick by. We don't look at one another but I can feel this whole brainstorming session drawing to a close. The night's various shocks have worn off, if not entirely then enough to be at least partially supplanted by embarrassment. Any second now one of them is going to bolt for the door and then that'll be that. I'll have missed the window. In the morning cooler heads will prevail and that means no trip, no clinic, no cure. I have to go for it now. I didn't want to do this, it wasn't part of the plan or anything, but I've lost the room and nothing else will sway them.

'Look, I'm sorry,' I tell them. 'I know you both want what's best for him. I just don't know how much longer he can go on like this, you know? Between his heart and, well, the rest of it, I'm worried that he might, I dunno, I just keep thinking about Gabriel whenever I look at him. Of all the things we, I, maybe should have done.' It's cheap, and cruel, but that doesn't mean it isn't true.

She lowers her head when I mention Gabriel. I know she's been thinking about him too these last few days and I feel for her, how doubly terrifying this prospect must be as both a mother and a proper, God-fearing Catholic, but it's necessary. Baz is standing again now, breathing heavy, more upset than angry. We're miles away from wisecracks at the airport.

'This isn't like that, Karl. That was, I mean, he was *depressed* and he didn't tell anyone and it's not like we could have known.'

'I know, right, I know. Relax, I'm not blaming us. I just wish . . . I'm not saying we should have known then. But we know now, don't we? We know Tom is in trouble and I can't think of a single place in this country, a single person, we could take him to that'd be able to help him. God knows we're not equipped, but if you could just trust me when I say that this is our last good option. Please, *please* just give this place a chance.'

45

Over the next half an hour I wear them down. Tom's mam brews a fresh pot of tea and we drink it and talk logistics and I don't mention Gabriel again, though he's in the room with us now, backing me up. I tell them both that I know it's not perfect, that it's a risk, that I'm as clueless on these matters as anyone. After a while Baz relents and agrees to run with the plan as long as we can keep a close eye on things. Tom's mam says she does trust me, which, even though it's what I asked of her, gives me a little burn of panic in my chest when I hear it. It's 6 a.m. when we finally rise from the table, our forearms red from the warmed plastic.

*

Gabriel Hogan hanged himself from the rusty-as-fuck goalposts of our local football pitch. Where we shot penalties together as children. The idea of that won't ever leave me. None of us were where we should have been when he dropped. I was walking the beach less than half a mile away, trying to decide whether I'd leave for America with Clara or stay put, fancying myself a man who did his best thinking against the backdrop of dark sea swells. Baz was on what may or may not have been a date with a local girl called Helen – a prickly barmaid from The Goat who I'd always assumed was a lesbian. She could have been. She could still be. It was one of the many things that didn't enter our heads for a long time afterward. Tom was sprinting across a bombed-out street somewhere in Sarajevo, trying to dodge the sniper fire, maybe. Or maybe he was sitting in a windowless back room smoking an over-priced black market cigarette, or listening to crackling radio broadcasts to help him understand the language, or sleeping beside his girl. There were deep welts scratched into Gabriel's neck when they found him, like maybe he'd had a change of heart one split second too late. Probably it was just the instinct toward self-preservation that all creatures have when the noose is tightening.

I had questions in the wake of it. Big, pointless existential questions. How can you grow up alongside someone, love them as fiercely as if they were your own flesh and blood, and not see it coming? How can you share a home and a life and two decades of history with them, and not see the change happening? There was a time when he couldn't have hidden that kind of darkness from me. A time when it was just us; when there was no one else we needed. When he would have *told* me. That afternoon might never have happened. Myself and Baz standing silent in our suits and scuffed shoes with Eugene and Therese, girls he had loved and chased away, lads from the neighbourhood, from our school days, from football teams long disbanded and forgotten; all of us watching uselessly as they lowered his coffin into the damp ground.

He was buried in Glasnevin, in the sprawling garden cemetery that houses everyone from fallen patriots to unbaptised babies. Strategists and foot soldiers from opposing aisles of the Civil War lie side by side there, some of them brothers. People leave bottles of stout on the headstones of alcoholic writers, and flowers for generals cut down in their prime. There's a plot for the nameless cholera victims of a nineteenth-century tenement outbreak and a giant round tower to house Daniel O'Connell, the Great Liberator. There's every kind of death imaginable in that cemetery. And now there's Gabriel. As the ten of us gathered at his graveside took turns dropping fistfuls of soil down on top of him, I thought about how many suicide victims sleep in that earth, their official certificates reading 'Death by Misadventure', their newspaper obituaries vague and ashamed. Gabriel's was an open casket, but the make-up didn't fully cover the choker of purple bruising the rope left behind.

To this day, the only person to use the word 'suicide' in relation to his death – aside from Baz when he's six pints in or mid bout of nervous verbal diarrhea – is one of the two idiot teenagers who stumbled across him while downing stolen cans of cider in the park. They waited an hour before calling the police, shitting themselves over the prospect of being caught in a less than lucid state. The notion that these two gangly, panicked fuckwits were the only company Gabriel had at the end still makes my heart thump. Six days after the funeral one of them turned up on my doorstep – all pimples and greasy hair in an oversized Metallica hoodie – and started jabbering breathlessly about how he felt 'connected' to Gabriel since he found his corpse. The lad actually used the word 'corpse' like he was describing an extra from the 'Thriller' video. I let him finish. There is something about this kind of train-wreck speechifying that transfixes me. When he was done he blew some hair out of his eyes and made a move to walk past me into the house. I put a hand on his dandruff-powdered shoulder and looked at him, solemnly, for a long second.

'Get the fuck out of here, you ghoulish little bollocks.'

I have not, for one second in the two years since it happened, felt bad about this.

Meanwhile, the phones were still down in Sarajevo. Our first three letters didn't make it through. I couldn't stop imagining them stacking up in an empty post office miles away from anyone while Tom lay, unidentifiable, on a metal slab in a crumbling morgue in a crumbling city. Ash on every surface. Gabriel was buried two weeks before word finally reached Tom.

Sarajevo, August 26, 1992

Early this morning, when I arrived at the market, people were crying into their hands. Bits of burnt paper were falling from the sky. Like black snow. Money is getting tight already and I was hoping to sell some Marlboros for whatever I could get from the vendors at the Markale. I've been smoking too much anyway. I got up at dawn to avoid any questions from Mac, who never puts feet on the floor before nine because, and I quote, 'If those cunts up in the hills can sleep in, then so can I.' He still feels like he owes me since the Reuters thing didn't pan out, God knows why. It was always gonna be a long shot. I'm not even sure I can do what they do anyway, Mac and the others. Maybe it takes years to learn how. When we drink at the bar, or kick a dead football around the old meeting room with the wait staff, or strap on our flak jackets to leave, I'm quiet, or I say something weird, and the others all notice. But they like Mac, so they say nothing.

The stink of spoiled food and uncollected waste has been rising all summer but this morning all I could smell was the smoke. Like someone turned on the hob underneath the dry ground. They tell me the library has been burning since late last night, sometime around midnight. Blasted by mortars. Gutted by fire. The place where I found myself regularly hiding my first week in the city, when I couldn't stop my hands from trembling. All those books, all those novels and poems, letters and manuscripts. Records of how the city used to be.

No one dared approach from the river side. Too many snipers lying in wait, now with a giant, flaming torch to draw the eye. It would have been suicide. All those tens of thousands of gallons of water, close enough to cup in your hands and lash against the library's front steps. Useless. From inside the building I could hear the heavy crack of beams and bookcases breaking, the pop of windows blowing out. I pictured huge piles of ash dropping to the floor. I tried to sneak in through a side door but a pair of gloved hands grabbed me around the waist and wrenched me backwards onto the ground. I could hear him roaring at me as I got to my feet, and then he was gone. I joined a line of soot-faced men and we lifted boxes of singed books onto a truck. Two firemen were passing an oxygen mask back and forth on the stoop beside us. Yellow helmets clamped between their knees. Wide white eyes shining. One of them just stood there, staring into the flames. The pressure in the hoses down to a trickle. After an hour, there was nothing left for us to load.

'What happened?' I asked, like a fool. We were passing a flask around, wetting our cracked lips.

'What you think happened?' a voice snapped back at me. 'When I wake up in the night, I see burning pages falling from the sky into my garden. I come to save what I can but every minute more explosions, all night more explosions. How can we save anything when the sky is on fire above our heads? What is left now? What is left for us when it ends? We have nothing.'

'*Imamo naše živote; mnogo toga još uvijek možemo spasiti,*'

51

a woman to our left said calmly. My Bosnian is still shaky as hell, but I think it meant, 'We have our lives; there is much we can still save.' The man shook his head, spat onto the ground, and walked away. As he passed I noticed his age, and the bandages wrapped around his right palm. The thick white burn, cream seeping out from underneath. I made a move to follow, but she put a hand to my chest to stop me.

'Leave him. He was literature professor at the university,' she said in English. 'It is very painful for him to see this.' I nodded, because I couldn't think of anything to say. 'He is right. Without the books, the art, what proof will there be that there was once another Sarajevo?'

'So what now?' I asked, low, so that only she could hear me. She was staring at the black smoke pouring from the window frames above us. Like most of the women in Sarajevo, her hair was curled, her make-up perfect, her clothes clean and neat. Little acts of defiance. I watched the flecks of ash stack on the padded shoulders of her blouse while I waited for her to speak.

'Now we try to save what is left.'

'But, eh, there's nothing left.' Where would the people of this city be without my keen journalistic observations.

'Not here, perhaps. But elsewhere. There is much we can still save.'

'Where?'

'You want to see or you want to help?'

'Both.' She looked at me strangely, the way most people look at me here, like they can't quite understand why exactly I'm around. I'm starting to wonder myself. The colour in her left eye was darker than the right, and she caught me looking from one to the other. I hoped that my face was already red enough from the inferno heat.

'Both is OK,' she finally decided. 'You look strong. Are you strong?'

'I used to be stronger,' I said. She laughed, and nodded her head like I'd made some wonderful joke. 'Yes,' she said, 'very few body builders are living in Sarajevo at the moment. It is a short walk. If you want to help, we can use you.'

We walked quickly, heading west through side streets where emaciated dogs nipped at each other as they circled around us, yelping for scraps. On Bravadžiluk, someone had written *Love Sarajevo, Defend Sarajevo* in yellow paint. The colour of cheap mustard. Underneath it was a bright red drawing of a Bosnian soldier holding a rifle. The picture had no face. I stared as we passed, she did not. She looks nothing like my mother, but they walk with the same stride. Purposeful. It had been weeks since I'd tried to call home. A shell exploded somewhere in the distance. She muttered something under her breath that could have been a curse or a prayer.

'My name is Tom, by the way,' I said, stooping low to hear her reply.

'I am Fadila,' she said, not looking at me. We hung a right onto Ćurčiluk Veliki. The long white spire of the Gazi Husrev-Beg Mosque. Fadila stopped and stared through the railings into the courtyard. Green and grey domes. Windows like bells. A courtyard fountain with a slatted wooden roof. Everything looking delicate and doomed.

'Soon, this will burn just as the library has burnt,' she said, shaking her head. 'Beautiful things cannot survive in this city any more.' She led me on, past the mosque and its gardens, to the library around the corner. It looked to me like an embassy from a bygone era. We were buzzed in and greeted by a tall, thinly built man in his late-thirties wearing a grey suit. Dusted with ash, like us. I could see the purple rings behind his black-rimmed glasses. Fadila introduced him as the library director. There was a streak of soot on his neck. She spoke rapidly to him and squeezed my elbow. He shook my hand warmly and led us through the cool building. Up two flights of stairs. Past wall-sized tapestries and stacks of leather-bound books. As Fadila translated, he moved his arm over tables of ancient manuscripts, thousands of lines of Arabic calligraphy etched into golden pages so beautiful I was afraid to touch the wood they sat on.

'These books,' he said, 'are the most ancient part of our city. Some of them have never been read, never been catalogued, but they contain the memory of every generation from the past one thousand years. All cultures. All ethnicities. They come from everywhere. They destroyed the Oriental Institute. Now our National Library is dead too.' That is how he put it. *Dead*. Like it was a person gunned down in the street. His eyes filled up with tears that he then coughed away, apologising. 'All of those books, all of those memories, whole lives preserved in ink. Gone. Soon they will point more guns toward us. We must save what we can before that happens.'

'What can I do?' I asked.

'You are a journalist, yes?' I squirmed, and nodded. I still haven't figured out how to properly answer this question. Does anything I'm doing here count as journalism? 'Well, perhaps someday you can write about us. For now, we need muscle. Fadila and others have been helping us for some weeks now, but after last night I fear the worst is coming. We must move quickly. Today we move the rest to the ground floor. To-morrow we must bring the most precious manuscripts to the basement of Careva Džamija, the Emperor's Mosque, across the river. Past the snipers. It is the only way, I'm afraid. They will be safe there, for a time at least.'

The director walked us back downstairs, over the thick Persian rugs in the atrium to a back room where five of his staff were piling books into chest-high columns against a white-washed wall. We shook hands without exchanging names. They nodded and returned to their work. Above the stacks was a message written in simple black lettering. When I asked Fadila what it meant she spoke from memory, writing it down on a scrap of paper as she recited the quote.

'"Good deeds drive away evil, and one of the most worthy of good deeds is the act of charity, and the most worthy act of charity is one which lasts forever. Of all charitable deeds, the most beautiful is one that continually renews itself."'

She handed me the paper. I folded it so that the corners met, and tucked it into the inside of my wallet. We worked until the sun went down. Carefully placing the oldest of the books into cardboard Bonita banana boxes and sealing them up as tight as we could. We stacked twenty in the corner of the room, said our goodbyes, and went home to sleep. Tomorrow, Fadila tells me, we will rise at daybreak and gather in the courtyard. We will hold our breath, and sprint across the exposed bridge closest to the library, past the sandbags and burnt-out cars and coils of barbed wire. We'll cross back and forth three times until all of the boxes are safe. Like something out of a war film. I'll probably be the gormless character actor who doubles back for a dropped box and takes one in the neck halfway through.

My hands have been shaking for hours. Just a slight tremor, but it's there. I can feel it in my jaw when I unclench my teeth. Like something is trying to shudder its way out of me. Deep breaths through the nose, that's what they say. Deep breaths till everything slows down.

I need to get myself right by tomorrow. Calm myself. I've promised her that I'll be there.

Chapter 5

We're having breakfast in silence. The four of us, a frayed patchwork quilt of a family. I'm too tired to eat and that pow-wow a few hours ago has me drained. If Tom remembers what happened last night, which I highly doubt, he hasn't mentioned it. Chances are he thinks it was all a nightmare. We drifted down here in stages – Tom's mam rising and disappearing first, then me, then Tom, and, a good hour later, Baz. Now he's sitting beside me in his billowing Pennys boxer shorts slurping milk straight from the bowl and fishing around in the Frosties box for the toy at the bottom. He called it, so it's his. A tiger badge. Not Tony the Tiger, just a regular tiger, its eyes wild and green. He doesn't seem pleased.

'I don't get it.'

'Hmmm?' Tom responds.

My instinct is to remind Tom not to take the bait, not to encourage whatever nonsense tirade Baz is about to begin. But any speech whatsoever, even this mumbled inquiry, has got to be a good sign, so for once I find myself hoping Baz lets loose.

'I don't get what the point is.'

'The point of the badge?' Tom's mother lowers her news-paper ever so slightly at the sound of his voice, which is slow and deliberate.

'Yeah, I mean, what's it advertising? If it was Tony there staring out with the big over-enthusiastic head on him you'd say "OK, yeah, that lad has been eating Frosties, fair play to him on getting the toy ahead of his grabby little brothers –"'

Granted he's not a philosopher in the traditional sense, but to give him his due, Baz does probe certain choice topics with the same rabbit-hole zeal.

'"– maybe I'll go buy a box of Frosties myself now that I'm out." Boom: Tony makes another million dollars. But this is just a failure of imagination, is what it is. A failure of marketing. How is anyone supposed to know where the hell this thing came from?'

'Maybe it's a vintage campaign,' Tom muses. 'Maybe that was how Tony originally looked in the early years.'

Most days this would drive me up the wall, but the fact that Tom is actively contributing to a conversation instead of staring glassy-eyed at the robins in the hedgerows at the back of the garden again is borderline miraculous.

'You think?'

He shrugs, swirling the small puddle of milk in his bowl so that the last remaining flake moves in circles with the current. 'Maybe. I got talking to a Canadian guy a couple of years ago who used to work for Gillette. He said the company planned to release a new razor every four to five years with an added blade "for extra closeness". Then, when they get to the point where adding more blades would look ridiculous, they'll rerelease the one-blade razor and sell it as a "classic model".'

'Fuck off. Shit – sorry, Missus Dempsey. I keep forgetting about God and all that.'

He can't see her cracking a smile behind her *Irish Independent*, but I can. She wouldn't be the type to burst herself laughing, at anything, but this is a step. After last night, maybe we're all a little closer.

'Just go easy, Barry, will you. Lord Almighty, I would have bought a packet of porridge oats instead had I known.'

'You don't seem convinced, Baz,' I say, because I want in on this nonsense now.

'You're damn right I don't. Tom, you're telling me that Gillette's big long-term marketing plan is to just hit the reset button?'

'So he said.'

'Why?'

'Well, his thinking was that people don't actually want real change. All they want is the illusion of newness spread out over the same old comforting stuff. Real change is frightening. Threatening even.'

'And he told you this, just like that?' I'm curious now.

'Well, he'd had a few drinks.'

'Yeah, but still, isn't that, like, a magician giving away his tricks or something?'

'I suppose he figured I wouldn't tell anyone.'

'Why?' I don't know why I'm pushing this.

'Well, it was during a pretty dangerous period in the city, and I had told him I was staying.'

Silence. Even Tom's mam has stopped rustling the paper. I

can hear the gulping rise and fall of Baz's Adam's apple. We're all so wound up we can barely breathe.

'So he told you because he figured you were due to be shot or blown up before you got a chance to tell anyone who mattered,' I say.

'More or less, yeah.'

'Right.'

His mam is not pleased. *There was no need for that*, her sharp little eyes are saying to me. She'd expect it out of Baz, but not me. But I know he doesn't want this. All of us walking on eggshells for fear he'll crumble if the wrong combination of words falls, like three X's in a slot machine. At this stage what does it matter a damn if we mention the siege or not? After last night? Maybe this is the only way to handle it. To let the topic drift in and out of conversation, unobstructed, till we don't even notice its presence any more. Till he can deal with it in the cold light of day. But we're a while off that yet I suppose. The broken clock ticks nine times before someone else speaks.

'Is there anything you'd like to do today, Thomas? Something nice before you boys head off on your trip?'

'I was thinking maybe we could stop by Glasnevin for a bit? I'd like to see Da and maybe pay my respects to Gabriel.'

Joy.

*

'Is it weird to admit that I sort of like it here?' Baz asks me.

We're doing a deliberately languid lap of this section of the cemetery, overgrown with vines and brambles and lush green

60

thickets of grass dotted with wildflowers, while we wait for them to finish. Tom needs time alone with his parents. At the end of that first month of '93, the earth hadn't settled on top of his father's grave before he was back on a plane to the Balkans.

'Probably,' I say, for obvious reasons. 'Definitely if you're going to start in on that baby-killing thing again.'

Baz's latest mini obsession is with the notion of the Church burying thousands of unbaptised Magdalene laundry babies in unmarked plots around the country. There's been all sorts of rumblings since a hundred or so infants were discovered in a mass grave and reburied here a couple of years back. Baz, the macabre bastard, has been following developments like a train spotter, occasionally giving me unsolicited, finger-wagging lectures on the subject like I'm a defender of mass infanticide.

'Nah, it's not that. It's just, I dunno, peaceful here, but in a messy kind of way, y'know? Like you could wander off and find a place in the high grass to lie down and sleep, if you really wanted to, and no one would bother you.'

A pair of foghorn lummoxes wandering round a graveyard talking nonsense. This is what mourners want to encounter when they make their weekly pilgrimage. I move to one side and bow my head as a couple of blue-haired fossils float by, but they cluck at us like toe-poked hens all the same.

'I mean, it's still creepy,' Baz continues, not giving two fucks about the cranky keeners still in earshot, 'don't get me wrong. When you think how many skeletons we're walking on right now—'

61

'*You're* walking on,' I say. 'I'm staying on the path because I'd like to avoid hell if at all possible.'

'Ah that's only superstitious bullshit.' This firm declaration from the man who, according to himself, has successfully shaken off the few remaining vestiges of Catholicism he had left, yet still crosses himself at the sound of every ambulance siren. I've tried, on many, many occasions, explaining to him that this little ward-off-the-evil tic of his is straight out of the Christianity playbook, which makes him a walking, shouting contradiction, but to no avail. 'It's not like they can feel it,' he continues.

'But there's a path, see? I'm now standing on a path under which there is not a big pile of dead women and children muttering ghosty curses up at me.'

'But look at what you're missing out on. I'm having the full immersive cemetery experience right here.'

'And I'm not?' This is why no one invites us anywhere nice. Because of arguments like this one.

'Nah. You're like one half of those pensioner couples who go off on air-conditioned bus tours of Egypt and then tell everyone all about how they've "been to the pyramids".'

'Which makes you?'

'Which makes me Indiana fucking Jones, dodging pygmy arrows and rolling under doorways to find Tutankhamun's tomb.'

'Scarily accurate. And all this from the man who hasn't been on an airplane in five years.'

'What does that have to do with anything?'

'I'm just saying.'

'So now I'm supposed to be jealous of the three-quid bag

of peanuts you bought on your forty-five minute flight to Manchester last year?'

As I myself am secretly petrified of flying, I may have blown up the heroic significance of this round trip in my own mind. Just a bit. Maybe.

'It was a trip abroad, wasn't it?' I counter.

'England doesn't count as abroad. You can't compare drinking warm cans of Tennent's in the cheap seats at Old Trafford with your retarded cousin Frankie, who you don't even like, to fighting mummies and stealing Tutankhamun's gold.' Frankie isn't actually retarded, by the way, God love him. He's slow, and he might be functionally illiterate, but he's definitely within normal intellectual parameters. Just about.

'Have you ever actually seen *Indiana Jones*, Baz?'

'The important bits.'

'Look, all I'm getting at is, in my admittedly limited experience, the first step on the road less travelled generally involves leaving the city in which you were born and raised. Where exactly are you planning to carry out these monster hunts and archaeological desecrations?'

'Right here, Karly.' He's tapping his head now, literally dancing on some poor bastard's grave. 'Right. Up. Here.' He executes an awkward barrel roll onto another plot and cracks an imaginary whip at an ancient, crumbling headstone. The wingless cherub on its base stares back at Baz, deeply unimpressed.

'Ah c'mon, Baz, for fuck's sake! Get off that thing.'

The dancing has become more elaborate in its gracelessness. Baz is now twirling and dipping invisible women, swivelling a non-existent cane as he descends the non-existent staircase. I don't know who exactly he's attempting to emulate now that the last of the *Indiana Jones* dumb show has been exhausted. I think I see a bit of Fred Astaire in the descent, but the rootin' tootin' leg kicks he's transitioned into are more of the Yosemite Sam variety.

'All right, Baz, enough is enough. You're gonna get us booted out of here or fucking excommunicated or something.'

'Ha, excommunicated from what?' Still. Fucking. Dancing. 'The cemetery?'

'Damn right the cemetery. I don't want to be buried in some fucking haunted Protestant graveyard because you got us banned from the only decent bone orchard in Dublin.'

'Ah that's Tom's mam talking. Dead is dead. They can have me stuffed full of fireworks and lashed onto a bonfire for all I care. I won't be around to complain.' There's definitely something manic about him these days. I'm afraid to ask what's up.

'Are you not tired? This is more exercise than I've seen you do in years.'

That's stopped him, thank Christ. He accidently hoofs a desiccated condolence wreath onto the path, where it rolls laboriously through my legs and into a thorn bush to die.

'What? You know well I play five-a-side every Thursday,' says Baz. 'That's intense exercise right there.'

'I can imagine.'

From around the bend in the path, Tom shuffles slowly toward us with his hands and forearms buried in the pockets of his shabby black overcoat. Far too heavy for the warm day, though he doesn't seem bothered by it. Spending three sub-zero winters in frozen basements and bedrooms with bullet-peppered windows probably plays havoc with a man's internal thermometer. The way the sun falls on his face washes out everything but the flimsy eye patch. I wonder who made it for him. Who sat down with a pair of scissors and thin piece of felt, stood behind him in the mirror and fitted it around his battered head. Who scooped the remnants of his pulped eyeball from his skull and dressed the wound so it wouldn't fester. I wonder how it felt without anaesthesia, without painkillers. I wonder what state the others were in; the ones he shared a makeshift hospital room with that day. Was she there with him, his girl? How far were they from the end? Did he fight off his carers and stumble, with all the sure-footedness you'd expect from the newly cyclopsed, into the room where the shrouded dead lay in pieces, waiting to be ID'd by hysterical loved ones? Did he rip sheet after bloodied sheet from the bodies, waiting for her to appear, like a magician's reveal, underneath his outstretched arm? Was any of this even close to what really happened out there? I feel like I should bellow every sentence at him, like I'm trying to communicate through the chunky glass of a prison visiting area when none of the phones will work. I doubt he'd register it any differently if I did.

'Lads.'

'All right, Tom? Where's your mam?'

'She's a bit worn out I think. She said she just wasn't able for seeing Gabriel today.' Baz splutters quietly to himself. Remembering, I suppose, why we're here in the first place. Far as I know, he hasn't been to the grave since the funeral.

'So . . . we're still . . . I mean . . .'

'We don't have to. I can go alone. I don't mind,' Tom re-assures him.

'No,' Baz says, louder than he means to, 'it's fine, really. It's been a while since, I mean, I should come, too.'

So we walk on. I lead, since I doubt that Baz remembers where Gabriel's grave is, and we move in single file so that the silence seems less awkward. Slightly less awkward. The bright mid-afternoon sun beats down with an intensity I haven't felt in a year and from behind me I hear Tom remove his coat and drape it over his shoulder. Gabriel's coffin was the first, and so far the only, that I have been asked to bear. There have been other deaths of course, before and since, some of them young men, maybe some of them self-inflicted too. We hear things and we don't ask. But his is the only coffin I've carried. I remember our slow march up this same path two years ago, feeling the tiny vibrations of the wood against my neck as Baz tried to stop his body from shaking. I told him to relax, that it was OK. We were nearly there. We felt like frauds that day, nervously playing our part in the funeral rites – the coffin, the burial, the mumbled Bible passages from the pulpit – like we were men, and not terrified kids who wanted nothing more than to run away from all of it. I wondered if he would have wanted me there at all. I've told Baz over and over since that morning there was nothing we could have done, that I knew him better than anyone and that he'd kept it all inside. I've said it so often that he's begun parroting it back to me at a higher pitch like he did last night. But he doesn't really believe it, and I sure as hell don't. There were signs, of course there were signs.

We're close now, I can see the careful arrangements of

sunflowers that appear each week, the reflective black marble of his headstone.

'I'm sorry, lads, I can't do this. It's just . . . my head's not right for this today. I thought I could but I can't. I'm sorry, Karl.'

'It's fine, Baz, honestly, don't worry about it,' I say this as softly as I can, trying to catch his eye, feeling like a prick for making him come out here in the first place.

'We won't be long,' Tom says. 'Meet you back at the gates?'

'Yeah, OK. Is there another way back? I just, I don't want to disturb your mam while she's trying to have a chat with, well, not a chat obviously but you know—' Tom laughs. Not a proper laugh but as close as we've gotten out of him so far. We're all sort of smiling now, half-embarrassed at what a shambolic mourning party we are.

'Eh, yeah that might be for the best. Unless you have anything in particular you want to say to my aul lad?'

'Ah you know me, Tom, I was never great with an audience, and your mam is much too harsh a critic. I'll come back again when I have him all to myself.'

'I think that's a wise choice; and I'm sure he'll be grateful for the company whenever you're ready.'

'Thanks, man.'

'No worries. Karl, any notion of what way we might sneak Baz out of here?'

'Lemme see now. If you cut through that middle section there I think you can wrap around the tower and make a break for the front entrance. Stay low though, if you're caught you're on your own.'

'Aye aye.'

'Oh, and Baz?'

'Mmm?'

'Try not to trample on any more corpses on your way out, will you?'

'I can't make any promises.'

Tom and I watch him bulldoze his way across the graves, disappearing around the tower and out of sight. We're still smiling as we turn back toward Gabriel's headstone. We walk these last few paces side by side, chuckling softly to ourselves, until we're close enough to read the inscription:

GABRIEL PETER HOGAN

1968–1994

Beloved son, brother and friend

Tread softly, here lies our world

'It's nice,' Tom says quietly.

'The quote?'

'Yeah. I haven't heard that one before.'

'Anna suggested it.' I feel like I have to clarify. 'I've always thought it was a bit unfair that her role was never carved onto that thing alongside ours. She loved him too, even after they broke it off. Though I suppose they never put "boyfriend" or "girlfriend" on the headstones, do they? Let alone exes.'

'I suppose not. Why do you think that is?'

'Who knows. Religious propriety? In case people start thinking about sex.'

'Could be. Hard to get a handle on your thoughts at a funeral.' The way he says this, wistful, like he's running back over the God knows how many he has attended these past few years.

'True. Could be something more practical. Fear of over-crowding, maybe?'

'Mmm. Like it might cause people to get carried away with second-tier titling.'

'"Tolerated co-worker".'

'"Rabid Man United supporter".'

'"Reliably sloppy drinker".'

'"Enthusiastic public urinator".'

There's more of the Tom I remember in this exchange. The spark of humour that always danced around in that serious mind of his. It's something I want back for him. The lightness. Most people would roll their eyes if I told them Tom was ever anything but a silent, furrowed depressive. But then, most people never really knew him.

'A dangerous can of worms really, you can see why they avoided it.'

'Yep. Anna wouldn't be the type to make a fuss over something like that. Too nice.'

'Did you get to speak to her much, in the weeks afterward?' he asks me quietly.

'Not much. I called around once or twice before she moved back home, but she was finding it all pretty hard. She asked about you though.'

'Why I wasn't there?'

'No, no I mean she knew why. She knew you would have been there if you could. If you'd known. She just wanted to see if I'd heard anything, if you were OK.'

'I'm sorry I wasn't here, Karl. I'm sorry it happened this way.'

'Me too.'

'Baz is having some trouble with it?'

'How could you tell?'

'I'm sorry if I dredged this up for you lads again.'

'Ah it's not like it ever went away.'

I can't tell if he can hear me.

'You leave, thinking you're doing the right thing. Thinking that it'll be the most worthwhile thing you'll ever do. In the end though, they die just the same as if you'd never been there at all. All of them, and more.'

'You did the best you could.'

'If I'd stayed at least I could have spent some more time with him.'

'Do you miss him?'

'I miss everyone.'

'At least we're still here.'

'But I'm not.'

It feels now like something significant should happen, like his last pronouncement should cue a sign: a rumble, a sudden darkening, the opening of the sky to drench us, and Gabriel, and the whole damn cemetery in a heavy rain. But nothing happens. The world does nothing to indicate that any of this shite talk means anything at all. The sun keeps shining down like it has all afternoon – harsh, and blinding, and unnatural. After a few minutes I turn to walk away. Tom waits for a long beat, and follows.

Sarajevo, November 10, 1992

I don't know how long I was out for. It felt like night-time. Something between a whistle and static in my ears.

His dead face flashing in my head. This young lad, he'd been kicking a plastic football against a pillar when I passed.

When I tried to swing my leg over the side of the guardrail the whole thing tipped over. The clang of it echoed like mad. I lay on the ground and waited till it was over. The sound of muffled footsteps and cries coming from down the hall. I saw it in the blackened window of an empty conference room before I felt it. The bandage safety-pinned tight around my head. Thick, greyed wool. Where some debris had hit, I guess. I remembered looking up at two pigeons on a windowsill. Then a blast. Then the head on the ground facing mine, tethered to its body by two flimsy stands of flesh. Then nothing. At the other end of the corridor, an old man was shivering. I searched around for a blanket or a curtain to tear down, but there was none. Everything stank of bleach and blood. I took off my fleece jacket and the thermal I was wearing underneath. It smelled like sweat and was caked around the collar with bloody concrete dust. I shook it out, embarrassed that anyone but me would have to put this on. The way he trembled. So violent it could have been a seizure. I draped the thermal over his shoulders and wrapped the sleeves tight around his exposed cheek until his spasms slowed.

I walked through the large double doors and down another hallway where more shivering patients lay in cots against the walls. All but two made little plumes of freezing air as they breathed. Three more turns and I found myself at the entrance to the children's ward. Or what was passing for a children's ward anyway. The doors swung open and closed as staff marched past me carrying bowls of steaming water, sodden red bandages, trays with serrated medical instruments. I stepped through after a bearded doctor and stood in the corner, hugging my arms to my chest against the cold. It gets into your bones these days. Children, some of them no older than toddlers, lay in tiny beds, mewling for their mothers. Five that I could see were missing limbs. Tiny stumps, blood seeping through the bandages and gauze. One boy in a slashed blue Italian football jersey was being held down by two knackered orderlies. His left leg was burnt black, flesh and fabric melted together. I couldn't stop gawking at them, all of them. A nurse cooed something into his ear as he roared and pleaded for his parents, wherever they were. When the doctor approached, masked, in theatre scrubs, the boy fainted. The nurse wiped the sweat from his little forehead as the bed was wheeled out of the ward. The long halogen lights above us flickered and one of the orderlies emerged from behind a curtain with a box of matches. He moved quickly and silently from candle to candle lighting as many as possible before the flame burnt out between his thumb and index finger. On the bed nearest to where I was standing, a girl of no more than ten bit her lip till it whitened and bled. Tiny pieces of shrapnel were being removed from her arm with tweezers. I stood there gasping, the freezing air shocking my lungs, until the woman with the tweezers looked up from her work. Her black hair was tied back in a ponytail and her huge green eyes stretched wide at the sight of me. She looked sort of familiar, but I was still too dizzy to figure it out. She said something in Bosnian that I didn't understand.

'You should not be in here,' she repeated in English, 'wait outside for me.'

I waited against the wall, trying to place her. My whole head throbbed and it hurt to swallow. I was too ashamed to ask for water in a place like that, even though it felt like I might collapse soon – my huge, ungainly frame crashing to the floor and causing a traffic jam of child-sized stretchers. The lights in the hallway went dead and left me standing there in the darkness, feeling around for the wall. I fumbled in my jacket for a lighter. Inside the pocket was a clump of gravel, one piece as large as a pound coin. I've been turning it over in my hand for hours. My zippo was scratched, but not broken and with its high flame I lit up the entrance to the ward. Staff barrelled out, cursing the darkness. I could hear the woman with the tweezers trying to soothe the children on the other side of the doors. They whimpered and cried softly into their pillows, like frightened animals. She held one hand up toward them as the other opened the door outward, promising to return.

'You are awake,' she said, striding past me. I followed.

'Yes,' I said, 'I, what happened? Where am I?'

'The zoo.'

'Eh, excuse me?'

'Where does it look like you are? You were knocked un- conscious by a mortar explosion. You are very lucky to be alive.'

'And those children?'

'They are not so lucky as you. Many will die tonight.'

'Jesus.'

'More will die of cold also, in the days ahead.'

'What about the generator?'

'No diesel, no generators. Not today. We must operate by candlelight when the power fails. We cannot sterilise equipment properly. Children wake from anaesthetic in freezing cold. There is not enough antibiotics so some will lose limbs and some will die. This is the reality of the situation.'

When I asked if I could help, she laughed.

'Do you have any diesel?'

'No.'

'Antibiotics? Anaesthetic? Bandages?'

'No.'

'Oh, so you have friends in charge of the Relief Convoys? Or perhaps you are from NATO and you have good news for the city?'

'Funny you should mention that—'

She sighed, and pressed hard on the bridge of her nose with her index finger and thumb before finally asking, 'Do you have any cigarettes?'

'Yes!' I said. I had one box of Marlboros left from the six cartons I brought over. I took the flattened white pack from the inside of my jacket and handed it to her proudly. She took three out, gave one to me, put one between her lips, and the last she slid behind her ear. She leaned in to the zippo flame. The gold in her fleur-de-lis earrings glinted. She pulled on the cigarette and rested her back against the wall for a second,

74

closing her eyes. I watched the smoke seep slowly from her nostrils.

'You are a journalist, yes?'

'In the loosest possible sense.'

'So watch, and write, and maybe help will come.'

'Do you think it will?'

'I don't know. Nobody knows. I must go now, it will be a very long night.'

'Wait,' I said. 'I really do want to help.'

She stopped, pissed off. I mean really pissed off. 'You are not trained, and you have a concussion, you cannot help. We don't need war tourists here. Go back to the Holiday Inn and drink with your reporter buddies, the *back* way, in case you are too brain damaged to remember, and try not to get shot. I have work to do.'

'You're a doctor, right?'

'I am a final year medical student, and I am very busy.'

'Please,' I said, 'there must be something for me to do here?'

She finished the cigarette and stubbed it into dust under the toe of her blood-speckled slip-on shoe. I tried to hold her stare, but my vision wouldn't settle. From inside the ward, a boy screamed. Her eyeballs vibrated with exhaustion and I finally figured it out. The darker colour of her left iris, closer to brown than green. She turned to walk away from me and because I could think of nothing else, I blurted out, 'Fadila!'

'Excuse me?'

'Your mother, is her name Fadila?'

'Yes,' suddenly suspicious.

'And she works at the library? At Gazi Husrev-Beg?'

She approached and squinted hard at me, head cocked

slightly to the side. I could see her nostrils flare, hear the slow intake of breath through her teeth. She smelled of rubbing alcohol and stale smoke. I was afraid I would kiss her. I blinked. She slapped me. I blinked again.

'My mother is nearly sixty years old. You want your nearly sixty-year-old mother trying to run through sniper fire with a box of dusty old books in her arms, hmmm? I almost kill her myself when I hear this.'

'I . . . I . . . eh . . . we were trying to save as many . . .' Stuttering like a teenager.

'Books! You and my mother and that fucking director, talking about books as if they are lives. You think that screaming boy cares about some ancient history of Bosnia he will never read? Find me a hundred thousand helmets and bullet-proof vests and antibiotic injections and I will help you save as many books as you want, OK?'

I didn't answer, just stared down at the streaks of gore on my boots.

'You are not as tall as she said.' Her voice softened up for the first time.

'I'm pretty tall,' I said, straightening. 'It's just the bad posture.'

'Come back tomorrow if you want, but I am not here to babysit reporters or put on a show for ghouls. You come, you help or you fuck off, OK? This means standing in water lines, washing bandages, cleaning toilets, bringing patients to bathroom, bringing patients to morgue, going to UNPROFOR post to petition for more help from those useless fucking soldiers. You are willing to do this?'

I nodded quickly and handed her back the half-full box of cigarettes. She cocked her head and stared at me.

'I will consider this my fee for fixing your head, yes?' She smiled at me.

'That was you?' But she had already turned back toward the children's ward. 'I'm Tom, by the way,' I squeaked in that mortifying way you have to cough your way out of. 'Tom Dempsey.'

'I know.'

'What about you, Doctor?' Desperately trying to stop her from walking off.

'Jelena Djordjević,' she called in a sing-song voice over her shoulder. Then she stepped through the gap in the swinging door and out of sight. Outside the hospital's entrance, the moon was beaming down on the cemetery across the road. Holding the dozens of fresh burial mounds in this cold, white light. It should have been frightening – standing out on that exposed hillside with bullet-riddled ambulances screaming in and out of the complex – and it was, of course it was; but to be honest, the whole walk home, for the first time in months, I barely thought about the snipers.

CALIFORNIA

Chapter 6

Maybe it shouldn't come as a huge surprise that we took a wrong turn coming out of LAX and are now getting ready to bed down for the night somewhere in the outer reaches of the Mojave Desert, silent and sulking and feeling every ounce the shower of gormless fuckwits. Speaking for myself, I sort of just assumed that I possessed a keen sense of direction, owing to the fact that I haven't been lost in Dublin since I was a kid. It's only now occurring to me that maybe being able to navigate a small city – one which I've barely left in more than a quarter century – isn't really a special skill; more the kind of basic muscle memory you could drill into a dog over a long weekend. Still, it's a little disappointing to have to cross this off my ever-shrinking Life CV. It'd be a sparse fucking document if I ever gave it tangible form.

A college degree, or at least some manner of diploma, was supposed to have been on there. I somehow scraped a pass on the re-checks of my maths paper and therefore became eligible to attend one of Ireland's fine establishments of higher education. I had chosen Arts, reluctantly, for want of something more specific to focus on, but probably would have abandoned the notion entirely long before Day One had it not been for Eugene and Therese. Neither of them had stayed in school past fifteen, twelve in Eugene's case, and I didn't have the heart to tell them the truth, which was that I just wasn't interested. The idea of sitting in a desk taking notes on subjects I couldn't give a toss about while the rest of the lads were working seemed like the most incredible waste of time back then. They, unsurprisingly, did not see it this way. Eugene gave me a watch that once belonged to his father. He'd had it re-strapped and polished to a high shine just for me, 'to make sure you're on time for your lectures.' I could tell by the look on Therese's face as he handed it over just how much the gesture meant. Gabriel and Clara were worse, God love them – pouring over a thick list of courses to decide which were most compatible with my unique skillset, shooing me away from the table when I started griping or talking the whole thing down. Clara was preparing for her Leaving Cert that year and could be counted on to produce, from thin air as far as I could ever tell, an array of neon highlighter pens and Post-it notes and flash cards whenever there was a decision to be made. For weeks afterwards I'd come upon slips of rectangular paper, in the cracks between couch cushions or stacked up inside a kitchen press, with headings like 'Geography: Pros & Cons' or 'Practicality Vs. Passion' written in neat block capitals. They were all so excited, so fucking enthused by the whole thing; so naturally I ended up disappointing them by packing it in after six months.

'It's just not for me, Clara.'

'First year is always tough, but if you just stick with it you'll get the hang of things soon.'

'I have the hang of things, I'm just not interested.'

'Maybe if you finished out the year. Took some time over the summer to think about it more—'

'It's done, OK. End of story. Time to move on to something else.'

The day I officially dropped out I put Eugene's watch in a drawer, where it's been ever since.

I should, however, mention that I was the only one of the three of us to properly absorb the manic, florescent workings of Los Angeles International Airport before we left the place. If I can retain any of it, Baz will be grateful for this local knowledge in two weeks' time. As things stand, assuming we don't die out here in the desert, the plan for getting back to Dublin (inspired, as you'd expect) is to hang around LAX for as long as it takes a few last-minute cheap seats to open up. If those seats end up being on an Air Finland flight with four stopovers and no meal, then so be it. The return leg of this odyssey can take as much time as it needs to. Since no one has a job or a girl or, let's face it, any kind of social calendar worth mentioning, we'll be in no rush at that end. Baz is on an indefinite leave of absence from his lofty position as a porter in St James' Hospital. For the umpteenth time he was stung sleeping in one of the newly empty patient rooms, while across the hall a brood of grieving relatives waited for the family's bloated, bluing patriarch to be wheeled away to the morgue. I think he may also have been stealing altar wine from the hospital sacristy. We've never actually discussed this, but bottles of the stuff keep appearing in the kitchen cabinets and rolling out from underneath the couch, so I think it's a safe enough assumption to make. I don't judge him for it. Hell, he's paying for half of this trip, he can drink Holy Water from a hip flask if he wants.

I myself have been on and off the dole for the better part of a year, occasionally biting at wedding photography gigs when the chance arises, and despising myself for it. Once or twice a month I take my camera – without question the only item in my possession that is worth more than a week's social welfare payment – and bus it down to some god-awful midlands town to snap pictures of boozy, ruddy-faced muck savages as they lumber across a function room dance floor to a reverb-savaged version of 'Come On Eileen'. If I'm lucky, by the end of the night the remaining aul lads setting up camp at the residents' bar will drag me over for a few free pints and a meandering yarn or two. If I'm very lucky, there'll be a stray bridesmaid or cousin the wrong side of thirty who'll take a shine to me sometime in the early a.m. and I'll end up with a bed for the night. More often than not, though, come two or three o'clock I'll gather up my camera and gear bag, making heavy work of my departure in front of the late barman, before finding a couple of soft chairs in whatever lounge is furthest away from the night's dying festivities. I'll sit low in the darkness with my feet propped up and empty the pack of Camels before nodding off with a wad of sweaty cash pushed down into the pocket of my jeans. It's a glamorous life.

Still, a part of me lives for these nixers, even the most depressing ones. The sulky shotgun couplings in decrepit hotels. The terrified best men necking pint after pint in the build-up to the speeches, loosening their stained ties and shuffling crumpled bits of paper back and forth. The roar of colic-addled babies and the patter of mouthy kids racing around rickety tables, dodging cuffs from barking fathers. Even these jobs are worth the trip. And it's not just the money – though I'd be thoroughly fucked without that. And it's not just the welcome psychological break from thinking about Clara, whatever she's doing right now, while watching day-time talk shows and burning ash holes in the sleeves of my grubby dressing gown at two o'clock in the afternoon – though there's no real harm in that either.

No, they're worth it because regardless of the nonsense spiel I rattle off to confuse stingy farmer Fathers-of-the-Bride over the phone, the truth is that the only time I can snap a decent picture is when I'm wandering alone in these silent stretches of the country, when everyone else has cleared off. Depressed bastard that I am at heart, the only photos I have worth holding on to are the ones I take alone, when the world is catatonic: pools of still black water in sodden stretches of blanket bog; empty birds' nests in the crumbling stone crevices of derelict cottages; the wave-battered sea stack walls off the west coast. Three months ago I heard back from an editor at *National Geographic*. They were putting together an issue called 'Abandoned Places' and wanted to use a half dozen of the photographs I sent in. I told them that Ireland isn't an abandoned place. They said that my version of it is.

Baz's savings, and the relative windfall I got from selling my pictures, are the only reason we've made it this far.

*

I'm in no hurry to get back into that toy car, the traitorous hunk of shit. I've given up trying to get comfortable enough to drop off while Baz snores and Tom shrieks and I slowly go insane. I'd just as soon use a coat for a pillow and curl up in the dust outside. Take my chances with the wildlife. A tiny yellow lizard runs across my shoe and off into the night. It occurs to me that we wouldn't be stranded out here like this if Gabriel was at the wheel. To give him his due, for a man who regularly displayed pretty questionable judgement in most other walks of life, he had decent spatial awareness. Either his gut would have led us to the coast road, which, again, doesn't seem like a task requiring more than the autopilot setting of the basic five senses. Or, even if he did take my shortcut to the middle of fucking nowhere, he wouldn't have let group morale plummet to the point where I'm catching Baz mock throttle me in the rear view mirror.

'The sign said "Other Desert Cities", Karl. How many deserts are connected to the fucking ocean?'

'I thought it was just a name.'

'What kind of demented fucker would put up a sign like that unless there was a desert nearby?'

'Look, it's a totally different culture out here. How am I supposed to know what every random billboard means?'

'It said "desert". The fucking sign had the word "desert" on it!'

'Shut up and let me concentrate, will you?'

'Well maybe if you'd gotten a bit of sleep on the plane . . .'

'Baz, I swear to fucking God if you don't pipe down back there.'

I may, *may*, have overindulged with the whiskey miniatures

on the flight when we hit a vicious bout of turbulence some-where over the Midwest, as many would in the circumstances. It's an unnatural form of transportation. Honestly, though, I don't know which was worse: the plane's make-your-peace-with-God convulsions or the shit-eating grin on Baz's face as he watched me dissolve into a gibbering puddle of nerves while two infants slept on soundlessly in the row beside us.

The lads are still rustling and rocking about in the passenger and back seats of the convertible, head to head at a right angle, Tom's ankles dangling from the open door. The desert air is cool now. I might as well do a lap of the perimeter.

*

Gabriel and me were pretty much on our own from the beginning. Before Baz and Tom and the rest of our intrepid dysfunction brigade came on the scene, it was just the pair of us racing each other back and forth from one tapped-out foster home to the next. We were neighbours, more or less. Just three streets apart. His father died the same year as my own. Single car accident on the Malahide Road. His blood alcohol three times the legal limit. It was no great shock to anyone. Gabriel's mother had bled out in childbirth and his aul lad just couldn't keep it together after that, hard and all as he tried. In a way, his mother's death turned Gabriel into an orphan; it just took another seven years to make it official.

We lost my own da to pancreatic cancer when I was five. It was all over in a few weeks. I think I recall a sterile white hospital room and a man breathing heavy underneath a web of clear tubes, but in all likelihood that came second hand from

Gabriel years later. After he died my mam and I lasted eleven months together. She all but froze to death one bitter night in November of that year. Had it not been for the groundskeeper doing his last rounds of the cemetery she would have. Even after he managed to shake her awake, it took two Guards to pry her skeleton arms loose from the headstone and drag her to the squad car. One of them sat in the back with her, frantically rubbing her shoulders through the emergency blanket till the blue tint faded. That's the version I heard, at any rate.

After Da died, Gabriel helped me fill in the handfuls of hazy, rose-tinted memories I had of him: still frames from Christmastime trips to the live animal crib at the Mansion House, slow-motion footage of the swaying of blue and navy flags the size of bed sheets above his head – Dublin colours from Leinster Championship matches on The Hill. Outings Gabriel had tagged along to on the days his father didn't come home. Pretending he'd joined another family. People would address us as brothers back then and we never bothered to correct them.

Some years later, when I was fourteen and Gabriel sixteen, not long after the third and final parental funeral we attended together, I was given a story about my parents:

An old neighbour of ours named Annie McCabe told me that Mam had struggled with the drink for years before she met my father. Friends spoke to her about it, or tried to, but it wasn't something she was interested in confronting. Not for a long time. Not until she found something she didn't want to lose. He dropped her home, swaying, from a charity dance in town one night, Annie recounted in that dreamy way of hers. Gave her a peck on the cheek and left her to fumble about with her keys till she fell on her face in the hall. I imagine him hiding behind a pillar, waiting to make sure she got herself in all right, agonising as to whether or not he should run back up the steps and help her to her feet. She swore off the stuff for good after that. No exceptions. She never made a big show of the decision either, the way every preachy AA wreck-the-head seems compelled to do these days. No, Annie said; Mam never avoided pubs or refused a glass to clink with at New Year's or sat in her local staring at the illicit golden liquid at the bottom of a tumbler till someone noticed and spoke up. And my father certainly never pushed for that kind of performance, Annie assured me of that:

'He was pure gentle with her always, that man. You'd get these stinking local bowsies, fellas who hadn't been sober a day in their lives, pushing hot whiskies or half pints into her hand at Christmas like they were being dead chivalrous. And God love them I suppose they were, in their own way. But your father would say nothing; he would never be one to lose the head or embarrass anyone for their heedlessness, you see. No, all he'd do in that quiet way he had, would be to slide it toward himself and order up a glass of fizzy orange or red lemonade for your mam. Then he'd put his hand down soft on hers and they'd wink at each other like movie stars and that'd be that. It got to be a kind of game they shared, I think. I always thought it was fierce romantic altogether.'

Annie's a sweet woman, kind of soft-headed in the way she goes on, but nothing but goodness in her. I still see her the odd time, usually at the obligatory Easter Sunday or Christmas morning masses. The ones where I spend post-Communion prayers debating with myself over what I believe, if I believe in anything at all, while trying to work the host down from the roof of my mouth like a bloody kid. I see her sitting there, front pew, with her sister and her nieces and nephews, and *their* little ones, crawling under the benches in their tiny dungarees, staring up at aul lads muttering away to themselves under their breath. Annie's getting to look shook enough since her own husband died last year, but at least she has the extended family to keep an eye on her. I think she would have taken the pair of us in back then, had circumstances been different. She never did have children of her own, for whatever reason. Mam would have seen it as the worst kind of betrayal though. The most she'd permit was Annie's coincidental appearances on our doorstep the rare weeks I was returned to the old house. When the state decided that Mam had cleaned up her act for good this time – not like the last time when she only *claimed* she was back on the wagon, or the time before that when she certainly *seemed* lucid during the interview. Annie would stay up next to the stove in the kitchen reading *Ireland's Own* till Mam came home from the pub. She'd take the curses and the how-dare-yous with a resigned nod of the head, and be banished back to her own 'barren fucking museum' so that Mam could tear the house apart looking for a hidden naggin of Powers she'd finished off the previous night. I'd wake up then, shit-scared of the noise of clinking bottles and the unnatural pitch of Mam's voice talking to herself. I'd pretend Gabriel was there, that he had climbed into the bed next to me and the two of us were reading player profiles from his old issues of *Shoot* till Mam KO'd on the sofa and I drifted off to sleep, head swimming with images of Johan Cruyff and George Best banging in wonder-goals from outside the box.

The next day my mother would throw herself at Annie's feet, me reluctantly in tow, and keen for her former self. She'd wail and choke and fall into Annie's arms till the poor woman had no choice but to forgive her. Once that was all sorted, Mam would ask for one tiny favour. 'Could you keep an eye on Karl for me, Annie? Just for an hour or so while I run a few errands. You know he's too much for me too handle out there, with my nerves.'

I still remember the hot swell of shame I had then, flushing up my neck and into my grubby cheeks, and the look on Gabriel's face when I told him, his tough little fists clenched white. It was all too familiar to him.

We had five sets of foster parents over the course of ten years. Always a 2-for-1 deal; Gabriel refused to go anywhere without me. Said we'd drown ourselves off Dún Laoghaire pier if anyone tried to split us up. No one dared call his bluff. He even convinced them to keep him back a year in school so we could be in the same class together. None of the foster parents were bad people really; one or two were rough tempered from hard living, most were well-intentioned but chronically dull. All but one pair were woefully out of their depth with the likes of us. We were wild, mouthy scuts who resented them for their pity and their charity and the humiliating rigidity of their daily rituals. The way the breakfast table was set and cleared by their train of mute bastards and orphans. The order of the school lunch boxes on the kitchen counter every morning. The watery eyes of the women and the awkward gruffness of the men and tight-lipped smiles from neighbourhood church-goers as we were paraded up and down the aisles in order of our decreasing height.

Being the angry little pricks we were back then, it was always Gabriel and me who'd start fights with the other kids. If ever someone looked crooked at me at school, Gabriel would start swinging digs faster than they could turn back around. In the middle years we got in the habit of saying nothing that couldn't be snarled through bared teeth, and spent more time sulking outside of classrooms than we did sitting at desks. At least once a week we'd shrink down low on the bus seat until all the other kids had gotten off, and ride the thing into O'Connell Street, where we'd sneak into the Savoy for a double feature. Gabriel always devised the most inventive ways of making a few bob disappear from the wallets and purses of any authority figure foolish enough to get settled in his presence. A fake parent, a real parent, a principal, a social worker – Gabriel didn't give a fuck whose money he was liberating for our social fund. He'd buy us bags of salty popcorn and big red Cokes and we'd stay there all day by ourselves, high on our own boldness, practising our excuses between films for when we eventually did have to return home and face the music.

Then it changed. One retired couple – Eugene and Therese Brogan – were far too long in the tooth to still be in the business of domesticating feral pups like us, but I suppose it takes a while to figure out how to do it properly. We were shipped off to their bungalow in Irishtown within a week of Gabriel shot-putting his school bag through the dining-room window of our fourth holding cell in seven years. Dermot – our jailor *du jour* – was a bloated, hen-pecked little fucker who was forever whinging and griping about some perceived slight or another. He threw a wild, off-balance haymaker that missed Gabriel's head by millimetres and connected instead with the edge of the wooden doorframe. Dermot fractured his hand in three places, cursed us out as 'little knacker cunts' and expelled us with a boot swing from Home Sweet Home No. 4.

We've been strong-armed out of an unfortunate number of establishments down through the years, but I still rank that early one as our most dramatic of exits. Stepping into the Brogans' some weeks later, we expected the usual 'stern but fair' warning that they all use in an attempt to lay down the law right away. I had a scowl on me that deserved a clip round the ear, and I was kind of hoping I'd get one too before the day was out, to show Gabriel that I was as every bit as fearless as he.

That wasn't Therese's style though, and it certainly wasn't Eugene's. We got no orders or finger-wagging or reminder of our less-than-exemplary track record. Therese brought us into their pokey little kitchen and plonked two bowls of jelly and ice cream down in front of us.

'Eat away, boys,' she said. 'Yous are like a pair of greyhounds standing there with the drawn faces on ye.'

I looked over at Gabriel with my eyes big as hubcaps. He smiled and shrugged and nodded for me to work away. I barrelled through two helpings while Therese leaned against the stove, waiting for me to take a breath.

'Easy, Karl, you'll be sick all over the woman's clean floor.'

I nodded vigorously and continued inhaling the wobbly slivers of lime jelly, slurping the melting ice cream off my spoon and wiping the dribble from my chin with the sleeve of my jumper.

'Now there's a hungry man,' were the first words we heard Eugene say in that fantastic Dublin gargle of his. He spoke like Ronnie Drew from The Dubliners, and could sing like him, too, when called upon.

'Would there be any of that left for me, *a ghrá*?' he said to Therese, Gabriel and me transfixed by the easy way of them. It was strange not having adults eyeballing us like zoo animals, asking us stupid questions about topics we didn't gave a shite about.

'Don't be giving that "*a ghrá*" business, Eugene Brogan. I had three packets of that stuff in the press at the beginning of this week. Raspberry, strawberry, and lime. Now we've only the lime. Can't you explain a mysterious disappearance like that for me, now?'

'Three packets, you said? –' winking at us '– And two just up and disappeared on you? Well that is a *terrible* thing, Therese, a shockin' thing. Do you think we might have been robbed in the night?'

'Funny now, Eugene, I don't think that, no.'

'Or could it have been the kind of thing where you only *thought* you bought them, but in fact all you did is stand in the shop thinking about buying them and then not end up buying them at all? Maybe you got distracted by a woman's magazine or a nice ironing board or something?' Winking at us again.

'No.'

'Right. Well, you know what must have happened then?'

'I do.'

'Some of those gurriers we do be housing from time to time must have stole them away. We only keep the worst kind of bowsies under our roof these days, lads. Terrible knackers of fellas altogether. Any one of them liable to steal your jelly, *and* your ice cream if they were given half a chance.'

We were beaming up at him at this stage, giggling at the pantomime of the whole thing.

'Thank the sweet babbie Jaysus that Therese does be keeping the ice cream under lock and key underneath the peas in the big freezer at the back of shed, and the *good* ice cream under the bags of sprouts in the far corner of the big freezer at the back of the shed.'

'Ah, for the love of God, Eugene.'

'If word ever got out about those hiding places, we'd be fucked altogether.'

'Language, Eugene! Jesus wept!'

'I've gone too far, lads. Leg it now before she gets the wooden spoon out and tears the arses off all three of us!'

We were in peals, running out into the garden, ducking under the clothes line and over the back wall with him, Therese making moves like she was chasing us till we were round the corner and out of sight. We spent the evening kicking clumps of muck around the football pitches and pucking stones out into the sea with a cracked hurl Eugene had grabbed from against the shed wall as we made our daring escape. When we arrived back that evening, he had us enter the kitchen in a silent *eyes up* manoeuvre, shushing us to keep quiet after his exaggerated system of signals set us off. Therese appeared from behind the fridge, lamped him over the head with a tea towel and announced that he was worse than a kid himself.

Eugene gave a few wolf howls of submission before pulling her into his arms and two-stepping them both around the kitchen floor and out into the garden.

That night Therese served up a feed of steak and chips that even I couldn't finish. Eugene told us about working in London during the Blitz, and how he'd sat on a pub stool staring at an unexploded bomb that had crashed through the roof and onto a pool table in the centre of the room. We were transfixed.

We had four good years living under Eugene and Therese's roof. Great years, really, to give them their due. Job himself couldn't have been more patient with me after Mam died, letting me stay holed up in our room and throw tantrums out of nowhere and curse them out when I needed to.

When I finally wore myself out from roaring and sobbing and punching walls, they talked me through it all in a way that never felt condescending or forced. And they had all the right words. They treated us then, as they always had, like we were real brothers, made us both part of the grieving process because they knew I couldn't do it without Gabriel. When they took us to matches in Croke Park, or into Bewley's on Grafton Street for breakfast, it wasn't to distract us, to buy themselves a few hours reprieve from trying to figure out what to say. No, they did those things because they were kind, and because they knew we were less likely to feel under interrogation wolfing down a fry or screaming at the referee from the Cusack Stand. Eugene told us about alcoholics he knew: decent, hardworking men and women who lost themselves to the drink when a loved one was taken unfairly. *Unfairly*. I remember the two of us nodding our heads furiously when he explained it that way. The way we felt about everything that had happened so far. Like it was some karmic injustice that had been visited upon our families. That's what we had always railed against, I suppose, if we had stopped to think about it. We needed to hear it from an adult though, to have the affirmation that it was nothing we did or didn't do a decade previous that might have helped set it all in motion.

They didn't give us any of that *God works in mysterious ways* bollocks after the funeral either, even though both of them prayed every night before bed. Still do, I'm sure. But they knew it wasn't what we needed to hear then. It was their wisdom we believed in anyway, not God's. Therese just sat us down and told us that things wouldn't always be that way. 'Life will get easier,' she said, 'better, as long as the two of you keep minding each other and don't harden yourselves to the good things in the world.'

We could have gone down a much darker road without them there, Gabriel especially. He was on the brink the year they took us in. I could see the flames leaping around behind his eyes when he was forced to interact with anyone but me. He'd laugh off all his scuffles with foster fathers and local lads once they were done, but there was a rage building inside him that he couldn't hide. Eugene and Therese went about soothing this – covertly, as was their way. Therese once described it to me as 'cutting the briars back so the flowers could grow properly'. Probably the only time Gabriel has been likened to a flower. She brought him to plays in The Abbey, Shakespeare and O'Casey mostly, whenever they could afford it. At first he'd pretend to me like he was only going for her sake, to keep her happy, and that the texts I caught him reading

– *Coriolanus, The Plough and the Stars, Translations* – were 'more shite I have to do for school'. That farce only lasted a few months. He knew well I was on to him and decided to own it before the slagging started, leaving big stacks of books on my bed when he was done with them, pointing out which had the most sex and violence, making every ancient play sound like a spaghetti western.

Eugene took us both out to enough matches in those first few months that when the time came to actually join a club, we didn't need to be asked twice. The thinking was, I suppose, if they've an unusual amount of pent-up aggression, let them exorcise it on the pitch and not in the schoolyard where they're liable to get themselves expelled. And it worked, far as I can remember. By the end of his first year with the U16 team, Gabriel had burst his way through so many tackles, left so many defenders winded and bruised in the muck, that they had to tell him to go easy in training or fellas were gonna stop showing up altogether. We met people through the club too, people we didn't instantly align ourselves against, which was a welcome change. Baz, Tom, older lads who hung out with lads who hung out with girls. We went to teenage discos stinking of aul fella cologne and smoked in big groups behind the club house and hung around the pier at the South Wall, talking about the World Cup and what birds we were gonna get with and who could list off more stupid facts about Thin Lizzy.

Eugene knew Tom's father well from his time working at Guinness, and our two families got to be close on the back of it. Myself, Tom, and Baz – three only children back in the days when this was all-but unheard of in Irish families – played in the same team of unskilled brick shithouses, traipsing around the city trading black eyes with small, sinewy little fuckers who couldn't care less about the score line. Scrotes in tracksuit bottoms riddled with hot rock holes who were more concerned with sticking their heads into our blunt instrument of a backline, which was comprised of fourteen-year-old lads with stubble that'd put grown men to shame. It made for some interesting off-the-ball incidents. Gabriel went out with Baz's cousin, Rebecca, till they got tired of shagging and arguing – two activities which, toward the end of their time together, became inextricably linked. Rebecca lived four doors down from Tom, so Gabriel would drop in before and after these daily lovers' tiffs to give us all the gory details. He once turned up with blood pumping heavy from his nose having been too slow to duck a snow globe. Those pack a wallop, apparently. The fright poor Tom's mam received when she opened the door to find himself looming over her like a sloppy fucking vampire, asking if she'd seen his brother. Goofy, barber's pole grin on his face.

After she'd cleaned him up and told him to try to find a nice girl who wasn't so *volatile,* Gabriel went straight out and plundered a neighbour's flowerbed till he had enough for a bouquet. I think Tom's mam was quite touched actually, entirely justified suspicions aside.

I still can't properly articulate how gutted we were when Eugene and Therese sat us down to explain why they were moving over to Liverpool, at least for a few months. Their second child, Donal, had just been diagnosed with testicular cancer and they needed to be near him till he got the all-clear. There were two young grandkids to be minded while Donal and the wife tried to keep things from falling apart. The guilt those poor people had burdened themselves with, thinking they were somehow *betraying* us by leaving. As if they hadn't enough to be worrying about without losing sleep over the feelings of two long-faced lumbering apes like ourselves. It tears the heart out of me just thinking about it. 'We want you to stay here while we're away,' Eugene said. 'We've put aside a few bob that we want you to have till you both finish school.'

'And we're only a phone call away, boys, you know that, don't you?' Therese said, her hands squeezing ours.

Donal did get better, and then worse, and then better again, thank God. Losing him and Gabriel would have been far too much for their old hearts to take. In the meantime, the two of us, and later Baz, who moved in on Therese's urging after we lost Gabriel, did our best to keep the house in semi-decent nick while we waited for them to announce their return. They call about once a month now, and I give them embarrassingly sparse updates on my life in Dublin, how I'm holding up. We were the worst type of clucking hens in the early years, on the days leading up to their visits home – screeching at each other for dropping food on the carpet or stinking out the bathroom, buying Madeira cakes that no one was going to eat, tearing down the black and white Page 3 girls we had stuck to the fridge door.

They're the wrong side of seventy now though, and Gabriel's funeral was the last time they last made the trip over. The way they looked that day; I'd do anything to forget it.

There've been times since when I should have visited them, times when they dropped hints on the phone that there was plenty of room in the house in Liverpool. I've always bottled it at the last minute though. The thought of showing up at the door, awkwardly invading the home of people I've never properly got to know, people who probably think I'm some shiftless, traumatised chancer squatting in a gaf that could have been sold years back if it hadn't been for their parents' soft hearts.

No, it was too much.

Certainly too much for me to attempt without backup, and backup was gone.

*

'So they tell me your snaps of the old sod are about to be famous?' It's the first time I've heard Gabriel's voice in two years. The first time I've dreamt about him alive. It's comfort to know that there's more of him squirreled away in the vaults of my memory than I thought, but that doesn't mean I can bring myself to look just yet. It's eerie enough out here with the stray howls in the distance and the crescent moon illuminating the contorted limbs of these freaky trees. The way they stand there in their hundreds, like a zombie army waiting to wake up and lurch around the empty desert.

'You heard about that?'

'I hear about everything. We get the news long before any of you fuckers have even made it. One of the many perks of having a seat in the skybox.'

'And?'

'And what?'

'And what do you think?'

'Well, like I've always said to you, landscape shots of fields in Bally-go-backwards aren't really my cup of tea. Seems like a load of bollocks, to be perfectly honest. I'd be more of a connoisseur of the Cindy-Crawford-with-her-tits-hanging-out school of photography. Granted it's a bit of a niche interest but I've always been the discerning type, as you well know. I am proud of you though, sneaky fucker. Stay at it and there might just be hope for you yet.'

Gabriel and I sit side by side in the dust. I'm staring out into the distance, waiting for the creeping reddish-orange haze to push up through the cloudless sky of the pre-dawn desert. I know it's a dream – I can feel the wobbly instability of this landscape, conjured up in heightened tones from recent memory – but that doesn't matter right now. I'll keep it going for as long as I can.

'Now *this* would be some spot for a funeral,' he says. 'You fuckers should have cremated me instead of leaving me to rot in the muck. It's a classier exit. Sprinkled a handful in Dublin, a little bit in Old Trafford, and the rest out here. Well, not *here* here, because this is the middle of fucking nowhere. Out of curiosity, how do you get lost trying to find a coast road? Surely you just drive toward the ocean?'

I just nod, keep looking forward. I'm half afraid he'll have that big purple bruise around his neck, or worse. After nearly two years in the ground. Though, if he does, it'll be by my invention.

'Fine machine you've picked up there though, Karl, it must be said. Mustang convertible, fire engine red, leather interiors. A real "Look out world, here I come with my tiny penis" type of car.'

When I finally do let my gaze flit sideways, he looks the same: ginger-tinted beard; shaved head; over-sized body splashed with Celtic crosses and Maori patterns and winding scrawls of Shakespeare quotes in black cursive; kitted out in a fraying Dublin football jersey, the sleeves rolled up and the navy number 15 on the back peeling off, and a pair of baggy tracksuit bottoms. He's talking again, rambling about the disappearing stars in the brightening sky, pulling on an everlasting cigarette. His slurred loquacity just as charmingly nonsensical as it ever was.

I look back toward the car to make sure they're still sleeping. I'm worried about Tom and what the harsh babble of men and machines that soundtracks LA has done to him, even in the brief time it took us to speed through. In one of the half-dozen tomes I checked out from the library, *The Shell-Shocked Mind*, I read that a car backfiring, a pneumatic drill, the slam of a heavy door – any of these noises, even muted by distance, can serve as a trigger. I think about the traffic on the 405, the effort it took for him to shake away whatever he was seeing in his mind's eye. How he jumped out of his seat when Baz touched his shoulder. Maybe getting lost in the desert isn't the worst thing that could have happened on our first night here. It's peaceful at least. Like camping.

'I'm really afraid this has been a mistake, Gabe.'

Gabriel is slugging something from a label-less green bottle. He grimaces and coughs into his closed fist. He offers it to me but I'm afraid to reach for it in case the whole thing dissolves, so I shake my head no.

'How's he holding up?'

'Not great, but he's surviving, more or less.'

'He looks rougher than you described, Karl. That creepy fucking eye patch for one thing.'

'You don't think it's cool?'

'I think depth perception is cool.'

'Overrated.'

'Seriously, what's the plan here? I mean, it's fucking good to see you – been too long – but Tom doesn't look like he's in great shape over there.'

'Why do you think we're doing this?'

'Yeah, but doing what, exactly? How do you know this Rambo shaman fella isn't a complete quack? I mean, I'm all for making nonsensical decisions on the strength of my gut, but we're talking about a man's sanity here. I've seen more than a few grizzled army vets stumbling through the big double doors up there and trust me, most of 'em are wearing that same expression Tom has on.'

'Yeah, but after that the eternal bliss kicks in though, right?'

'Whatever keeps you going to mass every Christmas.'

'So what do you want me to do? Leave him to sit around on his own at home with only his mam for company? Visiting graves and making excuses as to why he can't meet us for pints once a week till he ends up . . .'

'Like me?'

Silence.

'I dunno, maybe. I'm just trying to do the right thing here. For a change. Who the fuck knows what that is.' I think about holding back with this ventriloquism act, keeping him light and breezy, but then what would be the point of that? Why conjure him up at all just to cut the balls off the whole conversation?

'I am sorry about what happened. The way it happened. I know the three of you still blame yourselves for it—'

'We don't—'

'You do, and there's no shame in saying it, but sooner or later you'll all have to snap out of that way of thinking. Doesn't matter if it's true or not. It does no one any favours. "That way lies madness", as the fella says.'

'Still confidently misquoting the Bard, I see.'

'He's got a phrase for every occasion, brother.'

'Is he up there?'

'Who?'

'Shakespeare?'

'Fuck if I know. The place is a bloody cattle mart, they'll let anyone in. Too busy for manhunts anyway, I've a bar to run up there.'

'Seriously?'

'Damn right seriously. That was always the plan, wasn't it? I've been quietly honing my craft up there these past couple of years, you see; reading up on all manner of recipes for complicated concoctions and elaborate, multi-tiered, flame-enhanced libations. I've been sniffing out rarities from the moustachioed barmen of Manhattan's most famous speakeasies, taking business trips to craft breweries in the Boston and Portland and Milwaukee clouds, sampling Appalachian moonshine from backwoods' stills. I've been wetting my beak with rakija from the Yugoslavs, rum from the Cubans, limoncello from the Italians, akvavit from the Scandinavians – honing my palate with ancient ethnic brews and infusing them together to create super variants. I'm the only game in town on my patch of cloud these days, Karly. The punters are queuing up ten men deep to get in the door.' Who knew I had such detailed and long-winded imagination.

I feel like fucking crying. Why am I doing this again? What do I say to him, this ghost: that the bar was never anything but a pipe dream? That there was a reason we only spoke about it drunk, why we never saved a pound toward the project, why we avoided talking logistics like the plague? How would we have ever acquired the money, the visas, the fucking *wherewithal* to open a bar in America? It was never real. I wonder now if he knew that. Gabriel is out of breath, on his feet with the excitement of it all, but his smile keeps slipping, because how could it not. He flicks his cigarette toward a huddle of cactus plants, pinging it off the top of the tallest, and releases a growl into the night.

'Oh yeah, man, the works: huge live music stage, beer garden on the roof, food menu as long as your arm. Proper food. Not just pub grub and crisps. Every last thing we planned, I have it running round the clock. Well, technically there are no clocks up there but you know what I mean. And guess what I've called the place – you ready?'

'I am.' I wish he'd stop this. I'd stop this.

'The Blarney Stone.'

'Eh . . .'

'You like it?'

'Well . . .'

'Ah, I'm only messing,' he bursts, slapping his thigh and winking. 'I haven't a notion what we're gonna call the shaggin' place yet. I'll think of something. If you've any ideas don't be shy. Puns seem to be the order of the day.'

'Puns?'

'Yeah, you know, like Tequila Mockingbird or Pour Judgement or The Stickit Inn.'

'"The *Stickit* Inn"?'

'Yep.'

'Well the search is over so, you won't find a classier name than that.'

'Sadly that particular gem is already taken. Dive bar a few clouds down; piss-flavoured peanuts and roaches the size of your big toe scuttling across the sawdust floor. You'd be wise not to stick it into anyone you pick up in that place.'

'A crying shame. Back to the drawing board I suppose.'

'You'll come help me with the place though, yeah? Someday down the line I mean, like you said? It's not easy running the show all on my lonesome.'

'Stop, Gabriel, please.'

I can't bring myself to look up at him after I mumble this into my chest. I can feel him standing behind me, waiting for me to meet his stare. I hear the flint strikes of his lighter, the barely audible sound of paper crackling in the stillness.

'I'm not doing anything. This is your show.'

'I know. I get it—'

'No, you don't. You know why I didn't come over here sooner, Karl? To California like, not, y'know.' He jabs his index finger up to the sky.

I sigh and rise to my feet, still not catching his eye.

'Because you pissed away your plane fare on pints and colouring yourself in like an unsupervised toddler.'

'No, well, that was part of it. But I really did want to make it happen, the way we always talked about. I thought we could still do it. I figured I'd take a tour of the coast on my own, scout for locations, see if I could pick up some decent tips. Then I'd come home and you and me and Tom and Baz, we'd make a real plan – a business plan – for how it was gonna go. We could have pulled it off, y'know. The girls would have understood. Christ, part of me was hoping they'd tag along. Clara and you. Me and Anna. The lads and whatever smiley surfer girls can stand them over here. We'd have the run of the place. Dublin to California, Karly, who wouldn't want to try that out for a while? I know you and Clara always dreamt about something like that.'

Now that midnight has come and gone, it's officially eighteen months to the day since I dropped her off at the airport for the second time, in stony silence because of the way we had left it the night before. Because of the roaring and cursing and hands flung high in the air, the frustration that exploded from me a day too soon, and because six months of vague, impossible promises had been exposed for what they were. I wasn't able to follow after Gabriel died, and she was a fool for thinking any different.

'This isn't about Gabriel, Karl, and you know it.'

'Are you fucking serious? How can you *possibly* think that anything happening right now isn't about Gabriel? Seriously, name a topic, name any fucking topic under the sun and ask me if I feel different about it now that Gabriel is dead.'

'Karl, I'm just trying—'

'Name a topic.'

'Fine. You want to play this ridiculous game? Then that's what we'll do. Me?'

'What about you?'

'Do you feel differently about me?'

'Jesus, Clara, I'm trying to make an actual point—'

'And I'm trying to ask you if you still want to be with me. If you want to come to America with me like we've been talking about for the past three years. If you ever meant any of it. If you ever intend to actually *do* anything again.'

We went back and forth with letters once things calmed down. Civil, romantic even. She sent me a picture of her in a tie-dye T-shirt and yellow bike shorts, dwarfed by the fog-obscured grandeur of the Golden Gate Bridge. She was beaming at someone I hoped was a passing tourist. She sent it to me with a note that read: 'It's really not too late for us.' After that I took down her picture, and the fold-out map of California, and all those other things – photos, match tickets, pin-up calendars – that seemed sunny and beautiful and jarringly insensitive in the wake of what had happened. Like even the idea of planning a new life when his had been snuffed out was an act of disloyalty. Another betrayal. I stopped answering her letters after that. It was all too late. We were so far away from one another then. Now, if I hopped in the car and put the pedal down, I could be on her doorstep in seven hours.

My hands tremble and I can feel the vomit rising up at the base of my throat. I gulp huge breaths of stale air into my lungs as if to push back the expulsion, but it's no use. I take off my shirt, knowing it's coming, and wait. Within seconds I gag and hack and spit a tiny blob of brownish phlegm onto the ground between my feet. Between retches, I try to speak.

'This isn't, I mean, this is just me talking to myself here, man. It's not doing anyone—' But Gabriel doesn't stop.

'—I left it too late though, that was the problem. Never made it to the travel agent's. Just couldn't. Anna gone. You lads off wherever. Sitting there alone in the room or on lunch break at work or even just taking a piss in an empty pub jacks, and my heart would start beating like crazy. I'd start to sweat and shake and this fucking black haze would dissolve in through my line of vision and it'd be all I could do to grab the sink so that I didn't pass out. For the life of me I couldn't figure out what was wrong.'

'But you, you never said anything at the time.'

'Ah sure, what was there to say? I tried to a couple of times but you weren't, I mean, it's not our way, you fucking know that as well as me. I couldn't even articulate what was wrong. We're not built for long dark nights of the soul, Karl, they're not in our nature. There's never any solution at the dawn of them, anyway.'

'So, I mean, what's your point?' I have to end this. It's time to wake up.

'Christ you've got to be a moody bollocks since I left. My *point*, if I have one, is that you can't half-ass this. Sometimes the distraction, the change of scenery, can do wonders for a man's psyche. Maybe that would have been enough for me, the state I was in. This distraction might be good for you, and for Baz, and who knows, Tom might well get something out of it too. But it won't be enough. Don't expect miracles from your doc on the coast either. There's no magic cure-all for the kind of thing he's going through. You need to be in this for the long haul and let go of all the rest of it, the stuff you've been stewing on. For him.'

'And what makes you such an expert?'

'Nothing, I'm an expert in bullshitting, booze, Man United, and fuck all else. But I'm happy now, and believe me, as gregarious a bastard as I am, that wasn't always the case, you know that as well as anyone. That has to be worth something, right?'

'Yeah, maybe.'

'I'm also your surrogate older brother and psychological mentor and as such it is my sacred duty to guide you through the rough terrain of modern life.'

'Mentor.'

'Yup, death has made me sage. I've got a shitload of wisdom stored up in this brain. If you had sense you'd be taking notes.' He takes a huge slug of his concoction, a stream of it trickling down his chin and bouncing off his knee.

'Well you certainly look the part anyway.'

'C'mere, speaking of the tats, check out this one I just got finished.' He pulls the front of his ancient Dublin jersey up to his Adam's apple to reveal an impressively detailed constellation of stars inked, collarbone to hip, across his entire torso. They pulse and swirl and seem to expand out beyond the canvas of his body till a wide chunk of the universe fills my entire field of vision. It's like he's chameleoned himself into the infinite desert sky behind us.

'Eh. What do you think?'

'I think if the bar business doesn't work out you can always join the circus up there.'

'Fuck off.'

'Are you happy though? Really? You're not just saying that?'

'Does it matter?'

'Oh course it fucking matters.'

'Why? So you can let him go too? Clear your conscience? What if I told you there was nothing at all?'

*

In lieu of a rooster, I'm interrupted by the familiar hacking sound of Baz's lungs stuttering back to life. I'm lying in the dust, neck aching, sweat beads inching their way down the sides of my face. Gabriel is gone. Baz stretches against the body of the car, snorts his nose clear and gobs an enormous green blob as far as it'll go.

'Charming,' I murmur, beating the dust from my clothes. Tom emerges from the brush, wading through prickly vegetation as he fastens his belt. I can see the bags underneath his eyes from twenty paces.

'Morning, girls,' Baz announces blearily, cracking the bones in his neck. 'Will we try this again?'

Sarajevo, December 15, 1992

'We will play cards and drink and talk. We will not be having sex with each other tonight.'

'Tonight?'

'Perhaps not any night. I am still making my decision.'

'About me?'

'Yes. About your, how you say, "moral fibre".'

'Ah.'

'So there will be no sex until I have decided.'

'Understood.'

This conversation, or to be more accurate, clarification, occurred between short, breathless sprints as we made our way toward the hotel. We heard the crack of a rifle shot in the near distance and dropped low behind the back wheels of an abandoned van, blanketed with fresh snow.

'Is there anything I can do to improve my chances? On the moral fibre decision front, I mean; not, you know, the sex.'

'You do not want to have sex? This is the Catholic guilt I have heard about, yes?'

'God is always watching, Jelena. Especially sex, he loves watching people have sex. Can't help himself.'

'And he does not approve?'

'Outside of marriage? No, he's very old-fashioned that way.'

'An old-fashioned pervert, then, your god?'

'In a nutshell.'

'We will go on three, yes?'

'To which car?'

'To the hotel.'

'You think we can make that?'

'We will soon find out.'

As we passed through the bar, Jelena made a point of removing her ski jacket to reveal to the assembled masses of shivering drinkers her clean, white doctor's coat. It turns out she went to school with the new bartender. They congratulated each other on still being alive, which I caught, and then traded two lines, which I did not, before dissolving into peals of laughter.

'Tom, this is Goran Halilović. He has asked me if I am intending to steal your organs like I did to the other men.'

'And?'

'And I tell him, no. I am euthanizing all of the war correspondents so that we will have food for the winter.'

'I see. And that doesn't violate the Hippocratic Oath?'

'It is a, how you say, "grey area", but this is wartime, Tom, we must all make sacrifices. Even you.'

'Do I at least get a plaque or a statue for my sacrifice? So that future generations will know about my contribution to the war effort.'

'Goran will name a drink after you.' Goran nodded sagely, as if already settled on the recipe for my post-cannibalisation cocktail.

We went upstairs with two Tasty Toms, which as far as I could tell was just a heavy pour of whiskey and soda with a green umbrella hanging over the rim of the glass, and settled cross-legged on the floor between the beds. The sniper fire and low booms of distant ordnance were pretty much unrelenting throughout. Only twice, over the course of some three hours, did Jelena pause and release a tiny shudder, as if the accumulated weight of all those blasts and bullets needed to be shaken off before she could continue.

'Do you have any threes?'

'Go fish. Have you got any tens?'

'You can also go and fish.'

'Damn. I could have sworn I was good at this game.'

'It is seeming like that is not the case, Tom.'

'I hope you don't think less of me as a man.'

'Impossible. My opinion of you cannot get any lower.' She blazed a smile at me and scooped up one the discarded drink umbrellas, clamping the toothpick-sized wooden stem between her pressed palms, and twirled it back and forth so that the floral patterns became a blur of red on green. I picked up my own and, after carefully popping off the top, peeled free and unrolled the narrow length of Chinese newspaper that sits underneath the umbrella like a collar.

'Now, if you can translate what it says I will really be impressed.'

'Well my Chinese is a little rusty, but I'm pretty sure it's the secret recipe for Tasty Toms. Thought to be lost for centuries.'

'I knew Goran could not create a drink this complicated,' she said, sloshing the diluted whiskey around in her glass. 'I say to myself, "this must be an ancient Chinese formula".'

'And here's your proof. You'd better hang on to that scroll, we can start our own drinks company when this is all over.'

We flirted back and forth like that, trading easy nonsense

to make each other smile, until the drinks were finished and the cards abandoned in a pile by the bedside locker. And then I said something I should have had the sense not to.

'That was some rush, sprinting that final stretch to the hotel. Felt like we were in a war movie or something.' Her face changed then, turned cold, and she cocked her head slightly as though she was trying to figure me out.

'This is not the first time you have said something like that.'

'I'm repeating myself already. See, I told you I wasn't that interesting.' Nothing.

'This "war movie" expression. Is that what you are thinking?'

'No, I mean, of course not, I—'

'Because this is not a film, Tom. It is important that you understand this. It is not a Hollywood movie or a documentary or a news report. It is life, real life, for many thousands of people. It is real life for me and for my mother and Goran and for all the people you will never meet. I must know that it is also real life for you before we continue this.'

'It is, Jelena. I promise it is.'

'I hope this is true,' she said, squeezing my hand, and we left it at that.

Chapter 7

Below us on the desert floor is a camp. Or what I can only assume is a camp. Four tents – three near-identical khaki-green teepees and one a sort of rainbow blob, billowing outward from a straining central pole – form a wideish square, if you get liberal with the trail of yucca plants linking one corner to the next. In its centre is makeshift gazebo – a blue bed sheet with a hole in the middle stretched taut over four thick branches shoved into the ground – protecting a few lawn chairs and an extinguished fire. There's a mustard VW bus that's seen better days, and a few mysterious upright structures covered over with plastic sheeting. We are, to absolutely nobody's surprise, lost again. I refuse to take all of the blame for this second detour. I'm driving, so by the unwritten rules of labour division one of those other two useless lumps of shite should be on navigation duty. And by 'navigation' I don't mean Baz barking in my ear 'I still can't see the ocean' every ten minutes while the wind makes fucking origami shapes with our only map, may it rest in peace.

Anyway, we're thirsty and cranky and stiff as fuck from last night's campout, and this micro settlement appears before us like a sort of bargain basement mirage.

'Should we go down and say hello?' Tom asks.

'I dunno,' I say, 'they might think we're trying to rob them if we just sneak up at this hour of the morning.'

'Rob *them*?' Baz says, setting up what is sure to be another expansive tinfoil hat theory. 'They're probably part of a drug cartel, hiding out here after shooting up half of Los Angeles. I don't think they're worried about us robbing them.'

'What could you possibly be basing that on, Baz?'

'They're hiding out in the desert in the middle of the summer. Who'd be stupid enough to do that if they weren't on the run?'

'Who says they're hiding out?'

'What else would they be doing?'

'Camping, maybe?'

'Ah, don't be so naïve, Karl.'

'They've built a shagging gazebo, Baz. There's a bra hanging off the side of it.'

'I think I see a frisbee down there,' Tom says, amused. That seals the deal. My mouth is too dry to smoke and the backwash-heavy quarter bottle of near-boiling water we have in the boot is not going to be much good to any of us. On top of that, after whatever the hell the interaction with Dream Gabriel was last night, I'm too rattled to drive anywhere. Even if we hadn't gotten lost I wouldn't trust myself to navigate coastal traffic in this state. It was all I could do to hide it so far. Twice already Baz has asked me what's wrong.

We wave our arms back and forth on the trek downward,

trying to catch the eye of a bare-chested lad doing what looks like yoga, afraid to shout in case he gets the wrong idea, but he's happily ensconced in his own little world. Lids clamped shut, he's pushing the palms of his hands slowly through the air over his head, moving in exaggerated steps around the gazebo. He looks to be about our age, maybe a little older. All sinewy muscle and deep tan with a scruffy, sun-bleached Viking beard and triple-fastened dreadlocks slapping against the small of his back as he walks. Upon closer inspection, he's also bollock naked. Fantastic. We've reached level ground and are now only about ten feet away from the camp. Twice, Yoga Lad has moved within striking distance of us before turning back around, eyes still closed, dick still out, completely oblivious. I thought this shite was supposed to make you *more* aware of your surroundings. From a cluster of shrubs on the edge of the camp, a line of tiny baby quail scuttle along behind their mother, her top knot of feathers bending outward like a question mark. We exchange shrugs, open our mouths one by one to announce our presence, and then chicken out. This goes on for a minute, maybe two, before the half moon flap of another khaki tent falls forward into the dust and a girl, naked except for a silver bracelet and a pair of acid-washed denim shorts, steps out into the sunlight. She takes her tattooed left wrist in her right hand and reaches backwards with both arms until her shoulder blades make a muffled crack. If we had any decency, or cop on, we would look away at this point. We'd turn one hundred and eighty degrees, cough, and wait to be given the green light. Instead, we stand there slack-jawed, staring at the perfect curves of her body as she stretches away the night's cramped sleep. She leans forward, holding the toes of her foot till her head and heel are level. We're close enough to see the cracked callouses on her sole, the flaking purple varnish on her toenails. I'm about to say something, I swear to God I am, when she spins silently out of this position, her eyes rising on the turn till they're looking upward into mine.

*

The girl's name is Tina and, angel that she is, she has seniority here. She dropped off the grid some years back and others followed. Though we've been told time and again over the past three days that there is no hierarchy, no power structure, no structure of any kind really. Hard to form a respectable Council of Elders when you're shitting into a sawdust bucket, I suppose. Every year they break off, spend a month or two working – bartending, surf lessons, selling paintings, hauling fish out of the ocean – and then regroup to decide where to make camp next. The ocean, the desert, the forest. Anywhere they'll be left alone. They refer to themselves as 'Formers', as in: former high-school dropout and semi-professional skateboarder turned surf instructor (yoga lad, aka Eddie); former Ivy League business students turned painters and furniture carvers (Mia & Tyrell); and former Juilliard graduate and backing dancer turned bartender (Kim, who Baz, I can tell, has already fallen hard for).

I like these people. Even Eddie. They're at ease around us, I think, because we don't question why anyone would choose to live like this, to wander off the grid and stay there. We don't undermine their existence, and they assume it's because we're like-minded, or open minded, or at the very least non-judgmental.

We, I've come to realise, are none of these things. Not really. Not to a degree that anyone would go out of their way to commend anyway. What we are is afraid. Afraid of this back-story bartering, of being asked to engage beyond an observer level. We tell them things about ourselves, who we are, where we're headed, and why, but it's all vague half-truths. How can you tell an escape story when you're still exactly where you always were? No one wants to hear that kind of dour shite, even if we could articulate it. It feels pathetic just to think about. Not that we haven't tried to mimic their style. I even sort of like the idea of being able to condense your entire history into a couple of easily digestible sentences. The main problem is, we're very, very bad at it. Honestly, I feel like that midget out of a *Twin Peaks* dream sequence sometimes.

But they don't push, in fairness to them. Even Kim, who speaks at a rate of knots even when she's stoned, lets our explanations taper off into silence without pressing for more. I was going to venture a guess, I'd say we have Tina to thank for this.

Tina is different from the others. She's been nomadic a year longer than Eddie, two years longer than the other three, and there's a sort of shamanic quality to the girl. She tells stories about all kinds of things: the way the dawn noises change with the seasons out here in the desert; the time she spent hiding out on the Channel Islands off the California coast, just her and the miniature island foxes; finding a body half-buried in the undergrowth somewhere off the trail in Los Padres

National Forest; watching the gargantuan elephant seals splay out in their thousands across the shore at Piedras Blancas.

She listens to the others talk about the details of their old lives as if hearing it all for the first time. Something which, given the length of the days out here, I highly doubt. At night, when we're hunkered around the fire pit, Kim asks her for a nature story and the others, us included, cheer on the request. In three days I've never seen her wear more than the sparse getup she put on in the minutes after our intrusion. That's how she looks making coffee in the morning and that's how she looks telling stories in the flicker of firelight at night. Like a Victoria's Secret model wandered off a beach shoot, through a dust storm, and into the desert. I can't explain why exactly, but it doesn't seem to matter out here. She doesn't flirt, or entertain shitty attempts at flirting from anyone else, gamely as I tried in the opening hours of our stay.

Her role in the camp is maternal, and after the first night that's the way we see her, too. Textbook maternal that is; the *Little House on the Prairie* variety rather than the booze-sodden, amnesic version of my personal experience. Tina sits in the same uncomfortable pose for hours while Mia paints her aura in blues and purples, cooing praise from the corner of her mouth. The finished product always looks like someone exploded a Smurf and then tried to paint over the evidence, but then, I know sweet fuck all about art so maybe each one is a masterpiece. She argues with Tyrell about systems of governance, the two of them standing at invisible lecterns, lambasting politicians I've never heard of. Bob Dole? (When you find yourself getting chastised for being uninformed by a pair of bare-foot nomads out on the far reaches of civilization, it's probably time to buy a newspaper.) She indulges Eddie's wandering, penis-heavy yoga moves and Kim's all-cylinders diatribes about 'sleazeballs' of the music business with a level of benevolent patience I couldn't master in a hundred years. And she treats us like we've always been amongst them, like our clumsiness is actually contributing to this weird symbiosis, which feels nice, however misguided it might be (Tom in particular, despite the height disparity, has been placed snugly under her wing). In fact, pretty much the only thing she refuses to do, always with a soft shake of the head, is talk about where she comes from. Why she moved to California from whatever mysterious origin spot she hails from in the first place. Who she is.

'I've tried a few times,' Mia tells me, 'but she isn't interested in talking about it. Something happened, probably something bad, but she says it's all in the past now so it doesn't matter. I wouldn't get into it with her. You won't get very far.'

I won't. I haven't. Not really. Tina's origins are not our business. Just like Gabriel, and Sarajevo, and home are not hers, or anyone else's for that matter. Anyway, her gaps have set a precedent for ours. They've let us off the hook. Without them, everything about our weird fucking presence here, our ominous silences and knowing looks, would seem even more suspicious. Dangerous even. The kind of thing a group like this one might not want around them, throwing ungainly shadows across their sunlit utopia. We might be asked to leave, and we're not ready to leave just yet. Not when things are the brightest they've been in months.

Besides, I'm beginning to wonder if this might the best spot for Tom, long-term. If this kind of bucolic, kumbaya idyll is as good a place as any for him to get his head screwed back on. It's quiet and, as far as I can tell, sniper rifle and mortar shell free; the pace of life has been slowed to a sloth crawl, and God knows Tina seems better equipped to coax him back into the world of the present than we'll ever be. She knows when to engage him and when to let him rest. She's altered her elaborate task rota so that he shares her chores. She even washed his spooky, dust-streaked eye patch for him. There's no pressure on him to respond to any particular therapy, or dig through the wreckage of his memory for answers, or navigate the rough, loud terrain of 'normal' society. Whatever the fuck that even is. Out here, with her, it's stress free. Maybe that's all he needs.

Sarajevo, February 3, 1993

Of course I feel guilty. I know it'll be twice as hard without Da there to talk her down, to still the shaking in her hands with his own, distract her with stories she's heard a thousand times before. None of this is fair on her, I'm not going to sit here and claim any different. But I had to come back. Christ, on some level she must understand that. She still has her house and her routines and her faith. That's something, enough to keep her going at least. What the hell do these people have right now? If I'd stayed away, what would I have even accomplished here? A couple of months of running errands for the hospital, of standing around gawking at corpses and rubble. It just wouldn't be right. I know she hoped the money Da had squirreled away for me would go toward a house or a car or, God help us, a wedding, and maybe some of it still can someday. But the rates at the Holiday Inn are rising with every passing month and that has to be the priority now. I'll call home more often, send more letters, put more of myself into them for her. I'll be kinder when I get back, more patient. I just need a little more time.

*

Mac got in late last night. Shaking snow from his matted hair. I was in the centre of the room talking to Jake – his new producer. Mac and Jimmy sat at the far end of the bar. Goran poured them doubles each and they clinked and downed their glasses in one without looking at each other. Mac held two fingers in the air while he caught his breath and Goran refilled with a nod. I was excited. I hadn't seen Mac in a month. I wanted details about wherever he had been, the things he'd seen out there.

'Wait till the morning,' Jake said when I stood up to join them, 'you won't get anything out of him tonight.'

'Why?'

'They've been up north, at one of the camps.' I nodded and sat back down. I listened to the pianist play 'Sarajevo, My Love', a mournful cover of the ballad I've heard crackle through dying radios one hundred-odd times these past months, before turning in for the night. About an hour later Mac appeared at my door with a bottle of whiskey and asked if I was sleeping. I told him no and he side-stepped me into the room.

'I'm sorry to hear about your old man.' He poured us a couple of large measures and tucked himself into the corner, resting his head against the stained mattress that keeps the light and the bullets out.

'Thanks,' I said, clinking his glass. 'At least he held on till I got home. I had a week or so with him before he went.'

'How's your mother taking it?'

'She's pretty religious, which helps, I think.'

'And you?'

'Still above ground, same as yourself.'

'Wanna talk about it?'

'Maybe another time.'

'I wasn't sure you'd be back. Seven months is a helluva lot longer than most last.'

'You've been here eight.'

'Yeah, but I'm an old hand at this, Tom, a grizzled fucking lunatic who's spent years learning to repress all this senseless gruesome war shit, and I still haven't got it down. Believe me. But more importantly, I'm getting paid. You're just a fucking masochist getting baptised with fire for no good reason. If I didn't know better I'd say you get off on it.'

'You ever think about writing poetry, Mac? Or maybe pop songs? You've got a very lyrical turn of phrase when you want to.'

'Seriously, Tommy, do yourself a favour and get out of Dodge. I know I brought you here but I'm gonna feel like a real piece of shit if you get yourself blown sky high on one of your hospital runs. Think about it, will you?'

'I dunno, maybe. At least here I can make myself useful though, you know. When I'm not getting in the way, at least. I think if I went home I'd just sit around watching the news all day, feeling like I'd abandoned the place.'

'Would that be so terrible? You'd be part of a big fucking club.'

'I can hold on for a while longer. Who knows, maybe the NATO jets are fuelling up as we speak – cargo holds full of hope and feeling the need for speed.' We laughed like bitter old men and sat smoking in the darkness, listening to the gunfire outside.

'How was the trip up north?'

He shook his head and took a huge slug of whisky, finishing the glass and reaching for the bottle that stood next to my last dying candle.

'That bad?'

'Yup.'

'Wanna talk about it?'

'Nope.' I wasn't surprised. Why should I hold him to a different standard?

*

I woke to the sound of a fist jack-hammering the door. Jimmy. We'd only been asleep for a couple of hours. Mac was still comatose on my floor, a tiny pile of cigarette ash floating in the puddle of drool beside his cheek. Jimmy clapped a hand on my back and said sorry for your loss man but we gotta get going asap. He gave Mac a few light kicks and told him to wake the fuck up, that there was something happening in an abandoned nursing home in Nedžarići, a Serb-held suburb near the airport.

'Get up, Mac, you drunken jackass, I'm not missing another story to hold your hair back over the toilet.'

'Unless fucking Boutros Boutros-Ghali is standing on a tank, doling out free blow-jobs, I don't want to fucking know, all right?'

'Tom, help me out here, please?'

'Fine. You tie him up, I'll hold the pillow over his face.'

Between us we managed to drag him, swinging haymakers and releasing the foulest streak of curses I've ever heard from an American, to his feet. We perp-walked him to the bathroom where he hocked up some phlegm and squeezed a full tube of travel-sized toothpaste into his mouth, swallowing the whole thing in one gulp. Ten minutes later we were piling into the Land Rover. The driver and Jimmy in the front. Myself, Mac, and the boy who was to be our guide crushed together in the back seat. He couldn't have been older than eight, but the boy had run, alone and exposed, through the snow-blanketed field that sits across the road from the burnt-out Unis Towers. Past mounds of broken glass and rusted car parts and jagged lumps of shrapnel, until he reached the back door of the hotel. Christ only knows how he made the four-mile trek from Nedžarići alive. Six more elderly residents had frozen to death in the night, he said. The water and heating fuel and stoves that UNPROFOR had promised still had not arrived and there was nothing left in their stores except rice and rotting cabbage. One of the last remaining employees had been shot through the neck chopping wood this morning. The boy had been sent out to find a reporter. A staff member had written everything down on a slip of paper. It was damp from the sweating of his clenched fist.

The road to Nedžarići was in bad shape. Holes as large as kids' paddling-pools, some still smoking. We drove slowly, past soldiers in blue and grey uniforms who snorted globs of snot onto the ground. At an old police barracks we were told to step out of the car. Our driver detailed our credentials to a bald, heavy-set commandant who rubbed his hands together and rolled his eyes, issuing a warning as he waved us on.

'What did he say, Tom?' asked Mac.

'He said that this road will be closed to everyone soon,' I told him, 'and to do whatever we are doing fast.'

The nursing home faced out onto an exposed stretch of road. As we drove around the back of the building I could see the axe lying in a pool of blackening blood beside the tree stump where, till this morning, logs were split. I thought of Jelena, and how she said the birds have left the parks of Sarajevo, because all of the trees have been cut down for firewood. How silence follows carnage. We stopped the car, ducked out silently, and ran, single-file, toward the back door. It swung open before the boy's finger touched the doorbell. A gaunt, fair-skinned woman in her forties hurried us inside. Her hair was stringy and grey, hanging across her face, and there was a wooden crutch tucked tight into her armpit. '*Brzo, udite*,' she said to us, kissing the boy on the top of his head as he held her tight around the waist. She rubbed his shoulders, took the blanket from around her own and wrapped him up in it.

Inside, the smells of infection, and shit, and death. Dark, stained bed sheets covered the windows. A yellowed five-litre water container affixed to a sled. Death rattled from the shadows all around us. The still bodies of ten bundled-up geriatrics beside a tiny wood-burning stove. I thought of Eugene and Therese. How their joints and knuckles ached in the damp weather. A ginger cat nuzzled against the face of one of these crumpled forms. Her right eyelid was only half closed.

'She passed last night. We try to keep the others as warm as we can but it is too cold and we are all hungry. Shivering muscles waste energy.' Jimmy and Mac nodded slowly while I translated as best I could. Jimmy's camera panned across the bodies. 'It is too dangerous to find wood. I tried to tell Davor this but . . .' She trailed off like that, turned her attention to the stove. She lowered herself with a grimace, opened the latch and pushed two twisted-up sticks of newspaper into the tiny huddle of flames. Jimmy followed Mac from room to room, recording everything. I tore pages from an old copy of *Oslobodjenje* and scrunched them into tight cigars. The obituaries section made up two of the eight pages. The dead warming the dying. The woman carefully dripped water from a cracked china jug onto the moulded paper kindling and transferred it to an empty wicker basket beside the stove.

'When it dries and hardens,' she said, noticing my confused stare, 'the paper burns for longer.'

'Do you think the report will help?' I asked, because it seemed like the only question I could ask.

'Perhaps.' She was squeezing the hand of a pensioner whose laboured breathing rose up like chimney smoke from inside a makeshift balaclava of wool and tea-towel cloth. 'Perhaps not. We have petitioned the UNPROFOR soldiers many times to evacuate these people, to bring generators and food and men for the ones who must stay. They tell us that nothing can be done. Now it is too late for so many. Every night they die shivering. People who would live a decade more in another city, in another time.'

We'd been in the building less than half an hour before a soldier appeared at the door. The woman translated his barks, and told us it was time to go. She thanked us for coming and urged us to tell whoever we could about their situation. When I looked back toward the open stove latch, I saw that the fire had gone out.

Chapter 8

Relaxing as it's been here in sunny Middle of Nowhere, for the first couple of days I kept waiting for one of them – most likely Eddie – to let it slip. The real reason they were doing this. Were they waiting for the Mothership? The second coming? The end of days? Was this the period of downtime while The Leader went to pick up the keg of Kool-Aid? It took a solid forty-eight hours before I abandoned the notion. Tina could feel the cranky-fucker suspicion emanating from me and did her best to find reasons to turn inside out anything with even the faintest whiff of mystery about it: the bus cupboards, the bejewelled trunk at the back of her tent, the mechanics of the sawdust toilet (which I've had to empty *three* times, to Baz's one, by the way, even though we all know who's been making the largest deposits into that diabolical thing), even the chamberless innards of a replica pistol, kept on hand in case there was anyone they couldn't scare off with numbers alone. There were no sacred texts or animal bones or ceremonial robes. No oily Chosen One and his harem of child brides. No one asked us for any money or to swear any blood oaths. They're a tight unit, but they argue and tease and confide in one another like any ordinary group of friends. In her own words, 'there really is nothing to be afraid of here.'

In the mornings we drink coffee and eat spicy potato chunks fried in a spitting pan over an open fire. We hike languidly across tourist trails, making a show of hiding behind the stones and clumps of yucca plants when strange voices waft around the bends in the path. We watch the silhouettes of death-wish climbers as they scale mountainous rock faces in the middle distance. We eat picnics on the tops of huge boulders and smoke fat, baggy joints in the evening when the sun drops low. We pick our spots between the shrubs and cacti on the desert floor and wait for jackrabbits, kangaroo rats and camouflaged iguanas to make their moves. In the wee hours of the morning, coyotes chorus howl. During the high hot stretch of mid-afternoon, we lie in the shade and sup water from gallon jugs refilled from a tap in the hardscrabble town outside Joshua Tree. Baz and Kim poke at one another like teenagers through it all. More than once I've caught him giggling. I didn't think someone who both sounds like and weighs as much as a small tractor would be physically capable of giggling, but there you go. More power to him I suppose.

Tina takes Tom on long evening strolls, out toward the wavy horizon line. They start out and come back in silence but seem at ease in each other's company, which is a hell of a lot more than can be said when Baz and I are alone with him. Maybe she'll coax something out of him that we couldn't. A particular siege memory that's been wrecking his head or a recurring dream he can't shake or a plan to murder us all in our sleep. Useful snippets of info like that. We've slowly, very slowly, taken to revealing more about who we are and why we're here. Not everything, obviously, that would be impossible, but enough to let them in. It's the least they deserve, and the fact that everyone but Tina is so damn candid about their myriad skeletons – Tyrell's infidelity during his semester abroad, Eddie's father's jail time, Kim's drug issues – makes it stranger to be the ones holding back. On top of that, they've all heard Tom yelping in the night by now – the volume holding strong – and short of telling them he's possessed by the devil, the truth, or a version of it, seemed like the easiest option.

Mostly though we only go as far as we think Tom can handle. Mostly we just tell them ancient history from back home. Anecdotes about growing up in a place that bears no resemblance to anywhere they've ever been. These are the stories I like to think about, the ones I drift into to distract myself, so the telling comes easy. Sometimes, when I'm deep in the middle of one, I see Gabriel's washed-out desert form standing in the distance, tapping the outside of his wrist, shaking his head like I'm some terrible fucking disappointment, and I let Baz take over the narration and close my eyes. If he's so fucking wise then why'd he go and top himself, that's what I really want to ask him, the smug arsehole. It hasn't even been a week; the Restless Souls people aren't gonna turn us away at the gate because we missed our arrival date by a couple of days, for Christ's sake, and yeah, Tom's not getting any better, but he's not getting any worse either and maybe a spell out here will end up doing him the power of good.

Gabriel didn't have the answers when he was alive so why the hell would he have them now that he's nothing but an echo rattling around in my head?

*

'Broken.' That was the word Tina used to describe him this afternoon. We were dozing around the fire pit, half-watching the others play volleyball over the clothesline we rigged up between the bus and our car's antenna.

'Ah, just a little bent,' I said. 'And to be honest I'm pretty sure I did that on the drive down. I'll straighten it out with pliers before we return the thing. It'll be good as new.'

'Not the antenna,' she said softly, 'Tom.'

'What? No, he's just, he's been through some stuff, you know.'

'I do, and he needs help.'

'I know, and we're gonna, I mean, we're still planning on going, but I thought you and him talked things through a little bit.' She laughed at this, but not cruelly, just in that exasperated way people seem to do when we're caught stumbling our way through situations that would have benefitted from the application of a little more reason. I'm no stranger to the sound. There was a bird circling on the wing above us. A red-tailed hawk or a turkey vulture, I still can't tell the difference no matter how many times I'm told.

'He's sweet, Karl, and gentle, and yes, we talk about some things, but I'm not a professional, and he *needs* professional help. You're going to have to follow through with it, this plan of yours. Yesterday, out in the desert, he didn't know who I was. He kept muttering something in a language I didn't understand. Bosnian, I guess. By the time he came back to me he was so confused, so lost. I'm worried about him, and I know you and Baz are too.'

I'm ashamed of myself now, like we've inflicted something upon her. Something this entire new existence she's carved out for herself has been designed to avoid.

'Listen,' she says, 'we love having the three of you here, you know that, and you're welcome to stay for as long as you like. But if you really want to help him, I think it might be time for you all to move on. I've been around people like Tom before. Years ago now, but I remember. Most of the time it didn't end well. Those pages, I mean, I can't even imagine.'

'Pages?'

'The box he brought back from over there. You've seen them, right?'

*

I hadn't of course, though I had noticed the battered metal box that Tom has been lugging awkwardly around with him since we picked him up at the airport. Not often, just once or twice while he was transferring it in and out of that drifter's bag of his. It's about the size of a hardback dictionary, with a latch that has to be forced closed. There's no lock on the thing. I just assumed it held a few harmless trinkets, mementoes he picked up along the way: match books, shell casings, photos of his girl. That kind of thing. Tina said no. She said it was something we needed to be aware of.

For a few moments I thought about confronting her, getting up on my high horse about privacy or over-familiarity or some other transparently defensive bullshit. But I was embarrassed, and that embarrassment made me hate her a little bit. All that holier-than-thou perfection, how much sense the serene, psychiatrist's pitch of her voice was making. So instead I just nodded as she spoke, circling the sand around a hunk of singed wood with a tree branch I'd whittled down to a wand.

As I crept toward the car that night, I reminded myself to be pissed off at Baz for not being there to back me up in my obstinacy, my aborted attempt at righteous indignation. Pissed off at Tom for being so fucking mute about all this. Why couldn't he just have *said* something? Christ, the blast didn't destroy his larynx. I mean, I'm not a bloody mind reader. I don't have fucking X-ray vision. I shouldn't be faulted for ignoring something I never knew existed, for respecting a man's right to privacy, should I?

Regardless, rifling through his clothes till my knuckles hit metal, I didn't give two shits any more about his delicate fucking sensibilities. I could have been caught red handed popping open the latch and I wouldn't have blinked. But then I sat low against the back bumper of the VW and started to scan through the pages under the light of a tiny key-ring torch. When I'd read as many as I could stand, when I'd seen the dates written along the top twenty, thirty, forty times before disappearing entirely, when Tom's careful cursive became a maniac's jagged scrawl, I dropped them back into the box and forced it shut. I sat there on my hands, sucking air in through my nose till my heart settled and my Adam's apple felt small enough to talk through again. Then I crossed the campsite to where Baz was curled up foetal in a sleeping bag, and dragged him, groggy and grunting, out into the open desert.

*

'Will . . . you . . . stop . . . fucking . . . *pulling* at me and relax yourself. What in the hell is up with you? Why are you carrying around that thing?'

'OK, this is probably far enough. Even if one of them stirs, we're out of earshot.'

'Jesus, Karl, I don't know what has you so spooked but you could have at least let me grab my trousers. Kim is gonna think we're a pair of poofs if she sees me walking back like this. *And* I'm freezing my bollocks off. I remember you telling me that the desert didn't get cold. Another pearl of wisdom—'

'You need to get your stuff together and say your goodbyes to herself. We're leaving first thing in the morning.'

'Wha? No. Karl, I can't—'

'Of course you can, you've legs, don't you?'

'Yeah, but—'

'Look, we were planning on leaving in a couple of days anyway. Just trust me when I tell you that it's time to speed things up.'

'Karl, man, you're not listening. I'm – I'm not leaving.'

'Jesus, Baz, for once could you try to be just a little bit flexible? Two extra days making goo-goo eyes at Kim is not gonna—'

'It's not the two days, Karl. I'm not leaving full stop.'

'Excuse me?'

'I'm not leaving. I've talked to Tyrell about it and he said they could get me bar work no problem. Said that people go mad for the Irish accent out here. And Kim was thinking that—'

'Slow down. You're not coming with us to the clinic?'

'I'm not coming with you back to Ireland.' This takes a second to process. I'm stood there, catching flies, squinting at him through the darkness, trying to figure out if he's serious. Until last month I couldn't picture Baz even holidaying outside Ireland. Liverpool may as well have been outer Mongolia.

'What are you shiteing on about? I'm trying to talk seriously here.' But I can sense it running through him again. Same as it did in the graveyard. That pulse of desperation, of mania.

'So am I. I'm not coming home, Karl. Not for a good while anyway. There's nothing for me there.' This is a test. This whole day. The desert gods are testing me.

'A week ago it was like pulling teeth trying to convince you to *leave* Ireland!'

'I know.'

'Are you high? Is that what's going on? Because I told you we couldn't handle the stuff they smoke out here. It's not the same as the fucking Oxo-cube hash they fart out back home.'

He's hunched over now, eyes fixed on some empty square of desert floor, drawing and re-drawing an X in the sand with his big toe.

'I've been thinking about it since we landed. A lot. I've no job. No qualification. No girlfriend.'

'Join the fucking club. You just described half the shagging country, myself included. That's no reason to drop off the map.'

'There's something else too.' What in the name of sweet suffering Jesus is he preparing to tell me here? I'm not helping him fake his own death to get out of paying child support. That is where I draw the line. If there's a sprog on the way then he's just gonna have to man up and rear it as best he can. If we're lucky the kid might even avoid a life of substance abuse and incarceration. I told him, over and over again I told him, after he dodged the bullet with Sarah Dalton the first time around, to stop sniffing around that girl. The last thing she needs is your gargantuan spawn exploding out of her like the bloody Alien. Just shake hands and go your separate ways, I said, or, if you're dead set on carrying on these 3 a.m. trysts, at the very least bag up. It's the nineties, for fuck's sake, you can source a box of condoms without being married. I don't know which of them was more petrified that weekend, preparing for her doctor's appointment. Snapping and griping at one another, hissing blame back and forth for who forgot what. You'd think it was a jury they were waiting on. And now *this* genius solution to their latest domestic shitshow.

'Go on then,' I say, readying myself to tear him a new one. 'What it is?'

'I didn't mean to hurt him,' he says, 'not badly anyway. I just lost my temper, you know. The things he was saying . . . and now they're pressing charges.'

'Baz, man, what did you do?'

'You remember O'Loughlin? Locko?'

'Which Locko? Older or younger?' They're both odious little toe rags, same as their father, but I'd like to get it straight. My brain is melted as it is.

'Younger. Nasty little fucker . . .' He just trails off and stares at his bare feet, stretching his toes out into the cool sand.

'Baz. Look at me, please. What did you do?'

'He just wouldn't shut his mouth, Karl. Saying Gabriel was weak, that he'd always belonged in the nut house. That he'd be in hell now, with the rest of the ropers. So I hit him. Just once, just to shut him up. Broke his jaw. Knocked him out cold. They said the fall shattered his eye socket. Must have cracked it off the curb. There was all this blood, Karl, I've never seen so much pump out of a lad. I thought I'd killed him.'

'When? I mean – why didn't you say something?' Seriously, I'm well on my way to developing a fucking complex here.

'Couple of months ago. I don't know why I didn't tell you. Suppose I was a bit ashamed at dragging Gabriel's memory into something like this. Something so stupid.'

'We'll figure this out, Baz. Locko's brother used to play ball with us in school, remember? Maybe I can talk to him, explain things a bit.' He's shaking his head before I've even finished.

'No good, man. It's in the books. They're calling it aggravated assault. I'm supposed to be in court at the end of August. I can't go back to that, Karl. Jail time. People talking about me like I'm some sort of psycho, some sort of animal. That's not who I am.'

'I know that, Baz.' And I do, truly, but I also wonder when that stops mattering. What good does my knowing do in the face of something like this?

'That's not the way Kim sees me, you know? She says I'm gentle with her, kind, like. That she can't imagine me hurting anyone. Why can't that be me, Karl? The one she sees. The better version.'

'Who says it can't? I mean, we know who you are.'

'But you're the only ones. And that's not ever gonna change with a criminal record hanging over me, is it? Be honest.'

'I don't know. Honestly, I don't know.'

'I do. And I'm sorry, Karl, but I don't want to go home just to have that confirmed for me. Just to be told I can't ever come back here. Christ, I've been giving myself an ulcer trying to figure out a way to tell you this. But I think you two should just go on to the clinic without me. I can barely get my own head straight let alone prop up someone as far gone as Tom.'

'You don't mean that. Tom needs our help. Both of our help.'

'Does he? I mean, what the hell use have I been so far? What can I do other than muck things up even worse than they already are? Best he can hope for from me is a lot of awkward silence. At least here I can start fresh. And it's not like I wouldn't see you lads before you left. And you could come back to visit? You could come back to stay if you wanted! The pair of you will be the only thing I'll miss when I'm settled here.' *Settled here.* He's actually convinced himself that this fantasy is possible, God love him. All he wants is for me to nod my approval, to say OK, good luck to you, man, if you can dream it you can do it. He should know better. That fucking weasel Locko. I can *see* him saying it, sneering it through that cracked slit of a mouth, nearly wanting Baz to take his head off for the attention it'd bring. If there was any real justice in the world it would have been him dangling from the goalposts instead of Gabriel.

'You're not listening to me, man. All this, what you're proposing, it can't happen. Not now. Tom is in bad shape, worse shape than he's letting on even. He has to be. And he needs both of us. At least for the next few weeks while we see what the clinic is all about. Probably for a lot longer than that. You need to be there.'

'But, I thought . . . he's better now. He's doing all right, isn't he?'

'No, he's not. I know how you feel, I wanted to believe the same thing, but a little desert holiday is not going to do the job. A couple of good days, strolling around in the sunshine with a pretty young wan doesn't add up to much in the long run. He needs us there beside him while he gets some real help.'

'Stop saying "us". What good can I do? Why does he need me?'

I lift the box from my side and hold it out between us. Baz opens his mouth, sucking in air to propel another protest, but it's a reflex, and no sound comes out. He's afraid of what's inside, and he should be. Seconds pass without either of us budging. Eventually, he lifts the box gingerly from my loose grasp, cradles it in the crook of his arm, and reaches for the latch.

The moon is clear enough now, he won't need the torch.

Sarajevo, August 3, 1993

Every day it feels like more and more shells shake the city. I'd be surprised if there was a building left undamaged in all of Sarajevo. Sometimes I wake up to the sound of a blast in the distance, and I honestly can't tell if it was real or a dream

I didn't want to talk to anyone yesterday, let alone drink. Not that I had any say in the matter. I'd slept on and off for a couple of hours, maybe not even that. The rest of night was spent staring at the patterns on the peeling wallpaper, tracing their routes up and down, left to right and back again. Dawn broke. Even though I said I wouldn't, I peeked out through the crack of glass between the mattress and the wall. I could just about make out the edge of the blackened apartment balcony across the street. I knew there was still a tiny foot embedded in the iron of the burst-open guardrail stretching out into the dead air, unreachable. I knew that there was a toy fire truck lying in a pile of brown glass five storeys below it. I thought about Jelena's orphan kids, the two dozen or so waiting to be evacuated to England and America; the ones chosen for urgent care or adoption, and the thousands more passed over or barred from leaving the city – playing rat-a-tat-tat in dank basements with wooden guns and collecting hot shrapnel in empty ICAR ration cans between blasts. My chest ached all day and for the life of me I couldn't tell if it was just panic or something worse. I've been afraid to ask anyone about it.

I'm afraid Jelena will find out and treat me like a patient. I'm afraid of being robbed of what little ability I have to be of use to this city. I'm afraid of getting shot while I lie in the street. Grabbing my left arm like an old man. I don't want to die here, not like that.

When Mac let himself in I was sitting on the edge of the bed, my arms wrapped tight around my chest, staring at that crack.

'Tom,' he said. 'Tom . . . TOM!'

'What?'

'C'mon, Irish, wake the fuck up, it's four in the goddamn afternoon. Don't make me drink alone on my last day. I have enough of that shit pencilled in for when I get home to the family.'

Mac has taken to wearing sunglasses indoors these past few weeks. He hasn't slept properly since the football game. Jimmy told me the network heads aren't happy with his recent broadcasts. They say his style has become too aggressive, too condemning. 'You can't say "Četnik" on air,' they tell him, 'it's too loaded a word.' He's been instructed to return to New York and wait for his next assignment. He gives out to me for spending too much time locked up in my room, spilling the day's blood and guts into these pages. Says it's not healthy. I told him that if I've become obsessed it's only from following his lead. Last time I checked he had nine journals stacked on the floor at the foot of his bed, every one of them bursting with notes, drawings, polaroid photographs of the dead and dying, flattened Drina cigarette boxes inlaid with the pages of sacrificed books, phone numbers for homes long since abandoned or destroyed. His Happy Book, Jimmy calls it.

At the hotel bar, Jimmy and Jelena were deep in conversation. She was furiously rotating her opal ring, the one speckled with red flecks that she wore on our first date. I didn't realise at the time that it had, in fact, been a date. All we did was drink thick Bosnian coffee out of dented copper cups in the hospital canteen and talk about the logistics of transporting medical supplies across the city. Well, Jelena did most of the actual talking, her teaspoon twisting through the sweet black liquid, while I nodded and tried to think of something interesting to say; storing up what I hoped weren't egregiously stupid questions for the moments she drew breath. The ring, she said later, should have tipped me off. She only wore it on special days, days that merited a marker.

'How would I have known that then, though?' I asked.

'You didn't think it looked special?'

'No, I mean yes, yes, I thought it looked very special,' I spluttered, secretly grateful for my obliviousness that day in the canteen. I'd been nervous enough as it was, sitting there across the table from her, our hands almost touching, in what I assumed was a sort of informal interview. Being blindsided by a surprise first date would have instantly robbed me of what little cool I had left. I did notice the ring though; its slow orbit around the lip of her cup as she stirred. I noticed the tiny chip missing from her left front tooth and the way she held eye contact while sipping and how her nose wrinkled when she searched her brain for a misplaced English word. There were a lot of little things to notice.

She blew me a kiss as I approached on Mac's heels. She was wearing this flowing summer dress I've never seen before.

Cotton, the same colour as her left eye. Around her wrist was another new bracelet, this one a made of pink and purple twine twisted loosely together. She has so many on each wrist now that together they look like rainbow cuffs. I swear she'd wear a neon bulls-eye around her neck if those kids made it for her.

Jimmy and Jelena were arguing about the paramilitaries. Half soldiers, half gangsters. The ones who've been seen drunk-walking reluctant part-time troops from cafes and ordering them back up to the front lines to man the trenches. All summer the *kafanas* selling black market coffee and booze, liberated from UNPROFOR silos, have been doing a roaring trade. Smirking fixers sip espressos in the warm summer sunshine. Fed-up soldiers abandon their posts to drink and fuck and feel something that isn't fear before the city's last shaky defences crumble. Now the Powers That Be have had enough of it. As of this week all but the slyest of bars have gone black. Even The Bunker, everyone's favourite den of iniquity, has been boarded up. It's not fair, the radio broadcasts say, for able-bodied men to sit idle all day long while the army defends them; so they've made a show of taking away the temptation. But that's all it is. The army need the gangsters who supply said temptation to keep fighting, to keep rounding up the able bodies, numbing their terror in the shaky silent stretches between incursions with whatever works best, and then rounding them up all over again. At this stage, I doubt the government could rein in the gangs even if they wanted to.

Everyone has been waiting for Mount Igman to fall, and only the most unhinged want to catch the last bullet for a doomed city. But if the mountain corridor is taken, Sarajevo will be completely surrounded. The supply tunnel running underneath the airport will be all but worthless. The only trickle of arms into the city will dry up, and then it's game over. They won't invade straight away, probably not anyway; there are still too many unbroken people with magazine clips here to attempt that just yet. No, they'll just keep shelling the city back to the Stone Age. Then, when the time is right, they'll stroll in over the rubble. Either way, for now, that huge white sheet still hangs across the tree canopy in the mountains above us which means that the fighting goes on. Jelena's brother is still up there. Her nails have been bitten down to the quick for weeks.

'How can you say that?' Jimmy spilled half of his whiskey onto the bar slamming the tumbler down. 'Every one of them that abandons their post is one less trigger finger up there. One less pair of eyes scanning the horizon for JNA reinforcements.'

'Jimmy, you have been here too long to be so fucking naïve. Sarajevo is not Stalingrad. They are not robots, or professional soldiers, they are just young men. Students. Waiters. Whatever. They volunteer, they fight for a while, they get tired, they come home.'

'And that's right?'

'Right? Do not play the fool, Jimmy. Nothing in this city is right. You think it's right that the world has abandoned us here? That those animals rape and butcher and bomb while the world does nothing? It is what it is: better than nothing.'

'What about your brother? Why should he have to stay?'

'Abort, Jimmy, for your own safety,' I said. 'You won't win this one.'

'He shouldn't,' she said, ignoring me, nostrils flaring the way they do. 'If it was possible I would go up there and drag him home by the, eh . . .' She clicked her fingers next to her right temple, searching her brain for a word that wasn't there. So instead she grabbed hold of one of Jimmy's bushy copper sideburns and pulled him, howling, onto his feet.

'You understand now?'

'Ahhh! OK, OK, I fucking understand; lemme go!' She dropped him and tore a match from the remaining three in the book, staring off into space, smoking deeply while Jimmy grumbled away to pack up his gear.

'Pulling your pigtails means she likes you, Jimmy,' I called after him. Without looking back he raised one middle finger behind his head in our general direction.

'I tell him I do not want to talk about Hasan today,' she said. 'I tell him this as soon as we sit down, but does he listen?'

'Well, I'm sure he's learned his lesson.'

'He is lucky I do not grab him by the balls.'

'Glad to see your mood remains unaltered by this summer of love we've been having, my little fleur-de-lis,' said Mac. It drives her apeshit when he calls her that.

'If you leave him behind tomorrow, Mac, I swear I will come to America and tell your wife about your women.'

'What women?'

'Those pretty producers' assistants you give so many tours of the hotel. Short tours.'

'Goddamn, Irish,' he said, smirking behind those giant shades. 'You wouldn't hold up well under torture.'

'Sorry, Mac, I don't know how she gets it out of me.'

'I think I could make an educated guess.'

'To be fair, I never actually said they were short.'

'Personally, Jelena, I prefer to think of them as tapas-style trysts, entirely appropriate for our current situation. "A war zone is no place for foreplay". I think Lincoln said that.'

'You are an unusual man, Mac,' Jelena said.

'That I am, sweetheart, that I am.'

He planted himself down on Jimmy's stool, caging an army surplus bag inside its scuffed metal legs, and gave us a flash of that bristly Cheshire Cat grin of his. 'Well, sit down, both of you. We're gonna get roaring, stinking, maudlin drunk, right here, all of us. Then you three are gonna tell me how much you love me and how superb a journalist I am and how they'll be singing songs about my bravery and professionalism in the *kafanas* of Sarajevo for years to come.'

He turned to Goran before either of us could offer any kind of protest and asked for four glasses. From his bag he produced a litre bottle of clear, unlabelled alcohol, unscrewed the top, and poured out a line of sloppy, healthy measures like a man watering plants in a hurry.

'I don't think people sing songs about professionalism, Mac,' I said.

'Not yet,' he said, 'but give 'em a few months without me and the ballads will start to come thick and fast. Here, down the hatch. You too, Goran, don't give me any of that "I am vorking" bull either. As a paying guest of this establishment I am taking it upon myself to relieve you of your duties for the evening.' Goran shrugged, and raised his glass to us.

'*Živeli.*'

'*Živeli.*'

*

Mac wouldn't let us be until the whole potion bottle was empty. We drank long into the evening, slowly lowering the level of the liquid, listening to him fling insults at every passing journalist for their clothes, their accent, their 'fruity' country of origin – whatever leapt out of his mouth first, basically. Whenever someone took offence, which was about fifty per cent of the time, he raised his hands and bellowed, 'C'mon, man, it's my last fucking day,' loud enough to embarrass them into retreating back to the lounge. When that didn't work, Goran calmed down the hot heads with a free drink served up at the far end of the bar, on the condition that they lighten up. I suppose once Jimmy stormed off we all silently agreed to keep it breezy, which we did, more or less, for the rest of the night. Mac told us about some of his more unusual sexual misadventures and drug binges with the slurred stipulation that they were not to appear in any memoir or news article any of the three of us may end up writing. Goran polished the same countertop spot to a high shine while we listened to Mac's stories. Jelena flails her arms when she's had a few drinks. I've learned how to lean backward like a limbo dancer to avoid getting burnt by hot ash. So as not to fall backward off the high stool, she put her hand in mine and barely let go all night. Every so often, when I'd been silent a little too long I suppose, she rubbed the tips of her fingers against the inside of my wrist and smiled. To Mac's delight, she told us about an STI clinic she had worked at one weekend a month a couple of years back. 'I am now immune to embarrassment,' she pronounced, waving her cigarette in the air as if she were making a royal decree. Goran got all red, and admitted going in for a check-up, collar pulled high, only to recognise her walking down the hallway toward him, and hiding in a janitor's closet for half an hour until the coast was clear. He covered his face in his hands and hooted with laughter as on the other side of the bar we struggled to breathe.

'Pour him another one, Tommy! Help him forget!'

Jelena leaned over the bar and kissed him on the cheek, a smooch that left a perfect pair of chocolate brown lips printed on his five o'clock shadow.

'I never tell this to anyone before,' he said, slurping up another measure and shaking its taste away like a wet dog. 'I am confessing all of my sins!'

It was perfect last night, or as close to perfect as we're ever going to get out here. More and more this past year I've wished I could run my mind through murky water till everything fades, even just a little bit. Even for a couple of hours a week. At the end of each day over here it feels like I'm physically squeezing another set of bloody images into my brain, fucked-up details no one should ever hold on to that clearly, and all those images are stacking against the wall of my skull, pounding the bone, pushing their way back into my eyes every day that follows. Waking up just now though, sitting here waiting for dawn, I'm glad for the ability to play back last night, every little remark and gesture, all over again in my mind's eye. There's a warmth to it, a familiarity. Like the hungover post-mortems we used to have on Sunday afternoons back home.

Before he called it a night, Goran handed Mac three envelopes, carefully addressed and tied together with an elastic band, each one optimistically stamped with that doomed return postcode: Sarajevo 71000. They shook hands and Goran turned away toward the bar to clean a glass. Mac tried to slip these into the army bag without anyone noticing, but his motor skills weren't cooperating. The bag toppled through the gap in the stool legs and dozens upon dozens of letters spilled out on the floor at our feet. Mac sighed and made a noise like a rusty gate swinging open as he lowered his tired body down from the high stool to sweep them back in.

'So that's what you've been doing all week.'

He nodded without looking up at us.

'Could be the last messages some of these poor fuckers ever send,' he muttered. 'They deserve to know someone is gonna make sure they're delivered.'

As he was fumbling about with his room key, swearing like a docker in the dark hallway, Jelena doubled back and threw her arms around his neck.

'Take care of him, sweetheart,' I heard him say to her.

Jelena is still asleep. Her body stretched diagonal across the bed. I can barely hear her breathing. Mac's transport leaves in half an hour. I had better go say goodbye.

Chapter 9

On rare slow stretches, I steal a glimpse out to where the twin blues of clear sky and distant ocean bleed into one another on the horizon. For a few moments at a time, it's achingly beautiful. It's also pretty fucking terrifying from this vantage point. Of all the things we (I) neglected to properly research heading over here, this drive is perhaps the one most likely to get us killed. Well, so far anyway. I have my eyes fixed unblinking on the road ahead, trying not to glance at either the looming green cliff face to our right, or the four-hundred-foot drop to our left. The barely two-lane highway snakes in and out of itself for miles. We've been taking thirty mile an hour blind turns for over an hour now. It's beginning to feel like we're tempting fate. Every edge I look out over seems sheerer and more craggy than the one that came before it. My stomach leaps into my mouth and stays there till another hairpin manoeuvre has been executed successfully. Maybe I'm just shaken from last night.

The sun is high and hot, even with the breeze coming in off

the water, and I'd kill for a petrol station with a fridge full of ice cold anything. Fighting sleep deprivation with sporadic adrenalin spikes isn't doing much for my powers of concentration either. But I've chosen to drive Pacific 1 – instead of the safer 101 in this, my first time behind the wheel of an automatic, on the wrong side of the road – for a reason (the Pacific, the awesome fucking beauty of it all, or whatever nonsense I told myself before the car started moving), so we're all just gonna have to suck it up for now. Beside me Baz has been white-knuckling it for the past half an hour; silent, save for the obligatory elongated *fuuuuuuck* whenever an RV bulging with kids comes rattling past us in the opposite direction.

I think he was calmer before he realised how close I've been to killing us all this entire drive. By and large though, he's holding up well, considering. Poor fella was nearly in tears saying goodbye to Kim this morning. I told him he'll see her again, though he knows I can't promise that, especially if the charge waiting for him back in Dublin is as serious as it sounds. He may never be allowed back here. He hasn't looked at me since they waved us out. Tom has covered his face in the huge pair of gold-rimmed sunglasses Tina gave to him as a parting gift, so it's hard to tell how he's doing. By the twist of his head it looks like he's just admiring the view, which is what I hoped for when I picked this route out of a dog-eared seventies guidebook I salvaged from a 50p bin at a flea market in Smithfield. I cruise along slow, and choose to believe they're enjoying this.

*

He roars himself awake, unleashes a flurry of unintelligible Bosnian, and makes a grab for the door handle. It clicks and swings open as I haul the drifting car back into the right lane. One hand grasps the wheel while the other clamps tight on to Tom's ankle and holds on for dear life. Baz throws a forearm around Tom's neck and drops them both to the floor before Tom can leap out onto the road. A heavyset couple on the back of a motorbike roar obscenities at us as one of their chunky jackboot heels hammers the door shut. Tom is trapped in Baz's submission hold but their rocking back and forth is fucking with this Matchbox car's equilibrium. I can't keep it steady.

'Hold him still, Baz, for fuck's sake!'

'I'm. Trying. He's. Too. Strong.' Baz pants out a word with every new manoeuvre. All those months of watching WWF cage matches at three in the morning finally being put to good use. We've zig-zagged our way around the corner and into a rare straight stretch. There's an overlook turnoff about two hundred metres away, but the cars behind are too close to stop dead and turn in. I can't judge the distance of the truck coming against us at speed. I can hear that ridiculous panicked noise Baz makes when he's about to drop the barbell down on top of himself. If we don't pull off here we are well and truly fucked. Tom breaks free and rears up onto his knees just as I cut hard across the lanes in front of the wagon to the screech of straining breaks. The two machines dance around each other in slow motion. I can see the ash fall from the driver's cigarette, the mustard stain on the lapel of his checked shirt, the widening O of his mouth. I grab a clump of Tom's damp shirt and pull him downward as the car comes to a stop at an angle more flush to the guardrail than I could possibly have managed if I had all day to practise. Only when the honking dies down and the sound of stabilising tyres fades into the distance do I hear Tom's voice, his head resting on the seat next to my leg.

'I'm sorry. I'm sorry. I'm sorry. I'm sorry . . .'

*

'Still,' I bellow over the rush of salty air, 'it's one hell of a view, isn't it?' That's the first thing anyone has said in an hour. They both nod vigorously which makes me feel good, like things are getting back on track. Now that relative calm has been restored, I try to suck in as much of the landscape as possible. The red-tinted sagebrush and sun-scorched rocks on the inland border, the lines of pelicans gliding over stubby sea stacks, the shimmering dry heat and languid, lolling roll of the waves below us. We pull off the road to watch a trio of flattened surfers in slick black wetsuits paddle out into the rising tide, their powerful arms dragging through the water with such uninterrupted focus that it seems as if their final destination isn't a decent break, but some far distant shore. It's nothing like the Irish coast – how could it be? – but it reminds me of how we used to spend long summer weekends back home. Before all this real-world bollocks got in the way. The aimless June drives out to Howth or Wexford or wherever. Piling into Gabriel's shitheap of an Opel when the consensus call was made that the good weather would hold. Listening to matches we only half cared about on the radio, blasting tunes from the same three tapes in the glove box, parking by the pier to eat bags of chips and stare out at the boats in the harbour, maybe kicking a saggy football back and forth if we had one. The inevitable sprint for shelter when the heavens opened. Sunday carverys and pints at a hotel restaurant to finish it off. I want to talk about all this with them, to see if they remember it as strongly as I do, to see if it'll be of any use to Tom in fighting back whatever's taking over his mind. I believe, based on nothing but desperate optimism, that by resurrecting enough of these memories, and compounding their effect with a handful of positive, safe, *recent* images, images like the view which I hope he's absorbing right now, we can dilute or replace at least a few of the horror shots that dominate that perfect recall of his. It won't fix him, but maybe it'll help. Maybe it'll keep him together until the doc can. At this point I just want to buy him some time.

Just another few days, that's all I need.

*

It was his reporter friend Mac who booked him into the clinic on Wastwater Lake, miles from anywhere. The kind of place where the dawn chorus and the hammering of raindrops on water are the loudest noises you're ever going to hear. When Tom, who had been living rough, and damn-near somnambulant, in an abandoned apartment building on the edge of the city, finally resurfaced at the Holiday Inn, one of the barmen called Mac, who then called the airport, the clinic and, most impressively, Tom's mam for the final green light. He then sent the barman to pick up Tom's things and drive him to the airport, escort him to the airport really. Mac even had a driver waiting on the other side. Tom probably owes his life to that man.

It was almost two months before he let his mam visit him at Wastwater. She rented a room in a tiny B&B and every day walked the three miles to the facility gates in damp, howling north-of-England weather. I pictured her bundled up in her good winter coat and wellies, plodding along stoically as I've only ever seen her do, with all that unbroken time to think. Every morning the same doctor appeared – the Laurence Olivier-sounding one who spoke to me for half an hour on the phone one evening like I was a family member – and told her I'm terribly sorry, Mrs Dempsey, but he's just not ready to see anyone yet. She'd stand there for a minute, he said, decline a cup of tea from the receptionist, and leave for another day. No demands, no fuss.

We wanted to head over too, shit scared at the thought of it happening again. Of the guilt that oozes in slowly over the disbelief, and settles on top like oil slicks on water. But Tom's mam said there'd be no point. I can't speak for Baz, but I was ashamed at how relieved I felt when she dismissed us like that. I couldn't deal with it up close so soon after Gabriel. I asked her to send me a letter whenever she did get to talk to him. I assumed, correctly, that she'd be more inclined to discuss the details in writing than she had been on the phone. Something about analysing these things out loud that's always been too painful for her, too awkward. Not that we've ever been much better about it. Two years ago I would have dubbed a lad like Tom a psycho and thought no more about it – and yet I'm part of the first generation tasked with 'breaking the stigma' attached to this whole mental health thing. That's what we're told anyway. Whether anyone actually believes, let alone employs, all that proactive talk-it-out stuff is another story.

It should be us though. Christ, if it has to be someone it should be us. How can anyone expect a pensioner to get her head around ideas she's been taught to ignore her whole life? Jargon she's never heard, invisible illnesses too slippery to designate, solutions that don't include prayer, faith, a higher power pulling the strings in one direction or another.

She said she'd send me a letter when she had any new information to put in one. Curt, but then what else was I expecting? In February they went walking together on the misty lakefront where, for all anyone knows, she had spent the bulk of every frozen, drizzly day previous. I can't imagine how he must have looked to her, still so freshly beat-up and brain-addled. Unable to utter a single coherent sentence. They did this a few times a week until he asked her to go home. They were entering a new phase of therapy, he said, trying something new that might be useful in combating the nightmares and what they called 'hyper-arousal' – the constant panic that swelled in his chest and flooded his veins with adrenalin several dozen times a day, for no reason at all. He promised to come to the phone when she called. He told her that the doctor was free to pass on any information he couldn't say or didn't understand. So she left.

In April Tom had a heart attack. His second, apparently. There'd been an incident during the siege he refused to detail. An explosion outside a nightclub or concert venue or something. All he'd said about the particulars in the letter was 'she brought me back'. How she managed that, I don't know. At Wastwater they revived him with a portable defibrillator and had him transferred to whatever ramshackle hospital was closest for a night's sedation and observation.

By May the Wastwater docs had exhausted all conventional treatment options, and were pissing about with a host of dubious relaxation techniques more suited to pre-exam jitters than shell shock. Laurence Olivier, in fairness to him, refused to throw in the towel, even after the heart attack. He did everything short of swinging a pocket watch back and forth in front of Tom's eyes, but nothing took. Even if he'd had one last ace up his sleeve, the money from Tom's da's life insurance policy was all but gone. When I heard Tom was coming home, I sent the full list of procedures, tried and failed, along with a sizeable deposit cheque, postmarked for California, to a place I'd originally seen advertised in the classified section of a water-damaged American psychology journal I found in the library (perhaps the single most boring piece of literature I've ever attempted to read): Restless Souls. I put them in an envelope labelled EXTREMELY IMPORTANT and affixed an embarrassingly large amount of stamps to the front. I laid out my list – compiled from weeks of frustratingly dense and damn near unintelligible correspondence – in the same style as the inner section of the clinic's brochure; the one that proudly detailed Dr Saunders' 'famous' techniques. My list, Tom's list, was as follows:

- ○ Group Therapy
- ○ Trauma-focused Cognitive Behavioural Therapy
- ○ Psychological Debriefing

- Electroconvulsive Therapy
- Stress Inoculation Therapy
- Eye Movement Desensitisation and Reprocessing
- Targeted Exercise and Meditation Programmes.

Yoga and jumping jacks aside, these terms frightened me. I couldn't wrap my head around the stab-in-the-dark nature of their success rate. I worried about what would be left of his already-fucked psyche once it was all done. And yes, of course I thought about the drugs they were pumping into him, the name and descriptions I transcribed without understanding a word. *Benzodiazepines and beta-blockers for the panic attacks, amitriptyline and fluoxetine for the intrusive re-experiencing and avoidance, venlafaxine for the depression.* Antipsychotics when things got really bad. Which they did, far too often. In a way I'm glad that none of them worked, or at least worked well enough to be anything more than a stopgap, a way to temporarily straight-jacket his mind till it figured out how to burst free. All those tiny coloured pills; mind-altering compounds that belonged in the pages of science fiction scripts, not coursing through the veins of my mate, a guy I wanted back just the way I'd remembered him, not as some lobotomised zombie. Not numb to the world, inside and out. That's no way to live either.

*

'You're after missing the turn, Karl,' Baz says to me, jutting his thumb behind him toward the small oval sign we've just sped by. Carved lightly into the centre of the wood, in slightly lopsided summer-camp font, were the words *Restless Souls: Where the Wounded Come to Heal,* and a long arrow pointing down a dusty side road.

'Oh shit, did I?' I say, attempting surprise. 'Ah no worries, we'll turn back in a bit. There's something a couple of miles ahead I wanted to check out anyway. It won't take long.' Tom lowers his glasses slightly and looks at me in the rear-view mirror, intrigued. Baz is not pleased.

'Oh, I see. So when I want to take a half hour's detour to see an iconic piece of Americana, it's "too far out of our way", but when *you* want to spend an hour snapping black and white pictures of shaggin' tumbleweeds—'

'I don't care what that flyer told you, Baz, the World's Largest Donut is *not* an iconic piece of Americana. It's a fucking plastic donut on top of a donut shop in Inglewood.'

'It's a pop culture treasure.'

'Stop quoting that flyer like it's the Encyclopaedia fucking Britannica! It's a donut! We are not having this conversation again.'

'We could have gotten some food there, cup of coffee, maybe a key ring or something—'

'Look, you'll like this place up ahead. Trust me, it'll be at least twice as enjoyable as gorging yourself on stale donuts.'

'Says you.'

'Right, sit there and sulk so. We'll be there soon anyway.'

'Bloody dictatorship in this car.'

'You're just gonna make a point of not enjoying this, aren't you?'

He says nothing.

'Fucking hell. How about this, we'll swing by the giant donut—'

'World's Largest Donut.'

'We'll swing by the *World's Largest Donut* on our way back to LAX.'

'And we'll get out of the car for pictures?'

'If we must.'

'And actually buy some donuts?'

'Since when do you even eat donuts, Baz?'

'Well, if we're not even gonna do the thing properly we might as well just—'

'All right, all right fine. We'll see the donut. Then we'll take pictures with the donut. Then we'll eat a box of donuts and buy a World's Biggest Donut T-shirt and key ring and hat and whatever else you're after.'

'I doubt they have hats. Unless there's a museum or something. If there is—'

In the rear-view, Tom is smiling under his glasses. It is the single most heartening moment of the whole ride up.

'Yep. Absolutely. In the unlikely scenario that someone makes their living selling tickets to a donut museum, we will buy three of 'em. Tom, how does a trip to the donut museum when this is all over sound?'

'Would you believe,' he says from the back, 'I've never actually eaten a donut.'

'Fuck off. Really?'

'Really. I don't know why, just never really felt the need to.'

'Ah c'mon, what about that little hut on O'Connell Street?'

'Nope.'

'Jesus. You hear that, Baz? It's settled now, we'll have to go.'

'All right then,' he says, sounding genuinely satisfied. 'Work away. Are you gonna tell us where we're driving to?'

'It's a surprise,' I say, smug, though I'm not certain there'll even be one at the end of this.

'What's the surprise?'

'You are familiar with the concept of a surprise, Baz?'

'Fuck off.'

Just outside of San Simeon, about one hundred metres from an unspecified Point of Interest sign, I pull the car over to the side of the road and attempt to discreetly lift my camera bag into my lap from underneath my seat. Baz snorts. For the purposes of the reveal, I'm glad to see only a single car sitting in the dusty lot to the left of us. We climb over the wooden guardrail and onto the gangplank that leads down to the beach. I talk loudly over the voices of a couple of tourists passing us in the opposite direction and the lads look at me like I've been sneaking swigs from a hipflask. A long, guttural staccato call sounds off from somewhere below us on the still-obscured beach.

'What the hell was that?' Baz says. I shrug and nod us forward along the winding path. Clumps of yellow flower pods sit bright amongst the scrub brush on either side of us. As we round the corner, two bald crimson heads pop into view. A pair of buzzards – freaky-looking bastards with Red Skull domes and sharp yellow beaks – sit side by side on top of a blue sign that reads:

WARNING
HELP PROTECT OUR WILDLIFE
DON'T FEED, TOUCH, OR DISTURB
MARINE MAMMALS

Their thick brown plumage rustles with the ocean breeze. Baz takes a step closer. The planks below his foot groan and the birds rotate their heads toward us. Wary. One readjusts his footing on the sign, spreads his wings outward with a shiver, and takes off across the beach. His partner follows a split second later. Our eyes follow the birds' flight over the sand and that's when we notice the elephant seals. Lying there in their hundreds the entire length of the beach, just as Tina described them – massive and hulking and impossible to miss. A whole colony of them, great grey-black monsters, their thick blubbery coats rippling in the sunlight as they worm their way across the sand. Five-metre-long bulls with bulbous, whiskery snouts rising tall – snarling and grappling with one another, rocking backwards and forwards as they trade blows, belching forth war cries while the rest of the group lie in disinterested dog-piles all around them. Young females and black-coated pups scoot out of the way as the combatants bulldoze past them. Eventually the battle runs its course and all participants collapse – exhausted or bored, it's hard to determine – into another amorphous pile. And there's a stillness then, a near-silence, as everyone naps or lazily tosses damp sand up onto their sun-warmed bodies with an unconstrained flipper. When the fighting stops, we duck underneath the wooden railing and creep through the succulents and gorse bushes till the only thing separating us from them is a low ledge of sandy earth and a few feet of beach. We sit there, cross-legged in the undergrowth, as the sun drops low in the sky and the tide moves in over the black rocks. Maybe fifteen minutes pass before anyone says a word.

'This is really nice, Karl.' It's Tom.

'Yeah. I mean, a poor substitute for the World's Largest Donut but I thought it'd be better than nothing.' I nudge Baz with an elbow and he smiles.

'Apples and oranges, you smart bollocks. But yeah, I like this. A man could get used to living here.'

'You think?' Tom asks.

'Sure. Why not, like? We just stay, you know? Like Gabriel always talked about. Open a bar or buy a fishing boat or whatever. Figure it out as we go.' Tom nods and looks out beyond the beach to where eyebrow silhouettes of seagulls are disappearing into the soft orange horizon. I'm snapping pictures as unobtrusively as I can, pretending I'm not paying attention. Maybe Baz is sulking, maybe he just needs to speak the notion aloud before he lets it go. Either way, I don't say anything.

'C'mon,' Baz says, weary, after another stretch of silence. 'We'd better go if we're going, it'll be dark soon.' He's right; close as we are, I don't want to navigate these roads at night-time.

'One second,' I say, 'just let me grab one of the three of us.'

I lie flat behind the camera, perched precariously on top of a little mound of pebbles, and look through the viewfinder.

When I've tweaked the angle so that the seals and the sunset are both visible, I set the timer for four seconds and crouch back down next to the lads.

'One for the mammies,' Baz says as we rise, arms still locked around each other.

Sarajevo, October 15, 1993

I got a bear hug from Goran when I arrived back this morning. Apparently gunmen in Grbavica opened fire on a crew of journalists just before sundown. Last he heard, one was dead and the others were pinned down in an abandoned tram carriage, waiting for the assault to subside. When I didn't come home last night he assumed the worst. Somehow this led to him explaining that the Sarajevo tram system is one of the oldest in the world.

I met the rest of the family last night, God help me. I was so nervous walking up to the door you'd think there was a gallows on the other side of it. That kind of thing has never really been my strong suit.

Jelena informed me at three o'clock yesterday afternoon that I was coming over for dinner. She snapped her fingers in the air, remembering suddenly what she had been told to pass on days ago and rattled it off without looking at me. Her mother was cooking a special meal in honour of Jelena's favourite cousin, a surrogate sister really, who is spending her thirtieth birthday with her husband and four-year-old son in Stuttgart. It's been almost eighteen months since they fled the city and Jelena is never brighter than when a letter arrives with a German stamp affixed to the front. She spends her break poring over the photographs of the little boy in his dungarees, sitting on his father's shoulders or staring upward at the polaroid camera from his mother's lap. It's hard to describe the look on her face in those moments. A kind of painful joy I suppose you'd call it. She never wants to talk about it, so I try not to disturb her.

'Tonight is a special night for us and my mother would like you to be a part of it,' she said. Apparently her father and brother have been itching to meet me for a while now and the fact that I turned down their last two invitations (???) has made them suspicious.

'Why didn't you tell me they wanted to meet me?'

'I wasn't ready for you to meet them until now.'

'I just assumed I'd done something to offend your mother last year. Pronounced a word wrong and accidently called her a bitch or something.'

'No. She likes you. But my father and Hasan want to know what's wrong with you.'

'Who said there was anything wrong with me?'

'I did. I told them how you are.'

'Wait, what? How am I?'

'You know, quiet, strange. Not really a journalist, not really an aid worker, someone who should not be here but will not leave. I told them that you help me move corpses and then we make love in the room beside the morgue.'

'Jesus fucking Christ, Jelena!'

She cracked up then, leaving me sweating in the hallway while she changed the bandages on a twelve-year-old girl's neck wound. The girl, Abida, whimpered as Jelena gently applied what was left of a rolled-up tube of antiseptic cream and patched her back up again. Abida was flicking through a dog-eared copy of *Vogue* from 1991. She and Jelena began the game they have been playing for a week now, ever since the girl arrived on a stretcher from the Hrasno neighbourhood: Jelena points at a beautiful fashion model and tells Abida that she has the same cheekbones/eyes/neckline etc. Then she looks in my direction for confirmation, which I enthusiastically give. Abida blushes and waves it away, but turns the pages for her doctor to continue. The pair had lived one street over from each other before the fall of Grbavica, and the targeting of Hrasno that came afterward convinced Jelena to move back in with her family at the end of last summer. Thank Christ. She told me once that her old apartment building was blasted to rubble in the week after New Year. Abida's mother had refused to leave the neighbourhood. They came to Sarajevo as refugees a year ago because there was nowhere else for them to go. Abida had been standing at the kitchen sink when a shell blew her grandmother's tiny back garden away. A shard of glass had sliced through her neck, missing the carotid artery by millimetres. Half a minute later, she said, and her mother would have been back in the house. Maybe she would have even been through the kitchen, into the boarded-up living room, and completely out of harm's way. Her father is still fighting up north somewhere. It's been weeks since anyone has heard from him.

'How's she doing?' I asked. Jelena scribbled something down on one of the Holiday Inn stationery pads I brought over last week. Another of the dozens of indecipherable notes she writes herself throughout the day, each one to be reabsorbed by candlelight before bed.

'Physically, she will be fine.'

'You think her father is alive?' She scowled at me. 'What? There's a chance.'

'You see this is what I'm worried about. You say this optimistic shit in front of my brother and he will kick you out of the house. She told me where her father was fighting. Unless he is hiding under a pile of bodies, he is dead, same as all the others.'

'Sorry.'

'Me too.'

'What's your brother like?'

'Hasan? I don't know. Smart. Bitter. Angry. He was in the trenches on Igman all summer. Nineteen years old. You know what I was doing when I was nineteen years old?'

'Do I want to know?'

'Fuck you. I mean drinking cocktails, skiing, going to movies, listening to music, sitting in *kafanas* all day with friends. Talking shit, talking about nothing. Laughing. That's what he should be doing. Not digging tunnels and firing guns. He isn't a soldier, Tom.'

'He won't have to be one forever.' She scowled at me again. 'What?' I said, defensive now. 'That's not optimism, that's reality. It will end. It has to.'

'Even if he lives –' she feigned spitting on the ground as she always does to ward off karmic jinxing '– he will never be young again. He will never be like he was. None of us will.' I put my hands on her waist and kissed her then. She dabbed at the corner of her eye and asked me if her make-up had run. It had, just a little bit, but I told her no.

'Liar.'

'Did you really tell your father and brother that?'

172

'What?'

'You know, about us, and that morgue office?' I held my breath. She cackled and told me I'd find out tonight. Then she skipped away down the ward, carefully placing individually wrapped pieces of Cunga Lunga bubble gum on the night-stands of her sleeping patients.

I turned up at what I hoped was their doorway on Logavina Street just before six. It stood across the road from a dilapid-ated pink mansion. The Djordjevićs' home sits in its shadow; just a modest yellow house on a slope, the boot-sized holes in its tiled roof patched by red tarpaulin. Paint job chipped and scarred like all the others. Broken front windows covered by the plastic sheeting the UNPROFOR has been handing out for months now. By way of a gift, I put together this shabby-looking parcel made up of the bits and pieces Mac left me, as well as what I could find at the shops in Pale: two boxes of Marlboros, a bag of vodka and whiskey miniatures, some batteries, a quarter pound of coffee, a small piece of cheese, and an orange. I stood there on the doorstep, twitching at sounds of blasts in the distance, shit scared that these offerings would offend them somehow. Fadila answered and threw her arms around my neck before I could splutter out any sort of greeting. She kissed me on each cheek, and pulled me through the dark hallway into the living room where the rest of the family were leaning forward on the sofa, staring at a flickering television set. From a large brown armchair in the corner of the room, Jelena blew me a kiss and pointed her outstretched toe toward the screen.

They were watching a home movie, from October 1990

according to the time signature. On the screen, just above a thin strip of static, was a long dining room table covered with steaming food. Lamb kebabs, bulging spinach and cheese pies, meat sausages, rich red pepper relish, flaky pastries decorated with walnuts. The camera moved to a chocolate cake decorated with fruit slices in the table's centre. I had to wipe my mouth to keep from drooling. It's been a long time since anyone has seen a chocolate cake around here. Jelena's brother caught me, and grinned, before turning his attention back to the TV. From off-screen a voice called out and the camera pulled back to reveal a dozen or so smiling party guests – Jelena, Hasan and Fadila tucked in amongst them, their arms waving wildly at the cameraman, their faces full and young and tanned. There were red and blue balloons hanging from the lampshade. A little boy in dungarees was shifting in his high chair, his pudgy fingers trying in vain to reach them. Jelena stretched upward and untied the knot keeping one of the balloons dancing out of reach, and handed it to the child, who held it in front of him, staring into its shiny centre as if it were a crystal ball. And then the power was gone. The picture shrunk to a single white dot and disappeared and the room was dark again. Hasan, Jelena, and their father roared together, grabbing fistfuls of neon orange table tennis balls from a box at their feet and pelting the screen until Fadila scolded the three of them, pointing across the room at me. Me, standing there like a spare part in my rumpled, oversized shirt, waiting to be told what to do.

For a second or two we were, all four of us, silent in the near darkness as we stared at each other. Or I should say, they stared at me while I stared at my shoes, stealing glances upward in an awkward, jerky motion. Jelena lay across the armchair, her long bare legs crossed, smirking; Fadila hovered in her apron; Hasan, stood long and gaunt in his vest and khaki trousers, sized me up through narrowed eyes; while the father, Vuk, looked up at me with a tired smile from the edge of the sofa. He was frailer than Jelena described. A scratched wooden cane leaned against the wall behind him.

'So this is the Irish boyfriend.' Hasan's voice was slow and deliberate, like he was making sure I didn't miss a word. 'The one who saves books and children and kittens for Sarajevo.'

'Eh, something like that,' I said. 'Though I'm actually allergic to cats, so the kittens generally have to fend for themselves.'

'So why haven't you come to visit us until now? Are you an alcoholic?'

'Hasan!' Jelena and her mother squealed in unison. Jelena sprang up from her chair and slapped her brother over and over across the back of the head. She jabbed the poor lad, hard, with the spear-tip of her index finger, reading him the riot act in one long, sweary rant. The whole time her father did his best not to crack up laughing. When she finally stopped to take a breath Hasan raised his palms in surrender, moon-walking his way across the floor until he was using me as a human shield. He peeked out over my shoulder while Fadila tried to defuse her daughter. I reached into my crumpled bag, palmed the lone orange, and slipped it to Hasan when Jelena was looking away.

'Fuck, man, where did you get this?'

'Give it to your sister, *quick*,' I hissed.

'Aw man.'

After staring at the orange for a moment, Hasan launched

himself across the room, dodging Jelena's swipe as he dropped
to his knees and held it above his head. An olive branch. She
took it from him, drew back like a baseball pitcher, closed
one eye, and laughed.

'Come on,' she said, stepping over him to tip toe across the
room and take my hand.

Dinner, which Fadila had put together from the family's
latest tiny ration package and some clever haggling with a
Markale vendor earlier that afternoon, was the best I have
eaten in the city. We toasted to our survival with tiny glasses of
plum rakija – a gift from Vuk's brother in Belgrade. We spoke
about how thin I was getting, and Jelena's recently evacuated toddler patients, and Fadila's sheltered books, and Vuk's
straining heart. I hope Jelena didn't notice my Adam's apple
bobbing up and down as they read the poor man the riot act
for taking his walks round the neighbourhood. Seeing her face
twist with worry for him makes me all the more convinced
that telling her about my condition will do no one any good.
He brushed their advice aside with a long shake of his head.

'I have lived in this city for twenty years,' he told me. 'Those
animals in the hills will have to blow it from the face of the
earth before I stop walking these streets.' Fadila tut-tutted and
called him a stubborn fool. He kissed her fingers one by one
and made a joke I didn't understand but I laughed along with
the others all the same. They looked exhausted, and beaten,
but with no other options, what else can they do but plough
on? Trying – with their horseplay and teasing and memories of
feasts – to keep the siege out of their home. For a few hours
at least. We ate and drank and smoked together, ignoring the
distant sounds of gunfire as best we could, until our last candle

had lowered to a puddle and Vuk had drifted off to sleep in his chair. Fadila announced to the room that I was staying, insisting that I would not make it home before the curfew and that she would never forgive herself if anything happened on my journey back to the hotel. Jelena and Hasan nodded their agreement so I didn't protest. To be honest, the last thing I wanted to do then was leave that house, that family.

Before I left this morning, early, while the others slept, Hasan appeared and stood beside me, leaning against the bannister in the hallway while I tied my shoelaces against the second step of the staircase, which, far as I can gather, has been pretty much unused for over a year. He picked up the overly formal thank you note I had left on the hall table, scanned it, and put it back down without saying anything. He hadn't said much at dinner either. Not rude, just distant. Distracted. I wanted to ask him about the fighting on Igman all summer: whether he'd lost many friends, what he thought about the soldiers who had put down their guns and returned to cafes and clubs where some of their old friends still fiddled, how he felt about the Green Beret paramilitary leaders and the tactics they employed, if he planned to go back to college when it was all over. But I didn't. I just held up my blank packet of Drinas and made room for him on the stoop. We sat there as the light came in through the cracks in the window boards, and smoked those harsh cigarettes in silence.

'Your hands shake,' he said to me, in English, some minutes later.

'Hmmm?'

'Your hands. I notice last night at dinner.'

'Yeah.'

He held up a flat right hand, palm down. It trembled for a second or two before he clenched it and shoved it back into his pocket.

'Mine also.'

I nodded.

'You love my sister?'

How do you answer that first thing in the morning?

'You look at her like you do. Maybe it is a good thing. Maybe she loves you too. Do you think she will listen if you say to leave Sarajevo? To go to Stuttgart, or to Ireland?' His voice was hopeful, and I felt like shit answering so quickly.

'No,' I said. 'I've tried, but she won't leave the hospital.'

He sighed and rubbed some sleep from the corner of his eye.

'And you will not leave her.' I said nothing. But he was right.

'It is the same for my parents. You see my father, how he is. Every time there is an explosion I think maybe his heart has stopped. I tell him I know people who can get them through the tunnel and all the way to Split. Safe. But he will not listen, and my mother, she will not go without him. My family are – *kako se kaze* "*tvrdoglavi*"?'

'Stubborn.'

'Yes. Stubborn.'

'And you? Why do you stay?'

'I am not a political man, Tom. I do not like politics and I do not like to fight. At university I study mechanical engineering. I stay because I love my city and if you love something you have to protect it. Before this war, I have thrown one punch. Just one. When I was fourteen I hit my friend Bojan over a girl. For weeks afterward I feel like shit. I can't sleep. Now, I pull the trigger like it is nothing. If I am close enough to reach one of those fucking Četniks up there, I kill him with my bare hands like it is nothing. That is life here now.'

I thought about what it would be like to stand under the radio masts on the summit of Three Rock and look down at Dublin City as it crumbled, and burnt, and cried out to the world for help that would never come. I thought about what I might do.

'I hope you and I can be friends someday, Tom.' Hasan switched back to Bosnian when he said this.

'Someday? Not now?'

He laughed. 'I am afraid now is not the time to make new friends.'

We rose, smiling, and shook hands.

'Good luck,' I said.

'You too.'

I wonder if he's right. If it's been a mistake getting close to people with things the way they are. But then, how is anyone supposed to survive here alone?

Chapter 10

This car, slick and all as it looks, isn't built for anything even resembling off-road terrain. I worry about the tyre strength and whether or not the transmission will drop out behind us as we bobble slowly along this narrow trail. Even at this reduced speed, clouds of dust plume around our flanks, obscuring strange wooden shapes that jut out crookedly from the bushes. It's dusk now, I can see the moon coming into focus above our heads, and there's an eerie desolation to the landscape that I hadn't noticed before.

'You ever see *The Texas Chainsaw Massacre*, Karl?'

'That was in the woods.'

'You can buy chainsaws anywhere though. Also, snakes.'

'Baz, for Christ's sake . . .'

Since we're driving in the general direction of a watery grave, I crawl up the hill rising in front of us, and turn the headlights on before we hit the summit. As we make our way downward a sprawling wooden facility appears some five hundred metres away at the road's end, hanging out over the churning ocean as if it's levitating. Save for the high wrought-iron gate separating it from the rest of the world, the compound looks just as it did in the brochure. Five windowless bungalow units, each about the size of a tennis court, surround a central three-storey facility. This facility is shaped like a grain silo; rust-coloured cedar wood and huge oval windows through which I can just about make out illuminated pupil-like orbs dangling in front of a spiral staircase, which seems to wind its way from atrium to roof. The gate is about ten feet high, the metalwork an intricate pattern of swirls, birds, and vine tendrils. Fastened to the tops of the red brick columns that hold the structure in place, two security cameras point downward at our car. They beep and shift focus inward as we inch closer. We stare at one another, unsure how to proceed since there doesn't seem to be a bell or intercom. I open the car door slowly, covering the seat belt buckle with my hand as I click it open, as if the cameras are rare nocturnal animals I'm trying not to startle.

'What are you doing?' Baz whispers.

'I'm gonna go see if it's unlocked or automatic or whatever.' I take two steps forward and raise my palm to push against the metal.

'Wait!' Baz hisses, standing up over the windshield now.

'What?'

'What if it's electrified?'

'What? *Why* would it be electrified?'

'I don't fucking know. Why would it have motion sensitive security cameras?'

'Security.'

He thinks about this for a second or two.

'Electrified fences are a pretty effective form of security.'

'Yeah, so are guard towers, but it's a clinic, Baz, not Jurassic fucking Park.'

'Fine, go ahead and touch it if you want. Don't say you weren't warned.'

'Well,' I say, taking a half step back from the gate, 'even if it was electrified, and again, there is absolutely no logical reason why that would be the case, we'd have seen a sign. Like "Danger: 10,000 Volts" or something.' Tom has stepped out of the car and is staring upward into the lens of the camera on the left-hand pillar. A tiny red light blinks.

'Maybe we missed it on the way in.'

'*Look*—' I start, but before I can begin my rant in earnest a low whirring noise cuts me off and the moulded metal begins to move. At its centre, the outline of a felled sparrow turns a slow 180 degrees, wings clicking outward until its formally supine frame is soaring upward in flight. At the point of full revival, the gates swing open, just wide enough for our car to pass through.

'Well, this is already freaking me out,' says Baz, more to himself than anyone else. 'Hop in quick, the pair of you, before that yoke turns into the Terminator and blows up the car.'

As soon as our back tyres pass over the threshold the gates close, locking with a *click*, and the tumbling sparrow centre-piece plays dead once more. The drive toward the clinic is remarkably smooth, as if this stretch of road has been swept clear just for our arrival. The ditches on either side of us are lined with unlit tiki torches, held high by huge pikes ham-mered into the dry earth. It's almost completely dark now, and twin flames have appeared just outside of the silo. These are followed by six more, three on either side of the compound's front façade. There's movement in the high grass to our right, the rustle of dry stalks and what sounds like the slow clump of hoof falls.

I photographed a married couple as they left the church on horseback in some slurry-stinking midlands shithole about six months back. Mairead and Gerry: awkward, mouthy fuckers, both pushing forty, whose aged parents were fed up with them living at home. They must have weighed thirty-five stone between them and that poor, beleaguered creature, whored out for the day in a white feather headdress, looked fit to buckle under their expansive arses. I could have shot them in a blizzard through a stained glass window and it wouldn't have been a kind enough filter. Anyway, it wasn't anything special as horses go. Just an ancient piebald mare that should have been left to live out its remaining years in peace in a quiet back field somewhere. But looking at its soulful face through the viewfinder in my camera as it plodded in the mucky gravel toward the hotel at the end of the village, getting jabbed again and again and again in the side by the sharp corner of Mairead's Barbie-pink wedge, I felt that awful feeling you get sometimes as a kid. Those moments where you find yourself sitting there at the back of a free class, silent, or maybe even laughing away with the others like the nasty little bollocks you could be at your worst, while some geeky young lad – whose parents should've taken a bit more care with their school selection – gets the piss thoroughly ripped out of him in front of thirty other boys because his way of speaking is a bit off or he's still waiting on puberty to kick in. You feel like shit in the wake of it because even at that age, even softened by all the convenient deniability that comes with being at the lazy tail end of a mob, part of you knows you've been complicit in something ugly and cruel. And there's no hiding from that.

That's how I felt about photographing those inbred hippos and their ancient horse. So when I hear the sound of trotting hooves growing louder, I slow the car to a crawl, hoping to catch a glimpse of one still in the whole of its health – shiny-coated and strong and left to its own magnificent devices out here in the darkness. Two of them approach cautiously and stand staring at us, their tails swishing back and forth behind them. Except they aren't horses. They're zebras. Now, granted, I've never actually seen a zebra in the flesh, so a part of me wonders if this isn't some special breed of pony indigenous to California. The product of some wealthy designer breeding programme perhaps. But no, I tell myself, I know what a shaggin' zebra looks like and these are definitely zebra. Right?

'Is everyone else seeing zebras?' Tom enquires.

'Yep.'

'Yeah.'

'You think it's possible we took a wrong turn somewhere?' he continues, diplomatically.

'And ended up where? Kenya?' says Baz. The zebras are staring at us, chewing lazily.

'Maybe this is some sort of wildlife park.'

'You mean like Fota Island?' says Baz.

'Maybe.'

'That's impossible,' I say, confused. I take the Restless Souls brochure from the glove box and hold it up against the compound. 'See? We're here. Here just appears to also be a zebra . . . farm.'

'Sanctuary, probably,' says Tom.

'Well I for one am relieved that the good doctor will be able to focus one hundred per cent on helping Tom and not be distracted by the well-being of his private zebra herd.'

'For all we know they could be part of the therapy, Baz.'

'Ha, even better!'

'Don't be such a fucking cynic. People use anxiety dogs in PTSD treatment all the time. Isn't that right, Tom?'

'We did have two labs at Wastwater. Labrador pups called Iggy and Sam.'

'There. See?'

'You can't play fetch with a fucking zebra.'

'Animals are soothing, Baz, is the point I'm trying to make.'

'Well if that's all it takes we could have just bought a weekend pass for Dublin zoo and saved ourselves the plane fare.' As he says this, a long-horned antelope wanders past the zebras, hops over the ditch, and settles itself in front of the car. Nobody says anything. The antelope stares at us. We stare at the antelope. Eventually it gets bored and disappears back into the field.

'Karl.'

'Yes, Barry?'

'Any chance you can get us out of here before the fucking lions arrive?'

The zebras bolt as the car purrs back to life. At the turn in the road we pass a bare-chested older man walking in the opposite direction. In his clamped right hand he's holding a healthy flame, burning atop a black wooden stake, and criss-crossing the road to light each of the tiki torches. His head is shaved, not bald, and his silver beard stands out starkly against the coppery California tan of his skin. He wears faded cargo shorts and sandals. I watch his sinewy muscles move as his arm rises and falls. The stray embers float up into the sky like fireflies. We nod as he passes and his face crinkles into a smile under the light of the flame. I turn right into a large courtyard where three other cars sit snugly together. I park on the side most shrouded in shadow and kill the engine. The man is about a quarter of the way down the path, his torch moving diagonally at a leisurely pace.

'Why doesn't he just do one side on the way down, and the other on the way back?'

'Dunno. You'd think that'd be quicker all right.' We track his progress for another minute or two.

'I suppose we'd better head in,' Tom says. Baz twists his head backward to face him. His expression even more sceptical than usual.

'You know you don't have to go through with all of this if you don't want to, Tom.' Baz looks to me for support, which I don't fucking appreciate since he's fully aware that this is our last roll of the dice. Why he's chosen to float this now, five minutes from check-in, I don't know. 'If any of this mad alternative therapy shit feels too weird or extreme or whatever, just say so. Don't feel like you have to, just cause we're here. Right, Karl?'

My blood is rising now, but of course I can't say anything. 'Right. It's your call at the end of the day.'

'Thanks for saying that, lads. I know you mean it, and I appreciate it, but I want to try this. Really. I mean, it's either this or . . .' He trails off and I'm glad he doesn't finish it, whatever 'it' is. We all just nod our heads like dopes at a funeral and look away.

'Right.'

'Right.'

It's a reluctant shuffle to the silo's double doors. Now that we've actually arrived at the edge, no one seems particularly eager to jump. We're close enough to see someone ascending the staircase inside. A woman, her salt and pepper hair tied back in a tight bun, wearing a long lab coat and holding a metal clipboard. This snapshot of generic professionalism, after the robots and zebras and the wild man, puts a sliver of ease into me. I point her out to Baz so that he can log her presence too. The varnished wooden exterior of the building is carved with thousands of detailed nature drawings, from ground level all the way up to the top. They look like cave paintings. Stickmen hurling spears at buffalo, birds pouring out from leafy tree canopies, packs of scruffy dogs chasing nothing in particular, suns and moons passing midway as they swap shifts. This is impressive, objectively, but in truth I couldn't care less about wood carvings, and I doubt Baz or Tom have been harbouring a secret passion for them either. As I say, we're stalling. Eventually a receptionist spots us standing there like spare parts and gestures for us to come inside, his Hollywood smile gleaming out from across the desk. He looks to be about twenty, with a feather-garnished earring, wavy mane of surfer's blond hair, and a necklace of tiny blue seashells that rests snug against his collarbone. This can hardly be the polished robot I explained our days-long delay to over the phone earlier on this afternoon. We smile our comparatively yokel smiles back at him, gingerly raise our right hands in salute, and push through the doors into the atrium.

'Welcome, gentlemen, to Restless Souls, where the wounded come to heal. My name is Theo, I'm the night-time concierge here at the facility. How may I assist you this evening?' Unnerving. This blond kid has just exuded more charm and professionalism in this one auto-pilot greeting than I have in a decade of adult working life. His eyes are alert, but not scrutinising. His demeanour is business-like, but not unfriendly. If you told me this was one of the Kennedy flock – a law-school bound nephew on his final surfing summer break before returning to the real world – I would believe it. We can't talk to these people. I probably have more in common with a retired Maori fisherman than I do with Big Wave Theo here. Still, he's made first contact so it'd be rude not to at least try. I clear my throat, loudly, and approach his station.

'Good evening, eh, Theo.' *Good evening.* 'My name is Karl Sullivan. We're here to check-in our friend, Tom Dempsey. Thomas Dempsey. He's supposed to meet with Doctor Saunders tonight.' Theo smiles that blinding smile, nodding patiently as I fall over my words.

'Of course. One moment, sir.' *Sir.*

He punches a few keys, double clicks a cordless mouse.

'OK, Mr Sullivan, we have Mr Dempsey's room all ready to go. He'll be staying in the Coral Cabin suite. And according to our booking specifications you and Mr Connolly have requested to remain on the premises as guests of the clinic for the initial period of Mr Dempsey's stay, is that correct?'

'Eh, initial?' Baz pipes in. 'No, we'll be here for as long as he's here.' Theo's face registers no surprise.

'I was told that we would discuss a time frame for Tom's recovery with Doctor Saunders,' I say. In my peripheral vision, I can see Baz eyeballing me. 'So that we can all figure out *together* when we can take him home.'

'Very good, sir.' Still smiling serenely.

There's a long stretch of silence. I turn away from Theo's waxwork stare and zero in on the massive watercolour mural painted onto the wall to the left of us. Dwarfing the tasselled armchairs, dream catchers, and bejewelled cow skulls that populate the waiting area below it, the painting must be eight feet high and ten feet across. I'm surprised I didn't see it from the driveway. It depicts a long stretch of ocean with waves like huge, frothy speed bumps gathering steam in the distance. In the hazy, reddish purple sky clouds have taken on vaguely human shapes as they float toward a cliff top not unlike the ones we sped nervously past on our way here. Kneeling, arms outstretched at the cliff's precipice, reaching out toward a narrow column of light – more of an alien tractor beam than a ray of sunshine – is a man in combat fatigues with a dismantled rifle at his feet. It's striking, in a garish, ridiculous sort of way.

'Glorious, isn't it?' gushes Theo. The word sounds practised. There's no way 'glorious' is part of his off-duty vocabulary. We murmur various unintelligible noises of agreement. 'That,' he says, 'is an artistic interpretation of the exact moment when Doctor Saunders experienced his epiphany. Look at the play of light and darkness, battling for his future. You can really feel the struggle. Sometimes at night I just stand here and stare at it, for inspiration, you know?'

'Eh, yeah,' says Baz, mouthing *what the fuck* at me behind Theo's back. 'It's really something else all right.'

'Who painted it?' Tom asks

'One of Doctor Saunders' patients, about five years ago. A man by the name of Major Andrew Henderson. Poor guy had been haunted by night terrors and hallucinations since his return from Vietnam in 1975. Can you imagine it? Fifteen years of internal suffering after all that carnage and sacrifice. Anyway, he painted that for us in the summer of '91. Spent about three months working on it, day and night, but as you can see, it was worth it. We're always so stoked when he comes to visit.'

'Visit?' Tom asks. 'As in, after a relapse?'

'Hmmm? Oh no, no no no, nothing like that.' He sounds genuinely shocked, as if the notion of one of these brain-addled GIs falling off the wagon is completely incomprehensible to him. 'It's been over three years since Major Henderson suffered any kind of debilitating episode. He still utilises a personalised selection of our various meditative and relaxation techniques from time to time, but we actively encourage our former patients to do this when they experience echoes of their former trauma. We like to compare it to an athlete continuing a regimen of stretching after a successful operation.'

'So, he was cured?' Tom asks. Baz and I look away. There's a terrible hope in his voice that I can't bear to hear. I wonder how many other wits-end basket cases have heard the Major Andrew Henderson spiel.

'Well, insofar as anyone suffering from that type of

psychological damage can be said to be cured, yes, he made a full recovery.'

'Ah, there it is,' says Baz, erupting. '"Insofar as", I knew there'd be some type of bullshit happy-clappy Yank spin on what'll end up being the same temporary fix. Painting pictures on the wall and not sticking the barrel of your own army rifle in your mouth is all well and good, but I wanna know what kind of quality of life this lad has.' We're all a bit blown back by this, all except Theo of course. Normally, it pains Baz to even think about the final implications of this kind of thing, let alone roar them out loud. It's a fair question though, and Theo answers it like he's been trained to answer all questions.

'He has a new wife, Mr Connolly; an eighteen-month-old son; a managerial position at an auto dealership in San Francisco. He sells paintings from his own stall at a farmers' market on Sunday afternoons. The most debilitating aspects of his PTSD have subsided, and what remains is being managed by low dose medication and therapy.' Theo is looking directly at Tom now. 'He has a life again. That's what we aim to give people back here, Mr Dempsey, a life.'

We nod, sheepishly, and turn once more to the giant mural. It's blurry, the way watercolours are supposed to be, I guess, but not unhinged.

'This Major Henderson,' I ask, 'did he, I mean, was he the same afterwards? Was he his old self?'

'I didn't know his old self, so I'm afraid I can't answer that. I can tell you this though: we're not in the business of reprogramming people's personalities here at Restless Souls. Recovery requires sacrifice, often quite significant sacrifice, but given what you have already been through, Mr Dempsey,

I'm sure that comes as no surprise. Ultimately though, Doctor Saunders wants to *rescue* the individual from the rising waters of his or her own trauma, not create an entirely new, stable entity from the blown apart remains of an old psyche. But listen to me going on, parroting his mission statement like it's my own. Doctor Saunders will be able to talk you through all of this in far greater detail when he gets back.'

'Gets back?' Baz asks with what's getting to be characteristic brusqueness. 'Gets back from where?'

'From the lighting of the torches. Doctor Saunders lights every torch on the grounds each night at sundown. The flames chart a course across the darkness to our facility. They represent breadcrumbs of hope that lead those who are lost –'

'To where, a gingerbread house?' Baz interjects. Theo's smile is tight-lipped this time.

'– out of the woods. You need to revisit your fairy tales, Mr Connolly.'

'Yeah, that's why we travelled five thousand miles all right. To study up on Hansel and fucking Gretel.'

'Take it easy, Baz.'

'I didn't mean to offend you, Mr Connolly.'

'So, wait,' I say, 'just to clarify. That guy, the one with the beard and the bare feet and the rest, *that* is Doctor Saunders?' This can't be right. Our torch-lighter, he had to have been a groundskeeper. Some harmless local vagrant who completes the route once the real Doctor Saunders has finished lighting the courtyard torches and returned to his mahogany desk and government-quality internet access.

'That's him,' Theo confirms, proudly.

'And the animals?' Baz asks. 'Those lost-looking zebras and

antelope and god knows what else giving us the eye as we drove in. What's the story with that?'

'Aw, I'm so stoked you got a chance to see them at dusk! I find it to be the most peaceful time for observing the animals.' This seems to be a tic of Theo's. Moving back and forth between English butler-style formality and surfer-dude exuberance depending on his excitement level.

'Yeah, it was . . . nice, I suppose, but why are they here? Are they part of the therapy?'

'In a way, yes, I suppose you could say they are. Doctor Saunders purchased a number of small herds from a private reserve just a few miles down the road, on the former estate of Mr William Randolph Hearst.' He pauses for effect. We very clearly have no idea who Mr William Randolph Hearst is or why he would have enough zebras to allow for the sale of a number of herds, small or otherwise.

'Help us out here, Theo,' says Baz.

'My apologies. Mr Hearst was an American newspaper tycoon from right here in California. He was an extremely influential figure in both media and politics for over fifty years.' Again, nothing.

'You may know a version of him from the 1941 Orson Welles film *Citizen Kane*?'

I realise that it's almost certainly us who should be feeling embarrassed right now. This is likely one of those cultural touchstones of contemporary western civilisation that people just know. Still, since our ignorance out-votes his trivia three to one, I've decided not to even bother pretending we have a clue what he's on about. It could be my imagination, but for once it's Theo who seems shaken. If I didn't know better

I'd say he was a little bit embarrassed himself. A tiny, almost imperceptible bead of sweat has formed just below his hairline.

'Or from the *Simpsons* episode which parodies *Citizen Kane*? With, em, Bobo the teddy bear?' He grimaces slightly as he says this, though there is really no need.

'Oh yeah!'

'I love that fucking episode! With the big box of snow globes,' Baz exclaims.

'And the Ramones,' Tom chimes in.

'Yes! The Ramones, that was hilarious. Wait, Tom, you've probably seen about four hours of television total in the last four years. Where'd you come across it?' I ask. Theo looks thoroughly baffled.

'One of the orderlies at Wastwater was a big *Simpsons* fan. He'd sit down to watch the double bill on Sky 1 every Sunday evening in the dayroom.'

'You know,' I say, 'I think I do remember reading something about this Hearst lad. Not the full shilling, right? Used to keep jars of his own piss and build planes too big to fly?'

'That was actually Howard Hughes.'

'Ah.'

'Roughly the same era though.'

'Right.'

'So anyway,' says Baz, irritated at his own concentration span, 'the animals, Theo, why are they here?'

'Doctor Saunders will explain all aspects of the therapeutic process upon his return.'

'And when will that actually be?' I ask before a baritone drawl from the entrance shuts us all up.

'Gentlemen,' Saunders says, his muscled arms held outward

in greeting, singed wisps of silver hair stuck to his sweat-glazed chest. 'Please forgive my absence thus far. The fall of night waits for no one. I'm sure Theo has been taking excellent care of you, but as the man at the helm of this little ark, let me just say, on behalf of all of us here, zebra and antelope included, welcome to Restless Souls.'

Sarajevo, February 4, 1994

Hasan died on Tuesday.

His coffin was lighter than I thought it would be. As we carried it I wondered if he was in there at all. If maybe he was still lying on that freezing slab in the hospital morgue. Lips blue. Waiting patiently for fog to drop over the valley. No rush, Jelena said he'd been an atheist since childhood. I caught Fadila staring at the box like it wasn't real. Her only son – looking no different now than he did a week ago, save for a Golden Lily medal pinned to his chest, and a bullet hole through his throat – bundled into a plywood crate. Graffitied with old shipping stamps. Made me think of Da's. The pressure of it on my shoulder. Smooth and heavy. The slow walk to the grave. The shadow of Glasnevin's round tower. Everyone in their good clothes, heads bowed low. All the time in the world to mourn properly. To give him the respect he deserved at the end.

Snow had fallen heavy through the night and long into this afternoon. I pictured one of us slipping, dropping him. I imagined his shitty makeshift coffin shattering to kindling on the cold cobblestones. There'd be no more wood. No more time. No more energy. We'd have to carry him there in our arms. Stiff. Smelling of death. Tiny tunnel bored through his neck.

We moved quickly through the damp fog and the encroaching twilight. Stopped only once so that Vuk could catch his breath. He leaned on his hands against the backrest of a bench but refused to sit. That rattling cough the only noise. Fadila put her hand on his back, whispered something I couldn't hear. He nodded and spat a wad of phlegm into the gutter as discreetly as he could. Two mutts, all ribs, bared their sharp teeth at us. Matted fur wet and filthy. Too much effort. They trotted along behind us for a while, whimpering for scraps, then disappeared down a laneway.

We passed Groblje Lav, The Lion Cemetery, turned into a park in better times, and reactivated for service once the shells began to fall – too exposed these days even if it wasn't bursting at the seams with the recent dead. Like something from an old horror film. The chipped stone lion resting on its entrance pillar. Lying down to die. Fog leaking out like a river of dry ice. We walked on together toward the scorched Olympic stadium beyond. High above us, affixed to the tower, interlocking rings above a stylized orange snowflake serve as a reminder of better days, when all things seemed possible. Red terrace guardrails, flattened seats, panelling hanging by threads of electrical cable. Like punched-in teeth. Everything mangled now.

The former football pitches. The blight of fresh pauper's graves. Hundreds upon hundreds of makeshift headstones, crosses, planks, sticks, bare mounds. Black holes waiting to be filled. Gravediggers in ratty, snow-heavy jumpers. Trying to hack through the hard earth before it froze over. I recognised two of them from the last time. I wondered then how long a man could do a job like that – digging tiny graves – before he goes insane.

*

Hasan had only been in the ground for a few minutes when the firing started. There was barely enough time to say a prayer.

I bruised her wrist. Pulling her down as bullets kicked up dirt all around us. There was no time to be gentle.

Staggering home, her arm hanging unnaturally at her side. Purple marks spreading across the pale skin underneath her bracelets, ruined now. I tried to take her hand but she pulled away from me. Something in her eyes, like the broken parents at the hospital. She wanted to die. That's the truth of it. Meet their fire head on. Keep him from sleeping underground alone. And I took that away from her. But what else could I do?

The way she had screamed. Biting my arm till it bled while I pressed my body flat over hers. The pain, like my heart was trying to charge its way through the wall of my chest. I couldn't breathe. I tried to tell her stop, please stop this, Jelena, they'll kill you, he wouldn't want this, he wouldn't want this; but maybe I didn't say anything at all. I don't know. Something wooden exploded. Splinters flew past our faces. Fadila was wailing. A chunk of cloth and flesh bulging out of the wall of his grave where the diggers had disturbed an older plot. Three dull thumps, one after another. Hasan's mound absorbing the sniper fire. Another group screaming from across the cemetery. The fog probably only lifted for a minute or two, but I thought it would never come back.

Vuk was bleeding from a gash on his forehead. Fadila shaking in his arms. Her nice black dress all torn and filthy. A college friend of Hasan's propped them both up. I ran my palms over Jelena's head and body, checking for blood. When I found nothing, I pulled her tight into my chest and held her there. She was still and silent in my arms.

Chapter 11

When I let my mind wander unchecked, which happens far more often than I'd like in the stretches of silence that fill these long fucking days, it shapes Tom's future in one of two ways: entirely healed – the impossible return of my serious-but-functioning mate – or dead. In the former scenario, Tom re-enacts scenes from our teenage years, repeating lines in a voice without inflection, drained of all energy, as if to underline the fact that the whole thing is a sham, an echo of something real. In the latter, Tom swims out into the ocean and lets it swallow him up. I see his methodical plod from the shore to the water's edge. It's night-time and we're on a beach I have never been to before. He turns and raises a hand in my direction. It's not a wave of hello or goodbye, just a brief acknowledgment of my presence. When he turns back around, I see that his bare back is criss-crossed with long, raised scars. He doesn't flinch as the cold seawater rises above his chest. He power strokes his way out into the churning grey-blue and I watch the waves eat up the froth of his kicks like footprints in a sandstorm.

After a few minutes, there's nothing left to obscure. I watch him drop beneath the surface, his outstretched arm devoured inch by inch, and I do nothing. You can't be blamed for your dreams, I know that. But these aren't dreams.

To drive it away I play back scenes from invincible eras: clumsy tackles on frozen pitches in December; three-day benders in Galway City on New Year's weekend; hyperactive school tours to Lough Dan; warm summer nights in Scruffy Murphy's. Camping trips. Pub crawls. Principals' offices. County finals. I crush our careless, joyous shared past into an all-action highlight reel. It has no beginning or ending. No real plot to speak of. It moves backwards and forwards at montage speed and cuts out long before the tone can darken.

I started it after Gabriel died. I couldn't tell you why exactly. Eulogy. Therapy. Masochism. Denial. Probably all of those and more. What I do know is that it feels desperate now, like trying to reanimate a corpse, and that I need it. I need to do it while I still can, because with every passing month the old footage gets a little grainer, and precious scenes blur into nothing. I don't know what I'm going to do when this terrible fucking present overwhelms the past.

At Gabriel's funeral, I couldn't speak. I stood up there in St Patrick's and looked out at the faces of everyone we had ever known, crammed tight into the pews in their black suits and mourning dresses, and I couldn't say a word. I clenched my jaw and looked down at the single sheet of paper with its clumsy jumble of words; words that conveyed so little of what he meant to me, to us, that to read them aloud would almost have been an insult. Eventually I felt Eugene's hand on my shoulder, heard his soft growling voice telling me 'it's all right, lad, it's all right'. It would have been easier to cry then, but it'd been so long I think I had forgotten how. I sat in between Clara and Baz who draped their arms around me and held me there, tight, their heads almost touching mine, like they were preventing me from dropping off the face of the earth.

Eugene spoke beautifully, slow and soft and full of the things I wanted people to know about Gabriel but couldn't articulate. Not then. Not since. He said that he was proud to call Gabriel and me his sons, proud of how close we were as brothers, proud of the men we had become. Had we become anything at all? I could see the glisten in Baz's eye out of the corner of my own, feel the shudders running through his body as he tried to steady himself. Therese was sobbing quietly, her hand clutching Clara's, a trickle of rosary beads hanging over their entwined fingers. Eugene finished by asking us, pleading with us all, not to think of Gabriel that way. Cold and still and beaten, the way he never was in life. 'Pick a moment,' he said, 'something personal, hopeful, and make that your memory of him. That's what he would have wanted.' That, I could do at least. He stepped away from the microphone and put his ashen palm on the edge of Gabriel's coffin. I knew what words were running through his head then, the same ones that I had said aloud in the mortuary the night before: *I wish it were me instead of you in there*. The only difference being that in his heart, Eugene meant them.

So I did what was asked of me. I rewound the tape. Back before 'Be Not Afraid', before the identification, before the bloodshot eyes over the breakfast table, before the solitary benders that ended with him passed out against the front door, before Anna left. Before every needless street corner brawl. Before every ignored warning sign, to a time when things weren't so serious. I went back eight years, to our one and only foray into the heart of the Connemara Gaeltacht. Baz, who never had a head for languages, was struggling in class (read: couldn't give two fucks about class) and his mother decided that three weeks in Irish college that July was his last best shot at scraping a D in the Leaving Cert and thereby not totally disgracing his proud Gaeilgeoirí parents. Of course, as soon as we heard he was off to spend half the summer *ceili* dancing and splashing around the Atlantic with two hundred gamey country girls, our collective interest in achieving proficiency in the native tongue suddenly shot up. I'm not sure it occurred to any of the four of us at the time that the college might have some rules beyond 'good luck with the birds' that it was invested in enforcing. Still, Eugene and Therese gave us the nod, though I'm certain they knew full well where this newfound enthusiasm stemmed from, and Tom's mam finally relented when Gabriel told her about the college's tri-weekly mandatory trips to mass.

Our first major warning, for speaking English of course, came forty-five minutes into the introductory afternoon. Baz, with typical subtlety, asked a freckled, pony-tailed blonde in a Duran Duran T-shirt if she knew how long the assembly would be, because he was dying for a piss. That was the first time I set eyes on Clara, who looked to me like she belonged in a music video. She laughed, and shushed him, but it was too late. Some jowly aul lad in an Aran jumper dragged us away to the office and put our names in a huge black ledger and told us that we had two strikes left before we were out the door. I had to force a hand over Baz's gob to stop him from responding to this in English. We backed out of the office like deferent subjects of a mad king, and went searching for a hedge in which to smoke and figure out how we were gonna last the week. Getting sent home meant some mulleted mucksavage would be kissing Clara at the final night's disco instead of me, and at that age you could make more hay with a bird in three concentrated weeks in the Gaelic Gulag than you could in months of awkward 'dates' back in the real world.

Our second warning came five days later as a group of us were moving kayaks from the water's edge back up to the Republican-graffitied storage shed from which we had extracted them half an hour previous. In the interim, the skies had opened and the rain was screaming in sideways from the open sea. Marcus, the college's water sports guru and only Dubliner on the faculty, blew three short whistle blasts like a referee calling for full time, and bellowed *gach duine ar ais go dtí an tseid. Is é an fharraige ró-chontúirteach sa lá atá inniu.* To prove that this wasn't the case, and to show off to Clara and whoever else was standing around shivering themselves blue with us that morning, we dropped the kayaks and made a break for the water. Now, the fact that we were wrestling around the surf cursing at each other in the forbidden tongue was one thing; Marcus was one of us, to an extent, and would have let that slide. But Gabriel, never content to stay waist deep, decided to play chicken with the tide. Already into his stride he turned his head and roared a dare for us to do the same, and because we were all, on some level, forever following his lead, we shrugged and swam out after him. We could hear the fading voices on the shore change from Irish to English as genuine concern set in amongst the group, but we didn't care. The return leg was trickier than we thought, not that we had given it any consideration whatsoever, and by the time we felt the seabed beneath our feet again, it was all any of us could do to stay upright. My lungs were burning and after two wobbly steps on the wet sand of that beach at Indreabhán, I collapsed. The others fell beside me seconds later. Tom, the largest teenager at the college by some distance, looked like a prostrate Gulliver awaiting the Lilliputians. We turned over onto our backs, gasping and coughing and hoovering up the damp air while the others formed a white-faced circle around us. I couldn't read Clara's expression, but decided that she wasn't too pissed off. The sun punched holes through the grey clouds above us. I wondered if Marcus would let the rest of them kayak now. Baz rolled into push-up position and began to vomit, laughing like a madman between retches. It was glorious.

Three-strike policy or no, that little stunt alone should have gotten us all on the first bus back to wherever it was we were supposed to get a proper bus back home from. Instead, we made up some cock-and-bull excuse about mistaking a buoy for a drowning child and not hearing the whistles because of the direction the wind was blowing. They knew it was nonsense – how could they not? – but we pleaded with them in our pathetically broken Irish to give us one more chance and Marcus, for whatever reason, decided to back our play by claiming he saw Gabriel point to the buoy moments before we all made a break for it. After we were read the riot act in shrill, unintelligible Ulster Irish by the principal of the place, he booted us from the office and told us we were all on our final warning. On the way back to the bus, Marcus clouted us one by one across the backs of our heads with a rolled up newspaper, muttering 'fucking eejits' with a smirk.

So we wrangled ourselves another week's reprieve as a unit and it's still, to my mind, the best we ever spent together. We hissed passable answers back and forth to one another in the morning classes, cobbling together one functioning student from our collective scraps of vocabulary. Gabriel paired up with Baz in the two-man boats in the afternoons, teasing him and defending him and making him feel like he had an older brother, something we knew Baz had always wanted. Those hours gave me a chance to talk to Tom about Clara; about Eugene and Therese getting older; about his mother, and the rift that was widening between them that year. About the dark parts of the world he seemed so determined to wade into. He was never a big talker, even then, but for whatever reason, those slow, aimless ocean paddles took on the air of a psychiatrist's office. An hour or so a day to be slightly less inhibited versions of ourselves. For all I know Baz and Gabriel could have been doing the same thing. When we had said all that needed saying, and Marcus' new, extra-piercing whistle had been blown, we left the serious talk out on the water. In the evenings we pucked sliotars against the walls of the ancient stone house we were staying in and played football with our country doppelgangers on the soft sod of the uneven field beyond. We horsed down trough-loads of boiled spuds and rubbery discs of gammon ham at the long kitchen table, and fought over the one tiny landing mirror tasked with reflecting each of our over-gelled mops of hair

to despair or smug satisfaction. We piled into the shuttle bus
in a cloud of cheap deodorant spray and rattled back to the
college where the girls were waiting. We danced the 'Walls of
Limerick' and the 'Siege of Ennis' with Clara and her gang
and found out that they went to a posh private school just a
couple of miles from us back home. Easy walking distance,
for a fella with a reason to make the trip. Gabriel ended up
copping off with one of them, all lip gloss and peppermint
chewing gum, in the water-damaged former classroom above
the hall. Every night we snuck out of the house, creeping
stealthily past the old woman's bedroom window as she slept
in her massive buttercup-yellow nightgown, to the empty
field beyond. There, high above our whispers and plumes of
cigarette smoke, a million stars – more than I have ever seen,
before or, till very recently, since – blinked down at us, a stray
occasionally shooting across the dotted sky to a chorus of low
ooooohs and ahhhhhs.

A few days from the end we had come back to the house
jazzed after finding a litre bottle of Jameson stashed behind
the speakers in the main hall. Baz, with unprecedented stealthi-
ness, swiped the thing and bundled it up in a towel, which he
then crammed into Clara's bag.

'Karl.'

'What?'

'I need you to talk to your bird.'

'What? She's not my, we're just – wait, why?'

'I need you to talk to Clara.'

'I *was* talking to her till you dragged me back here. Why
are you so damn fidgety anyway?'

'No time to explain. The feds will be on to us any minute.

There's a bottle of whiskey in that big stupid-looking handbag she carries around. And before you say anything, I had to take it. It was just sitting there, looking at me like. It's done now anyway, we can't put it back. I can already see O'Riordain headed that way. Fucking hell, he's gonna hit the roof when he twigs someone has nicked it. The lad is a psychopath. Did I tell you I heard he was in the IRA? Jesus he's liable to batter us to death if he finds out. We're fine though, we're fine. They'll never check her bag. All we have to do is make it to the bus and we're home and dry. But you have to tell her to play it cool. Tell her she can split it with us later, she's just gonna have to be a mule for another hour or so. Ask her if she has any tampons she can throw on top just in case he does do a bag check.'

How we escaped that hall – with O'Riordain stomping between groups of clumsy teenage dancers, swatting hands away from waists and hurling accusations from that huge, reddening face, its booze-burst capillaries rising to the surface like forks of purple lightning – I'll never know. Clara actually took the whole thing in pretty good humour – said she admired our 'commitment to following the worst thought-out heist imaginable through to its inevitably tragic conclusion' – which only made me more determined to ask her if she wanted to stay together when we got back to Dublin. Three hours later the five of us (plus a mate of hers who, for the life of me, I can't remember a thing about) found ourselves nestled against the inside wall of a ruined cottage somewhere between her house and ours, sipping whiskey and red lemonade from tiny plastic cups. We had the soft whoosh of the ocean below us and that uncountable galaxy of stars above and we were happy as pigs in shit. Baz was holding court, detailing the art of the perfect grab as if he were a seasoned cat burglar. I can remember so clearly putting my arm around Clara, the feel of her whole body leaning back into my chest, smiling up at me in that way she would on and off for years afterward. I can see every tooth in the broad grin that spread across Tom's face – a rarity, even in those days – as Baz explained the art of reading a room for weak points. And clearest of all, I remember Gabriel's face as he watched us. That's when he was really at his happiest, when we were all so settled into something that we stepped out of time together. All those heart-in-mouth stunts he pulled were just a way to get us there. Looking back, it was as if a part of him knew it was all going to be over too soon. Like some whisper in his head had told him that those six or seven years were the only good ones he was ever going to have, and that he had to make them count for all of us.

So when he strutted back through the doorway of that ruined house having relieved himself a distance away out of courtesy to the girls, and O'Riordain's buzz-saw voice came pealing through the night air after him, I knew exactly what he would do.

'C'mon,' I said, 'he can't see who it is in the darkness. We'll all leg it together.'

He shook his head, smiling at our five faces bobbling up and down in unison, and downed the remainder of his syrupy concoction. 'He has the place cornered. Unless you want to scale down the cliffside and swim, Karly, no one's leaving here without him seeing us.'

'But you'll be expelled.'

'Ha, no shit, Sherlock.

'Then I'm going out there with you.'

'If you want to be choked into unconsciousness by your brother and wet your trousers in front of your new bird and all your mates, then sure, you should absolutely try to go out there with me.'

'Gabriel—'

'Look, it's fine, honestly. Stop fussing, you're losing your mystique. I came down here to have a laugh with you lads, and I've had it. Christ, it's a miracle we made it this far. But there's no sense in all of us, not to mention these poor *innocent* young waifs, getting the boot if we can help it. Anyway, I've been gunning for a showdown with this fucker for two weeks now and that piss above the parapet has just given me the green light.'

'You're sure?'

'Course I'm sure. I'm always sure. Now, as soon as you see him chase me round the bend in the road there, gather up those cups, get back to the gaf, gobble up a tube of toothpaste each, and hide under the covers. If all of you aren't tucked up tight in your beds by the time he drags me back there by the ear, well, we're quadruply fucked, and whatever unfinished business you have down here is gonna stay that way.' He winked at Clara and me and scooped up the bottle of Jameson, its dregs plinking round the bottom. 'Right, I'd better go return this to its rightful owner.'

Next thing we knew he had leapt up on the embankment outside the cottage and was waving his arms in the air like a marooned sailor, mock stumbling backwards and forwards while O'Riordain stood fuming on the roadside some fifty metres away.

'O'Riordain, ya terrorist bollix, do you want a drink?' Top of his lungs.

'You! Of course it's fucking you.' Funny how O'Riordain reverted to the colonial tongue in this moment of incandescent rage. He probably realised that it's trickier to put the fear of god into someone like Gabriel if they haven't a clue what you're saying. 'If the seal on that bottle is as much as fucking cracked, I'm gonna stick it up your arse and boot you till it shatters.'

'Now, now, *a mháistir*, no need for that kind of talk. Sure we're all friends here. And look, I saved you the last shot. Here, catch.' With that he took the bottle by its dark green neck and flung it high and long into the air. From our crouched positions we could see it arc its way across the stars and down into a nest of chunky rocks in the roadside ditch, where it shattered into a thousand brilliant pieces.

When I think of the eulogy, of Eugene's one request in the church that day, it's the sight of Gabriel sprinting off into the starlit night, his infectious laugh floating back to us as we scramble away to safety, that I hold tight to. It's how I keep him alive.

Sarajevo, July 17, 1994

I abandoned him.

I wasn't there to watch over him.

I wasn't even there to help carry him.

I'm sorry, Gabriel. I'm so sorry.

I nearly killed a man last night. I would have. A shell stopped my heart. It's been eight hours since the blast and I still have blood on my knuckles. Smell of his sweat on my forearm. Ringing in my ears again. Jelena is asleep on my chest. Holding on to me tight. I've never seen her frightened of me before. She flinched when I leaned over to snuff out the candle.

Obala was packed. Made me sick, the feel of the place. We watched this band, Sikter, from a corner. Snarling down at the pit of people. Punk prayers. Everyone's clothes a size too large. Soba, Sikter's front man. Sarajevo's renaissance man, back and forth from the frontlines between gigs. Planting mines. Power chords blasted from the fat mounted speakers. I closed my eyes, let myself vibrate in the dark. Tried to calm down. Jelena said something I didn't hear and smiled. Nervous. So I smiled too. She stroked the side of my face. Soft, like I was an addict coming down. Her hair the only thing in the room that didn't smell of sweat.

Soldiers in green fatigues leaned against the bar, arms

around each other's necks. Spit flecks sailing through the air. Singing. Their faces twisted. Draining dregs from their shot glasses. One grabbed the arse of a waitress as she passed. I saw her wince. I stared at a photographer from the Holiday Inn. Arrived a day or two before I left. Remembered the bald fixer who brought girls to his room. They couldn't have been older than fifteen. Scared little things. How they'd leave. Red-eyed and ashamed, but with wads of money bulging from their tight trousers. Photographer's stubby fingers were pawing at another one now. Young. Wasted. He fed her drink after drink. Rubbed the bare small of her back. Soldiers were banging palms down on the bar. He looked up and grinned at me. No recognition. I stared him down till he stopped smiling. He mouthed 'fuck you' and turned away.

All night long I saw faces of people I knew were dead. The buzz-cut kid with the mangled head. The mute toddler who went into septic shock and died in Jelena's arms.

Hasan.

Goran.

Gabriel.

Tried to shake them away. Clamped my eyes shut. Tried to slow my heart. The broken beats felt like a countdown timer. Shirt soaked through with sweat. Jelena felt the dampness and held my face in her hands.

'Tom,' she said. 'TOM, open your eyes. Look at me.' Strobe light flashes. Fat purple rope bruise around her neck.

'What's wrong?' she said, palm over my chest.

'Nothing,' I said, 'it's just boiling in here is all. Why don't you say hello to the others and I'll get us some drinks?' I said it like that. Formal. Waved at Amira and Marko. Tried to smile. Jelena rubbed my arm.

'*Volim te*, Tom.'

'I love you too,' I said. 'Go on over, I'll follow.'

Gabriel talking to a Japanese journalist at the end of the bar. Pulled three cigarettes from the journalist's pack as he spoke. Gabriel's hand on the back of his neck. Japanese scribbling notes. Gabriel putting one cigarette behind each ear. Third between his lips. He wore a long brown trench. Stroked a soul patch Gabriel never had. This can't be the last time I see him. It's not fair. I got closer. His face blurred and then it was someone else. I waited for it to turn back. The man with Gabriel's face was telling a story. A trip into enemy territory on Mount Trebević. Stealing through the trees in the dead of night. A convoy of patrol vehicles. I'd heard it before.

The band had stopped. 'Just Like Heaven' playing low. People catching their breath. Smoking with shaking hands. Marko and Amira talking to Sikter's drummer about something. I couldn't see Jelena. Too many bodies. I took a breath, told myself everything was OK. Bathroom door swung open. Her high heels. Her perfect smile. I watched her move though the crowd like she was the only one in colour. I watched him step out in front of her. His hand on her waist. That look, same as I remember. I was moving through people. Shouting in my ear. She pushed him away and said something. Around them people laughed. He slapped her hard across the face with that fat, filthy hand.

People tried to pull me off. Don't know how many I hit. When they stopped trying. I felt his face crumple under my blows. Cheekbone. Nose. Teeth. Glass from the table I threw him through. The pop of his shoulder. I dragged him through the shards, into the centre of the room. Blood from his burst eyes. Mouth pulped, gurgling at me. People screaming. Jelena screaming. Soldiers standing around us. I reached up to the thick black belt of one. Pulled it from the open holster. Jammed it into his mouth. The music had stopped. For a moment, there was only the blood in my ears.

'And *you'll* live.' Roaring at him. He couldn't even see me. 'You'll get to live!'

I told Jelena, leaning into her as we staggered toward the hospital, that it was her voice. Begging me to stop. That it brought me back before the shell hit. It was the right thing to say. But not the truth. Truth is, if the shell had dropped five seconds later I would have already blown a hole through the back of his head. Instead, while the others dropped to the ground, steadying themselves, my left arm went numb. I let the gun fall sideways from his mouth. Tried to scrape through to my heart. When I woke up, Jelena was crying into my neck. *Hvala bogu*, she kept repeating, *hvala bogu*. Never felt so weak before.

People looking down at me. Terrified. But no one stopped us from leaving. I don't know why. Maybe they felt sorry us, for her. Maybe the photographer's reputation. Maybe no one has any energy left. Maybe no one cares. A stocky paramilitary told me that I was lucky he was in a good mood. I nodded, leaned on Jelena like a crutch. Black smoke rising from fresh ruins outside. Still only nine o'clock. There was light left in the sky.

'We have to get away from here,' she said to me, hours

later, when we finally lay down to sleep. 'We cannot live like this any longer.'

'I know,' I said.

Another lie.

I don't know anything any more.

He was the strongest one. From the very beginning he was always the strongest. If he can't take it, what hope is there for any of the rest of us?

Chapter 12

It's been two and a half weeks and the Golden Coast is still every bit as golden as it was on our drive out here. Baz and I, on the other hand, feel a little more tarnished every day. We take the car out further each afternoon, just to sit on a different beach and chain-smoke Lucky Strikes swiped from the clinic's over-stocked tuck shop. Sometimes we swim. Well, I doggy-paddle. Baz wades out into the ocean till the water reaches the bottom of his chest, then drops onto his haunches and rests there. Sometimes we explore the rocky, lichen-blighted outcrops that separate one stretch of sand from another, the tiny tide-pools full of crabs and starfish and rainbow-slicked straps of seaweed. Once or twice a day we'll forget why we're killing time out there. We'll spot a group of bombshell blondes in their bikinis or the cresting fins of a dolphin pod and all solemnity will be suspended for a few minutes. We'll launch into one of our nonsense conversations – the kind I'm actually beginning to miss of late – about the importance of the Irish accent as a pick-up tool, or the odds of being eaten by a shark versus being hit by lightning, or the ease with which Baz could (probably) maintain balance on a surfboard, if he was arsed. But we don't talk about his court date, or Tom's future, or Gabriel. Mostly, the situation demands silence, so we're silent.

I really don't know what kind of mental state Tom is in right now. On Thursday he stormed out of Group and punched apart a section of the perimeter fence. Granted it's built more for privacy than security, but still, there's nothing flimsy about that fence. Baz was out watching the zebras at the time. He found Tom kneeling in the grass, staring at his bloody knuckles, violently sucking in air through his nostrils like he was trying to fight back vomit. I can't I can't I can't was all he would say. Baz took him to the infirmary for stitches and a sedative while I went to find Saunders. I spent forty-five minutes ranting at the (ordinarily) perky morning receptionists, demanding that they page him again, and again, and again, until he finally emerged from that fucking bunker of his. Relaxation Unit 5, as every chilled-out shitebag in the place calls it, despite the fact that A) it's the only building on the grounds with both a card and a code lock affixed to the wall, B) it's the only building on the grounds with a stainless steel door instead of a wooden or glass one, and C) I've yet to see Tom, or any of the other half dozen or so flush head-cases keeping this place in zebras and on-site chefs, actually *enter* the unit. It's like Willy Wonka's fucking chocolate factory. When Saunders did appear and amble across the courtyard to us, he was all sincerest apologies and assurances of progress being made. He said that outbursts like Tom's don't just disappear overnight and that we would have to be patient. 'We have been patient,' I said, 'but both our time and our money are running out.'

Saunders told me not to worry about either, but he said it in a kind of hippie, all-things-are-fleeting sort of way that only served to piss me off even more. I'm just glad it wasn't Baz waiting in that atrium; he'd have put a boot through those pretty glass doors.

*

I've phoned Clara's office twice since we arrived: the first to get her extension from the front desk, the second a day later just to hear her voice say 'Hello? Hell-o? Helloooooooo?' before hanging up. But that's it. Before we got here, I told myself I would let this lie, at least for now. Told myself that it was probably pointless, all this sappy daydreaming and rose-tinted revisionist bollocks. It's not like we were ever bulletproof at home. Christ, we'd broken up and gotten back together more times than I could remember by the time she left.

She bought me my first camera after one of those breakups. Something I'd had my eye on for months but was too broke or embarrassed to buy for myself. She turned up at the house after a month of stubborn silence had passed between us, and presented it to me as a peace offering, albeit with the card affixed that read: *if you're going to be such a moody prick, you might as well channel it into something creative.*

Of course there was every chance she'd changed jobs since our final letters or, it being summer, taken a holiday somewhere out of state. Not that I was plotting anything before we left Dublin. I picked the central California coast because it's peaceful, and sunny, and its roads hug the Pacific Ocean for miles; because it's the place we always said we'd go, the four of us; because it's basically the polar fucking opposite of a Sarajevo winter. It made sense. It *makes* sense. There were facilities in San Francisco I could have chosen over Restless Souls, reputable facilities. One of them is run by a guy who has his own nationally syndicated radio show. I could have booked that no problem and it would *still* have been for the right reasons, there wouldn't be a damn thing Baz or Tom or anyone else could say that'd discredit the place, or undermine my reasons for choosing it. I could have sent her a note a month ago saying I'd be in the area. I could have called from a petrol station along the way and organised an evening drink. Something casual. I could have told Baz I was going for a drive to clear my head, met her for an hour or two, talked some future stuff out, and come back without anyone being the wiser. It would have been a piece of piss compared to some of the logistical shit storms we've had to deal with so far. But I didn't, I haven't. I made no plans to see her. She still has no idea about any of this. Basically what I'm saying, if I'm saying anything at all, is that I haven't done anything wrong. Short of flying Tom out to Tibet and leaving him in a basket on the doorstep of a Buddhist temple, this is the last and best hope he has at finding some measure of peace in himself. We have to remember that, no matter how soft this place is beginning to feel.

*

Tom's days here consist of long beach walks with Saunders, group 'sharing' with weepy combat vets turned grief council- lors, oceanside meditation sessions, diet and lifestyle seminars, exposure therapy, creative writing classes, and, more recently, sensory deprivation hours in the clinic's isolation tank. On top of all this there are star-gazing nights, woodcarving classes, fishing trips, camping trips, nature hikes. Stuff we could be doing back at Joshua Tree for free. It's like they couldn't agree on whether the place was a summer camp or a health spa, so they settled on PTSD clinic and just continued about their business, same as before. I'd like to see more of Tom, pick his brain about what helps and what doesn't, find out whether some of the shit that looks ridiculous from the outside in is actually helping, or just passing the time till they figure out how to tell him he's a hopeless case (something which I still can't say out loud, but feels more like the truth every day). But I can't, not right now anyway. Almost every activity is Closed Door, which means no guests allowed; and since Baz and I are the only guests staying here at the moment, what it really means is *fuck off out of the way and wait for us to come get you.*

No matter how many freak-outs Tom has here, how many fences and bedside lockers and plates he destroys, how often his screams roar out like a lighthouse beam over the black ocean, Saunders keeps telling us to trust him, to trust the methodology of the clinic. But we've seen too much of what's inside Tom's head. I can't figure out how they intend to talk the memory of a bread line bombing, or some kid's limbless torso, or the brother's neck bursting, or whatever happened to his girl, out of the labyrinthine storage unit he has in there. It all seems like a Band-Aid for a bullet wound, as the Yanks are so fond of saying. Part of me feels like a fool for ever believing in all this. For being seduced by a fucking pamphlet. Baz tells me as much most evenings after dinner now, and instead of agreeing with him, like I should, I parrot back a version of what Saunders has said to pacify us however many days or hours previous. Usually he shakes his head at this and walks off to stare at the animals. Yesterday evening was different though. He wouldn't let it go.

'So you honestly think it's working?'

'Baz, c'mon, man. Don't start, not tonight.'

'I'm serious. This isn't me just having a moan. I want you to tell me if you think any of this talk-it-out, meditation, coffin-full-of-water stuff is having any effect, because if it is, for the life of me I can't see it. Far as I can tell, he's getting worse.'

'What do you want me to say?'

'Say you've noticed an improvement in him that I've missed because I've been too busy looking for the cracks. Say he's told you in private that he's on the mend but he doesn't want to jinx it by getting too optimistic too soon. Say what you actually think, something that isn't one of Saunders' fucking nonsense fridge-magnet slogans.'

'Look, I'm not an expert, I know as much as you about all this. That's why we came here. If Saunders says it takes more time then—'

'And how much time does that quack think Tom has left, hmmm?'

'I don't know.'

'Last night. Don't even try to tell me you didn't hear it. I thought someone was getting mauled by a fucking bear, the noises that were coming out of his hut.'

'That could have been any of them.'

'Ah would you stop it, for Christ's sake. When did it become part of your daily routine to bullshit me?'

'I'm not.' I am.

'Three more days. Then I'm taking him home.'

'There's nothing they can do at home. You know that.'

'I'll tell you what I know, right? I know he's getting worse. I know his mother is at home waiting for the bad news. I know that Irish pharmacies stock sedatives and anti-psychotics and heart pills just like anywhere else.'

'And that's the kind of life we want for him, yeah? A fucking doped-up vegetable?'

'I want him to be alive, Karl. That's my first and last priority now. The rest of this stuff – this *holistic* treatment – I went along with it because you seemed so sure it'd be a silver bullet, and I started to believe you because I'm a fucking gobshite, and maybe because I had my mind on other things, but not any more.'

'This stuff can work, Baz.'

'Maybe –' softer now, like I'm the one who needs to snap out of it '– for some people, but not for him. Not for someone this far gone. I'm not saying the trip was a bad idea. It was great to be able to come out here together and pretend for a while. It was important. But these people can't help him, Karl. That's the sad fucking reality. Explain to me why I'm wrong and I'll shut up about it.'

What is there to say?

'Three days?'

'Three days.'

The pale green glow of the clock radio says 3:47. Nothing good can be happening at this hour. There's a hammering at our cabin door, but it's what you might describe as a polite hammering. Like a gloved hand tapping Morse code. Across the room, Baz's arm is swinging over the bed frame, grabbing at something on the floor that isn't there. I get up and crack the corner of my kneecap against the bedside locker. I howl and hop across the room, swinging a petulant kick at nothing. Unfortunately nothing turns out to be the right corner leg of Baz's already straining bed frame. It pops loose and shoots through the air, connecting with the window proper because we have forgotten to lower the blinds. Before I can investigate just how badly the window has been cracked, the second of Baz's remaining three bed frame legs buckles, causing all fifteen stone of him to roll sideways off the bed, and belly flop the hardwood floor. It sounds like someone has wounded an already irate moose. The hammering gets more erratic. I look at the clock again. Still 3:47.

'Mr Sullivan! Mr Connolly! Is everything all right in there?'

'Karl? Karl? What's happening?' Still half asleep. 'Why am I on the *fucking* floor? Was there an earthquake or a volcano or what?'

Between the foot and the knee there are sharp pulses of pain running up and down both legs. My right arm is also limp with pins and needles from whatever contorted sleeping position I settled into four hours ago. I'm hobbling around like a fucking stroke victim who needs a piss. Baz's face and funny bone took the brunt of the impact so he isn't even attempting to rise.

'Yeah, a volcano is after erupting outside. Hop back up on the bed there before the lava gets you.'

'Fuck off, I'm in pain! What happened?'

'You farted and broke the bed. We should have reinforced the thing.' He lunges for my ankles with a growl.

'Mr Sullivan. Can you come to the door, please? It's an emergency.'

'Jesus what does this Ken doll want now? Just a second, Theo! C'mon, Baz, get up, will you?'

'I'm trying to figure out if anything is broken.'

'Ah wouldya stop, you've taken heavier falls off bar stools and only noticed when you couldn't reach your drink.'

'Help me up then.'

I lever him into an upright position and the two of us hobble across the still-dark cabin to unlock the door. Turns out it's open, Theo is just too polite to intrude without permission. Looking at him standing there in the full moonlight, the colour drained from his broad face, it's obvious that something is very wrong. He's frightened.

'I'm sorry to disturb you.'

'It's fine, Theo, what's happened?'

'It's Mr Dempsey. He's run away.'

'Excuse me?'

'I was at my desk. Reading, but facing the windows. I always make sure that my line of vision is clear you see because—'

'Yeah all right, Theo, we know you weren't off having a wank. Just tell us what happened quick as you can, OK?'

'Right, sorry. I saw him run past the doors. He was barefoot. He looked, well, can I be honest?

'Yes!' Mother of God where did they find this lad.

'Deranged.' Fuck. It sounds so much worse when someone says it aloud. 'I shouted at him to come back but I don't think he heard me.'

'Have you called Saunders? Is anyone looking for him?'

'I came straight here.'

'Right. Go find Saunders. I don't care if he's sleeping or meditating or howling at the fucking moon. Get him up. Raise as many orderlies as you can and tell them to fan out and find him. Baz and I will get started.' Baz is already half dressed. 'What way did he run?'

'North-east. Toward the closed trail. It starts behind the backup generator at the far end of the compound.'

'Why is it closed?' Baz asks. Theo looks down at his shoes. 'Theo, why is that trail closed?'

'Well, it runs across the high cliff edges. We felt that, considering the fragile mental state of many of our patients upon arrival . . .'

I grab my runners and a pair of crumpled shorts from the pile at the foot of my bed, and we start sprinting. The moon is bright enough that I can see the whole property as clear as if it were daylight: the caged grey generator some two hundred steps away, the flimsy wasp-striped barrier that forms an elongated X behind it, even the looming outline of Hearst Castle perched on a high distant hilltop. As we race through one of the fields, a herd of dozing antelope scatter in silence. Despite the pearly moonlight, I stumble as I'm cutting back up onto the path and drop my runners as I struggle against gravity. It's another ten yards before I'm back in stable equilibrium. I'll get them on the way back. Baz is staring straight ahead, holding his breath and pumping his arms like an Olympic sprinter on the home stretch. Our elbows graze as we vault the barrier in an unplanned, and unlikely, display of athleticism. Baz finally breathes as our feet hit the dirt on the other side. The trail slopes downward into a lush corridor of bright green ferns. Newly snapped tree branches litter the overgrown path. Afraid of stepping out into nothing, I lead us left into a dead end of tangled vegetation. We double back and pause to catch our breath at the base of an embankment.

'Tom! Tommy! Where are you, man?'

Nothing. There are huge footprints in the mud, sunken deep at the heel. We claw our way upward, digging our fingers into the imprints made by his toes to pull ourselves over the top. As we rise, I can hear the violent crash of the ocean against the rocks below, the whoosh of the tide sweeping backward after it pounds the shore. We wouldn't be able to bring his body home for his mother to bury. Baz makes it over the top first and pulls me up the rest of the way. The force of it almost dislocates my shoulder. At the top, we doggedly swipe our way through a few more feet of damp forest until all that's left in front of us is the ocean and the moon and a long, narrow ledge, upon which a lone, skeletal figure stands bare chested – his bowed face veiled by a curtain of lank hair, his pale toes hanging out over the edge.

Two weeks before he walked out into that field, before they found him, Gabriel tried to talk to me about it, whatever 'it' was. Must have been three, maybe even four in the morning. He had spent the previous two nights with Baz and myself, necking pints one after the other at the bar in The Bleeding Horse like it was the eve of prohibition. He wasn't himself, anyone could see it. All heavy sighs and silences and beer mats torn to damp confetti in his fidgety hands. We'd look at him sideways and he'd perk up for a half hour or so, rattle off an anecdote or two, but that was about as lively as he got that weekend. Then, on the Sunday afternoon, while we were still incapacitated, throats raw and heads split from the dehydration, he called up the stairs that he was going into town to watch the United match. That was the last I saw of him for about fourteen hours. When he finally did make it home, he'd lost his keys, his wallet, everything. I heard the rattle of his head knocking rhythmically off the bottom pane of glass beside the front door, his mumbled rendition of Bowie's 'Golden Years' slipping in through my open bedroom window, the words punctuated by his sad little chuckles. He didn't even notice when I unlocked the door. I stood there, looking down at his burst lip, his swollen left eye and the flecks of blood dried into the collar of his rumpled shirt, and waited for him to look up.

'Tom!' I blurt out before I can stop myself, but he doesn't move. He raises an arm outward, slowly moving his flattened palm back and forth in small circles, drawing a figure of eight in the air with the tip of his index finger.

'Tom,' I say again, calm as I can manage, 'can you step back from the edge for a second so we can talk? Please?'

He lowers his arm but doesn't turn to look at us.

Prostrate on our doorstep, Gabriel had taken on that extra poundage of dead weight acquired only by corpses and the paralytic drunk. I dragged him down the hall by his armpits, the way spies move security guards they've just concussed and relieved of their uniform, to see if the kitchen light would reveal any head wounds more substantial than what was already on display. I sat him down on the corner chair, its shitty wicker frame wheezing under his bulk, and turned his shaved head over in my hands. Softly, back and forth until I was satisfied there were no other bruises. We sat there for an hour, tea towel full of ice cubes pressed to his banjaxed eye, while he reluctantly supped water from a giant McDonald's cup. It was the worst I had ever seen him, which should have been enough. When he spoke to me it was barely comprehensible, bits of stray information from his stumble home bleeding into details from the United match bleeding into misheard song lyrics from a dance floor he couldn't recall. I slapped him awake every time he drifted and he'd cry out and swipe at me weakly. It was nearly dawn by the time he started making sense. He said he was sorry, that he couldn't get his head right these days, that he didn't know what was going on. It wasn't a confessional exactly, but it was the beginning of something. Something I was too weary to entertain at that hour. Something I chose to ignore. I told him to stop talking shite, that it was all right, that he just had a few too many. He lay into me as we ascended the stairs, the bristle of his stubble scratching against my chest. By the time I set him down on his side in that dank bombsite he called a bedroom, he was already asleep. I looked around at the tangle of bed linen, strewn like discarded tethers across the floor from whatever convolutions he'd gone through the previous night; at the ashtrays full of half smoked cigarette butts and the collapsed piles of dog-eared books and the blood-encrusted eyelash separating the bruise on his lid to the purple bags underneath. And I left him like that.

I can see Tom trembling, squeezing his scabbed fists open and closed to try and slow the rising convulsions. I hope this is fear. Fear means he might still back out. There are more slivers of scarring across his back. Not the long, scourging welts I imagined, but small splashes of smooth, burnt skin – the raised tissue a colourless archipelago. I move toward him a half step. He bends his knees ever so slightly. Baz grabs a hold of my arm. His shining eyes plead with me not to get any closer.

'I just . . . can't do it any more, lads,' Tom whispers.

'It *will* get better, Tom,' I promise, based on nothing.

'We've tried, Karl. Everyone has tried so hard, but it's not doing any good. In here –' he taps his temple '– it's fucking relentless. All of it. Every day. All night. I can't get rid of it.'

'It just takes time. It'll fade.'

'No. You don't understand.'

'What don't I understand?'

'It should have been *me*, man.' He raps his balled knuckles against his sternum as he says it, the moonlight hitting his wet eye as he turns. 'She'd done so much, pieced so many of them back together. Hundreds of little lives, and it wasn't enough. Wiped off the face of the earth like everything she'd done, like it all meant nothing. And I'm here. *Why* am I still here? A vulture. A fucking war tourist, travelling across a continent to gawk at half a million skeletons in a cage.'

'That's not what you were, Tom.'

230

'Wasn't it? You ever think that maybe this is the punishment? All that talk about needing to witness it, to see what it was really like in there. As if I had any right. Well, now I've got what I wanted.'

I could have made time for him the next day. Even half an hour would have been something. Christ, it wasn't as if I had anything desperately important to take care of. There was no job interview to bungle or remote bogland wedding to attend. Baz and the rest of the functioning adult population of the country were back at work. It was a cold, wet fuck of a Monday afternoon and I had absolutely nowhere to be, but I chose not to be there when he got up. I could hear him in the room above me – the creak of his bedsprings as he woke and rose, the clumsy rustling around for an inhabited cigarette packet and the repeated flint strike of his zippo. I could see him through the ceiling, sitting on the edge of the iron bedframe turning the sounds and shadows of his night over and over in his mind, letting the ash burn down toward his knuckle and then fall away unnoticed. It would have been the easiest thing in the world to knock on that door, announce that the place smelled like a derelict brewery, and then sit down beside him and wait. But that's not what I did.

'She wouldn't want this, Tom,' Baz says now, his trembling arm outstretched as if connected to Tom's retreating form by an invisible rope.

'I see it all as clearly now as I did when it happened, lads. Every body part, every burn and bullet wound. I see her face . . .'

'What about your mother, Tom? She won't recover if you do this. There won't even be a grave for her to visit. For us to visit.'

It'd be one of the better places to end it all, I suppose. Scenic, at least. Though I've never believed that matters to people in the way we imagine it does. Having something pretty to look at as the light goes out. It certainly didn't matter to Gabriel. They told me he died around sunset, as if the word, the soft orange time of day it conjures, should have meant something even if it were true. Even if the sodden grey skies had cleared that day, which they hadn't; even if there had been a gap through the cage-like tree branches and tagged industrial green fencing that he faced out toward, which there wasn't; even then, what significance would it have? Would the dusk twittering of birds and the play of light and shadow on the dewy grass have even registered as that fat fucking coil of rope choked the life out of him? As he jerked and scratched like a snared animal, eyes bulging, piss running down his trouser leg. I truly doubt it.

Tom is shaking so violently now I'm afraid he'll slip over the edge before he makes up his mind. The sea below is battering against the cliff wall. He presses his hands together in front of his face as if in prayer, though I know this can't be the case, and begins to sob. The moon's spotlight seems cruel now. I want to grab the guy, lead him back to the compound and let him break apart every building with his bare hands till all the pain and poison that's bedded down inside him has been exorcised. But that isn't the way it works. For an agonising second it looks like he's about to step off, but then he freezes, stumbles forward, and collapses at our feet. Baz props his head up in his lap, and holds him there. We wait, watching his face darken as the moon disappears behind a wall of cloud, until the voices of Theo's search party come wafting, useless, through the trees.

Sarajevo, November

Quiet today. Quiet and cold.

Jelena couldn't face the hospital. First day she's taken off in weeks. I watched her toss and sweat in the night. When she woke it was still dark. Hair tangled, stray strands glued to her forehead. Tried to explain her nightmare, telling me listen listen listen, Tom, please, but then she woke fully and it was gone. Everything gone but a flash of falling stone towers and the sound of barking dogs. We stayed under the blanket, pressed tight together. Every blanket we could find. Tucked Fadila up in a heavy quilt on Vuk's old chair. Waited till she fell asleep. It's been weeks since she's left the house. Days since she's said a full sentence. She doesn't talk about her books any more. She still bakes *kiflice* in the old wood-burning stove, just a little every few days, but never eats it herself. She looks a decade older than that day we met. An old woman waiting to die. If we left the city now, if we left her alone like this, I'm certain she would.

On the days Jelena asks me to stay home, I take Fadila's hand in mine as she sleeps. Sometimes she smiles. Pretending. Husband and wife. Mother and son. Shell blasts always ruin the make believe. But today was quiet. In the silence, I closed my eyes and pretended that Gabriel was sitting on the edge of her chair, the side of his shaved head tilted toward hers. The soft whistle of his sleeping breaths filling in the gaps between her own.

She slept through. Jelena and I listened to my U2 mixed tape till the last batteries died. Talked about California. New York. Berlin. London. Everywhere. Our plans are less specific these days. Easier to just be there. Hop from city to city, continent to continent. Close together as the folds in our blanket. We drew a trail from Hawaii to the Rockefeller Centre to the Galápagos Islands to Havana to Sandymount Strand and back to Sarajevo. A revived Sarajevo. The hardest one to reach. She lay with an ear pressed against my chest. Checking for missed beats through the thick padding.

Chapter 13

Technically just under one of the three agreed-upon days remain on mine and Baz's pact, but we're a long way from that now. We're breaking him out of here, today. We'll smash through the gates if we have to; check into a motel somewhere further up the coast where one of us can keep an eye on him 24/7. He can relax for a week or so – eat, swim, people-watch – without having to dredge up massacres for a group of unhinged, touchy-feely strangers. When he's stable, we'll drive back to LA and go home. Baz was right. What else can we do?

Propping up his long, limp frame between us, we bulldoze past Theo, two orderlies, and Saunders himself. The latter has to step off the path and into the ditch to let us through. He grimaces as he presses his forearm against a tree trunk for balance. We walk on without hesitating. They call after us, voices breaking as they inquire as to whether or not Tom is all right. 'Does he look fucking all right?' Baz snarls back. They catch up with us by the time we manage to lower Tom over the crest of the embankment. We allow Theo to pass us down one of Baz's escaped shoes, and nod our thanks. Saunders looks on imploringly, and is lucky that all he gets is a glare taken straight out of Tom's mam's repertoire. The compound is further away than I remember and Tom's dead weight slows us to a zombie stagger. I can feel their presence a half dozen paces behind us, hear the orderlies whispering something to one another. God, I hate these fucking people. By the time we get him back to his room, a layer of peach-coloured dawn is pushing upward through the sky.

We sit outside his open window, one eye on the sunrise, the other trained on each shift and arch of his body as the dreams start up again. I'm too exhausted to pick up the cigarette that's slipped through my unsteady hand. Baz is dozing, his head lolls back and forth in the warm morning sunshine. This place could be paradise. I must have nodded off too, because all of a sudden there's a human shadow separating me and Baz. I look up and he's standing there in his lab coat, waiting patiently for one of us to notice his arrival. I'm on my feet, staring down at him. He doesn't look up. I reach for the collar of his shirt, but stop when I realise he hasn't flinched. He's not afraid of me.

'What do you want?' Quietly, through clamped teeth, so as not to wake them.

'I want to help Tom,' he says. I almost laugh, hearing this now.

'Well you've done a bang-up job so far, Doc. Really sterling work. I think he'll be ready to re-join normal society any day now.'

'I wish I could have proceeded with the next step sooner, Karl, believe me, but it takes time to properly assess a new patient's needs. Very few people require such extreme therapy.'

'Bullshit. "Next step" my hole. You just want to keep him here long enough to justify charging three *fucking* grand for waking up monsters you can't kill.'

'We don't charge anything, Karl.'

'As if all this talking does – wait, what? What are you talking about?'

'We don't charge anything. Our patients' cheques are never cashed.'

'That's . . . that doesn't even make sense.'

'I can see how it appears that way, and I am truly sorry for what almost happened today, and for not being entirely honest with you, but I guarantee, when you next check your bank balance, all of that money will still be there.' I don't understand any of this.

'Why?'

'I will explain everything soon, I promise.'

'Too late. We're leaving as soon as Tom wakes up. Whatever game you're playing here, you can continue it without us.'

'You can't do that, not yet.'

'Watch us,' I say, turning my back to him.

'If you take him away from here now, he'll be dead within the month.' This time I do grab him. Both hands twisting the lapels of his shirt.

'What the fuck do you even know about it?' I hiss.

He still doesn't flinch. That measured baritone does wobble just a tiny bit though. 'I know that I have been working with veterans and conflict survivors for decades, and while each case is different, there are commonalities. I've seen this kind of behaviour before and I am prepared for what must come next. Yes, our sessions have brought certain traumatic memories closer to the surface, but that is how the process has to begin. He's more vulnerable than ever at the moment, because he *has* to be, but if you take him away in this tortured state, you are condemning him to complete mental and physical disintegration. I take no pleasure in telling you this, but it is the truth.'

'*Enough* of this cryptic shite. Explain to me what this is all about right now or we're gone.'

'Please, Karl. Just bear with me for a few hours more. Can the three of you meet me tonight at sundown by Unit 5? I'll do my best to explain it to you all then. Just one more day, that's all I'm asking for.'

*

'So, wait, back up, you're saying that this whole thing is what? A front?'

We're trying not to touch anything in this sterile corridor inside Relaxation Unit 5, and I have to be very honest: this is the least fucking relaxed I've been since we got here. Getting Baz to agree to this meeting in the first place took some coaxing, but nothing compared to the job I had keeping him from legging it when he saw what looked like a souped-up dentist's chair inside one of the glass rooms.

'No, Mr Connolly, there's nothing fake about what we present to the world here. All of our therapists are highly qualified, all of our therapies are drawn from the latest clinical research into PTSD and Traumatic Brain Injury. We have a staff pharmacist who left a prestigious senior position at Johns Hopkins to join our team; visiting social workers who specialise in reintegrating psychologically damaged veterans back into the workforce; and the most state-of-the-art diagnostic and therapeutic equipment available including functional-magnetic-resonance-imaging, MRI and PET scanning machines.' He gestures toward different rooms along the corridor as he lists these machines. 'I myself, under a different name, was a professor of neuroscience and psychiatry at Mount Sinai hospital before establishing this clinic.'

'You were a professor of neuroscience?' I ask. This just can't be true. No legitimate doctor in his right mind would abandon a gig like that for this fucking circus.

'Among other titles held, yes.'

'Bullshit,' says Baz. 'He's just saying all this now because we've rumbled the scam operation he's got going on here. He's probably no more of a professor of neuroscience than I am.'

'Look around you, Mr Connelly. If this is a scam, it's an extraordinarily elaborate and expensive one.' Baz reluctantly casts a glance around the facility and mutters something to himself. 'We can sit down together and pore over my degrees and credentials if that would put your minds at ease, gentlemen, but I assure you, I am who I say I am.'

'Then why not put that on the front of the shaggin' pamphlet?' My voice growing high, almost hysterical. 'Why all this spiritual epiphany bollocks? What's there to hide?' He sighs. I get the feeling this isn't the first time he's had to walk people like us through this.

'The research I and my team have been conducting over the past ten years has necessitated a certain level of misdirection, of secrecy. I was quite a well-known figure in my field until circumstances demanded that I step away from public life and adopt a persona which would attract less institutional attention.'

'What kind of circumstances?' I ask.

'Dr Saunders, the "spiritualist Vietnam veteran", may be a fictitious character; my doppelganger and I may be polar opposites in many respects, but ultimately, our goal is one and the same: to help heal those with wounds we cannot see. I'm not a mad scientist, gentlemen, believe me. I just want to help. This affliction you suffer from, Tom, it hasn't just been my life's work. It's been *part* of my life since I was a boy. If you'll indulge me for a few more minutes—'

'This should be good,' mutters Baz.

'One morning in the winter of 1950,' Saunders continues, 'my father rose early despite the cold. He dressed in his old army uniform, covered the back wall and floor of our basement in a plastic tarp, and put a gun in his mouth. No one understood it properly at the time – certainly not my mother and I – but the man had been struggling with what we now call PTSD for over five years. When he came home from the Pacific, I witnessed what I had previously known to be a kind, communicative, stable man collapse under the weight of his own anger and fear. He was in despair, haunted by what he'd seen and done, and there was nobody to help him. When I graduated from college, I realised that this same situation was playing out again and again in families all over the country. I visited them, hundreds of them. I interviewed returned soldiers and their wives – sadly, often their widows; holocaust survivors; prisoners released from super max detention facilities; trauma victims of all ages and circumstances, from abused and abandoned children to geriatrics who'd seen friends drown under clouds of mustard gas in the trenches of World War One. I wanted to see what connected them all. I wanted to learn how emotional memories are shaped, stored, and loosed upon us against our will. More than that though, I wanted to see if those memories were truly as fixed as we've always been told.

'Over the years we've had some breakthrough successes with both behavioural therapy and medication, and those successes have helped to transform lives. To save lives. But somewhere along the way it became clear to me that this wasn't enough, not for those who needed our help the most. Everything we did up to that point sprung from the foundational assumption that once memories are consolidated – once they are imprinted onto the circuitry of our brains – they cannot be altered. For those suffering under the severest forms of PTSD, the choice was a devastatingly simple one: medicate yourself into a permanent stupor, or succumb. We knew there had to be another way. Which brings me to the circumstances of my disappearance from the hallways of institutional medicine. At our primary research facility in New Jersey, after years of early promise leading us down blind alleys, we finally perfected a revolutionary, potentially game-changing method of treating extreme psychological trauma. Unfortunately, despite the almost one hundred per cent success rate of our animal trials, there remained, and remains, a dogged refusal to entertain the possibility that our memories may be more malleable than conventional wisdom asserts, and our request to proceed to the human trial phase was denied. But I refused to give up. I knew how crucial it was that we conduct these trials, and time was of the essence. If history has taught us anything it is that there will always be war, there will always be trauma, and there will always be those left unmoored and abandoned by the machinations of geopolitics and the abuse of power. This rising generation of Americans – your generational peers on this side of the Atlantic – have been fortunate enough not to be embroiled in a devastating and protracted conflict like World War Two or Vietnam, but relative peace like this never lasts. I've seen this first hand, and I vowed to do everything in my power to make sure we were ready for the fallout when the inevitable occurred.'

'That all sounds peachy, doc, but again, why the theatrics?' I ask him. 'Why not just walk away and set up your own clinic under your own name?'

'It's actually quite simple, Mr Sullivan: if we were to advertise Restless Souls as a place of experimental psycho-pharmacological research, rather than a solely therapeutic facility, we would be subject to excessive scrutiny from the American Medical Association and the FDA, scrutiny which would have resulted in our almost inevitable closure. I couldn't risk that, so I created a new, outlandish public persona to serve as a smokescreen, behind which my team and I could work unimpeded.'

'So what exactly is this place?' Tom asks, the words like syrup coming slow from his mouth.

'This place is why you are here, Tom. Over ninety per cent of our patients have no idea that this particular programme exists. They leave this facility having undergone *only* the rehabilitative treatments we advertise publically, and the vast majority of these patients have benefitted tremendously from said treatments. I know much of what you've seen here so far may seem pointless and unquantifiable, but, with respect, gentlemen, smarter men than you have devised these methods and they have saved the lives of countless damaged people. Much of what Tom has experienced throughout his various sessions these past weeks he will already be familiar with from his stay at Wastwater,' he looks at Tom – who nods, warily – and continues, 'and it is my hope that when the procedure I'm about to detail to you has been successful, he will be able to benefit from them in a way that has been all-but impossible thus far.'

I'm trying to absorb as much of this as I can. Tom doesn't look angry, just confused and thoroughly worn out. Two middle-aged lab technicians walk past us into a room full of blinking computers and file cabinets. The words Brain Imaging Core are emblazoned on the glass door.

'As you both know, when Tom first arrived we carried out a neurological scan to ascertain whether or not the injuries he suffered in Sarajevo resulted in any previously undetected Traumatic Brain Injury.' I didn't know this actually, though from his tone I think it's fair to assume that this particular piece of ignorance is my own fault.

'We conducted that scan here in this very laboratory, as we do for many of our patients. There is nothing clandestine about this unit, gentleman, only a certain procedure conducted herein.' This, again, is probably something we could have asked about earlier.

'Eh, yeah, right. And?'

'And thankfully the scan came back negative on that front.'

'Well that's something.'

'However,' he continues, 'what we deliberately failed to

mention at the time – which again, Tom, I do apologise for – is that we were also conducting a comprehensive scan of the *workings* of your brain.'

Tom looks around at us for a cue, which we don't have, and eventually turns back to Saunders and says 'That's . . . all right?'

'What we found, gentlemen, will surprise you.'

'What,' says Baz, 'you don't think we're surprised enough as it is?'

'Ha, yes, quite. Forgive me. Let me ask you all something: what is your present understanding of how memories are retained in the brain?'

This lad is really taking the piss out of us now.

'Honestly?' I say. 'I think I can speak for all of us when I say we have sweet fuck-all understanding of how memories do anything. Cheers for pointing it out though.'

'I don't mean to condescend. Let me try to explain.' And by God does he try. It goes on for some time. After the tenth pause-and-rewind request, I swear he's considering a fucking sock puppet show. It starts out OK; he sort of eases us in by setting the scene. According to Saunders, and, I presume, science in general: 'Every memory we retain depends on a chain of chemical interactions that connect millions of neurons to one another. Those neurons communicate through tiny gaps, or synapses, that surround each of them. Every neuron has branching filaments that receive chemical signals from other nerve cells and send the information across the synapse to the body of the next cell. A normally functioning human brain has trillions of these connections. When we learn something, chemicals in the brain strengthen the synapses that connect neurons. Long-term memories, built from new proteins, change those synaptic networks constantly. Some get weaker, while others – as they suck in new information – get stronger.'

After that, gibberish. Well, not complete gibberish, but it's like herding cats trying to get the three of us to follow together. Every so often, always before Saunders has finished the explanatory sentence, Baz stages a loud, poorly acted, Eureka! moment. Then he starts sulking when I say, fine, explain back to me how the amygdala works then if you're so fucking smart. That quiets him down, though obviously it takes us off track a bit too when I have to apologise for snapping at him and coax him back to the conversation. Anyway, Saunders says that memories take a few different forms, which, sure, doesn't sound like rocket science, but then he delves deeper into it, drawing pictures on a whiteboard with his right hand while the left one presses an index finger to the spot between his eyebrows. This, he says, is where emotional memories are stored. It seems fear memories are like tinned fruit – it takes a long fucking time before they expire. I don't know whether he's exaggerating for our benefit or what, but in his own words, 'Tom possesses perhaps the most exceptional power of recall I've encountered since I began this programme.' Tom, who throughout this impromptu lecture is so spent he can barely form words, apparently has a synaptic network that's working overtime, and it's driving his mind off a cliff (the Doc's poorly chosen words, not mine).

'The sheer number of horrific incidents you witnessed during that period has resulted in a situation where your mind has been completely overwhelmed by traumatic memories, to the point where the real world is slipping away from you. Even the most dogged stoic could only sustain this for so long. That is where we find ourselves. It pains me to be so blunt, gentlemen, but we are rapidly running out of time. Whether it comes in the form of another stress-induced heart attack or, forgive me, suicide, this relentless barrage of traumatic memories will eventually kill you.'

There's an awful silence. Worse than silence, a frightened, confused muteness broken only by the unnatural hum of medical fridges and the beep and whir of machines. My chest is tightening as if the organs inside are quietly imploding one by one. The technicians work on diligently, unaware of or unconcerned with this death sentence. Tom's eyes are downcast, Baz's look to me for answers I don't have. What can I do but ask?

'Can you help him?'

'Yes. Yes, I'm convinced we can.'

'How?'

Then he's back on what we're assured is the meat of this whole thing: 'memory reconsolidation.'

From what I can gather, conventional wisdom treats the process of long-term memory consolidation like wet cement drying on the footpath. Until it sets, its shape can be changed, re-moulded, but as soon as it hardens, sorry, soldier, but you're stuck with your demons for the long haul. Once a couple of hours have passed and they've bedded down in your subconscious – once the biochemical and electrical processes have been completed and the short-term memory has become a long-term one – you can fuck off to your happy place for as long as you like but they'll still be there when you get back. Forever imprinted onto the circuitry of your brain. Now this, I believe. This seems like the inevitable, unscalable wall we all knew we'd find ourselves at the base of sooner or later, and I'm cursing under my breath accordingly. Except that, somehow, it's not. That's what Saunders' Project X, or whatever he calls it, is all about:

'What we have discovered is that in order for memories, especially fear memories, to be recalled, they must retrace the neural pathways in which they originated, and, in certain instances, those memories can be *re*consolidated.' He seems super excited by this word. I still don't get it. I look over at Baz, he shrugs.

'So?'

'So, it's not cement, as you put it, that we're dealing with. It's more like a saved Word document on a computer. We can open it back up, alter the text, and re-save it. We can *change* it, Mr Sullivan! That is what we do here.'

'Jesus. So wait, are you talking about brain surgery?'

'You're not cutting up his brain,' Baz chimes in. 'I saw what they did to Jack Nicholson in that hornet's nest film.'

'Cuckoo's nest, Baz.'

'Whatever. He's not doing that.'

'It's not surgery, exactly. We don't destroy or remove any part of the amygdala, and we certainly don't perform lobotomies.' He chuckles at this. 'Ahem. Our process is relatively simple . . .' It's not, of course. It's like something out of a trippy sci-fi film, but maybe for Saunders and his team of po-faced savants this kind of procedure is as straightforward as re-wiring a plug. I'm not sure whether this scenario makes the whole thing more or less worrying. Either way, their *process* involves reintroducing old siege memories in as clear and powerful a manner as they can. For this very reason, Tom's little box of horrors has them all priapic.

Speaking of, Baz and I are forced to feign surprise when the doc's repeated mentioning prompts Tom to explain the pages he brought home – the how and why of their existence – though it isn't the sheepish, apologetic reveal I was still secretly hoping for. The one which, back in the desert, I had already decided I deserved. Instead it's clear from his first exhausted, monotone sentence that the lad had not gone out of his way to keep them from us. From anyone, really. Tina and Saunders both asked and we didn't. That was all.

Anyway, if I'm understanding the plan correctly, Saunders will use these pages to dredge specific memories back up to the very surface – one by one, a single incident per session, nice and clear and devastating. The risen memory will then retrace the same pathway as it has with every previous instance of traumatic recollection and, while it's still pinging around behind Tom's eyes, they'll stick a needle in his forehead and inject a miracle drug right into that spook house fear centre of his brain. Abracadabra, the wartime highlight reel gets a little bit grainier. Or, in Saunders Speak:

'The anisomycin prevents the neurons from producing the proteins necessary to store the full emotional impact of the memory. The memory itself, the sight and the sound of the incident, will remain, but its traumatic associations will disappear. If we repeat this process in response to the reintroduction of the most debilitating memories Tom has carried home with him from Sarajevo, I'm confident that we can save his sanity and, ultimately, his life.'

'You're confident?' Baz asks.

Saunders gets his back up a little at this. The old Official Doctor's Disclaimer impulse kicks in for a second or two. Not that I totally blame him. He's essentially talking to two large, angry children and a vegetable here.

'There are no absolutes with these procedures. Tom's is a special case. It has the potential to yield transformative results to an extent we have not yet witnessed in any other patient. However, it would be remiss of me not to mention that his weakened heart muscles put him at a greater risk of cardiac arrest during the focused recollection process.'

'So you're saying he could die on the table?'

'We are as equipped to deal with heart failure during the procedures as any major hospital in the state would be.'

'But he could still die.'

'Yes. He could still die.'

'We have to talk about this some more,' Baz says, his hand pressed against his temple, 'it's too much to get straight all at once. How do we even know this memory thing has ever worked?'

'We keep extensive, detailed video records of every patient who has undergone this procedure. Before, during, and after. Our technicians are currently in the process of editing much of the footage into a digestible visual aid to accompany a presentation I will be giving at a conference in New York later this year.'

'But you said it was all a secret?'

'It is, Mr Sullivan, but to be frank, I'm done reading suicide statistics over my morning coffee. This procedure works, but I can only help so many people from a bunker on the edge of the world. It's time to stop hiding.'

'We just want to help him get better,' I say. 'We're not interested in joining the bloody vanguard of a crusade we don't even understand. That's the last thing he needs.'

'I understand your concern, I really do, and I would never try to sell you on this if that were all it was about. Tom's case would be a compelling addition to our proposal, no question, but we have enough proof without it. I responded to your letter, I brought you here, I revealed to you a mission that only a handful of people in the entire world are aware of, because I knew, even before I laid eyes on him, I knew that we were the only ones who could help. That's all.'

'When do we start?' Tom has raised his head for only the second time since we stepped into this building. Till this moment, Baz and I have played the role of flustered parents, talking to the principal about our son's troubling behaviour while he hangs back silently in the doorway.

'Tom,' Baz says, reaching out with both hands and laying them on Tom's shoulders, searching to meet his eye, a gesture that would have been impossible at the airport just one month ago, 'you don't have to.' Tom pats one of Baz's hands with his own and smiles weakly, before turning to face Saunders.

'When do we start, Doctor?'

'Immediately.'

Sarajevo

It's only me here now. There's a kind of symmetry to that I suppose. I came here alone, people appeared and disappeared, and now it's just me again. Just me. I don't know how long I've been sitting here. If it's day or night outside. Isn't that funny? Everyone else is gone, or they might as well be gone. She's gone. That's all that matters. I don't know what happens now.

Can't do it.
    Not any more. Not on my own. Not without her.
    Nothing but ashes and rubble. Dead eyes and silence.
    Now it's all silent.
    Nothing left to save here.
    Nothing.
    Ničeg vise nema.
    Ničeg.
    Ničeg.
    Ničeg.

Chapter 14

Against all the odds, and our once-bitten disinclination toward optimism, it seems like Tom's treatment may actually be working. Every morning he looks a little more alive, his eyes rise to meet ours a little more often, as if a dense cloud of fog is seeping out bit by bit from inside his skull. He's almost a version of himself again. Having said that, this drip-feed success hasn't come easy. It's been more than two weeks since our first visit to the lab. As soon as Tom made his decision, we had three painful days of him and Saunders poring over the pages, carefully matching specific entries to the events that dominate his nightmares and waking visions. Things he has never spoken to us about. Horrendous shit no one should ever have to suffer through. Twice he had to be restrained and sedated. Once he almost hit Theo with a chair when the poor lad arrived with a pot of herbal tea. But he got through it. He knew what page detailed what event from the first sentence so they never had to delve too deeply. Saunders just marked each relevant entry with a blue Post-it note and moved on to the next. After that came two weeks of the treatment, split into alternating days of reconsolidation and recovery. On his recovery days Saunders has been testing Tom's responses to certain paragraphs, to see if the memories have been success- fully dampened. So far so good. No cloudy eyes, no panic attacks, no flashbacks.

Baz was wary from the beginning, and I suppose I don't blame him. The procedure itself is, well, intense. We stand on the observer side of a one-way mirror while savant lab rats scurry around behind us dotting i's and crossing t's on pages of their indecipherable metal charts. Nobody but Saunders gives us so much as a 'hello'. On the blind side of the glass, Tom sits bare-chested in the tricked-out dentist's chair. Hooked up to a heart monitor, a brain scanner, and two or three other machines the names for which I can't even pronounce. He's restrained, like an animal, to prevent him from tearing the wires from himself and breaking apart the lab. Saunders asks him if he's all right, if he'd like some water, if his chest feels tight. Tom shakes his head no. Then Saunders begins to read.

He starts with the date, and I watch Tom twitch. I watch his bones press against the pale skin of his torso and the rise and fall of his Adam's apple and the panicked flare of his nostrils as he tries to control his breathing. Underneath the florescent lights the little slashes of white scarring appear like the beginnings of some abandoned design. He's terrified. Then Saunders reads Tom's accounts, coaxing as much emotion from them as possible. If I didn't know what the end game was, the whole thing would seem depraved, like a protracted sneer. He carefully enunciates Tom's words summarising the day when a boy's near-decapitated head lay next to him on the cracked pavement, eyes open. The day nine children watching a street football game were brought in in pieces, screaming for their mothers, dying in hallways in their short pants. The day when his girl's brother took a bullet through the neck as they shopped for cigarettes at a market stall. How he could feel the warm blood running down his forearms as he cradled the guy's head in his lap, screaming for something to stem the flow. How he gurgled and spat and wet himself as he died in the street. The bullets that ate through his burial. All that blood and earth and screaming. Tom's knuckles crumpling the face of a man he all but beat to death on the floor of some club. The gun in his hand, the crazed intent. He scrunches his eye tight as Saunders reads. His voice rises louder and louder as he's ignored: 'OK, that's enough, that's ENOUGH.' I watch him squirm and curse, watch the spikes on his heart monitor rise, listen to the awful quickening background beep of its warning siren. Watch the slight twisting movement of the black Velcro straps that bind his wrists and legs. Watch Saunders move closer, repeat passages, bring the entry to a close, say, 'easy, Tom, easy, it's OK, shush shush shush, it's OK, breathe, just breathe.' Watch Tom sweat and scream and cry while we stand there and do nothing.

When about five minutes have passed in silent recovery, when his breathing and heart rate have slowed to an acceptable level, Saunders and his assistants inject Tom with the drug through a tiny hole in his skull. I can't watch them do this. We promised them all, Tom included, that we wouldn't try to intervene if we were allowed to observe. A bullshit promise we both secretly agreed to disregard if it looked like things were getting too hairy. For seven sessions we'd been true to our word, even when things looked pretty fucking bad. Last night though, watching Tom jerk and rage – thick blue veins bulging from his temples, the bottom rungs of his rib cage jutting out grotesquely, his dying heart running on fumes – Baz snapped, and tried to break down the door. Fortunately, it was both heavily fortified and key card entry only. By the time he managed to wrestle a badge away from one of the techs, Tom's attack had subsided.

'This is fucked up,' was all Baz kept repeating as we watched Tom sit there, unable to wipe away the tears that were building in the corners of his eyes. 'This is so fucked up.'

'It's helping him,' I said. And it was. It is. But looking at him crumpled in that chair, it didn't feel that way. 'He's nearly there. One more session, that's what Saunders said. Just one more.' Of course, the question I really want to ask the good doctor is the only one he can't answer: and then what? What happens when we're done? When Tom is all patched up, what are we taking him back to? I don't have a plan for the next year, or five, or ten. Maybe we watch Baz get sentenced to a year in Mountjoy for assault. Maybe he gets a suspended sentence and we all move in together, too broke or broken to set foot outside the door on a Friday night. Maybe it becomes one of those houses, one of those existences, built on silence and routine. Where football commentators and *Late Late Show* guests speak more words into the stale air of the sitting room than we do to each other, and we're sure of that fact because we're always at home watching. Maybe we'll look back on this as the last time we ever took a chance on anything. Maybe all we'll do from here on out is look back. I really don't know. Why am I thinking about this? I'm gonna give myself a fucking panic attack. Right now, all that matters is the procedure. I just hope he can last.

Chapter 15

I was planning on hanging up again. I don't even know why I chose this morning to call. I listened to her say it just as before: *hello . . . hello . . . helloooooooo?* but by the time that last syllable faded to silence, the receiver was still pressed tight to my ear. There was a long pause where all either of us did was breathe. Then she said 'Karl?' and that was it. We were tentative at first; it's been a while. She told me about her work at the gallery, her painting, the things she had seen and done and not done since the last time we checked in. She told me how much she was looking forward to seeing the *National Geographic* pictures. It occurred to me that, outside of the single night class I took in Dún Laoghaire six years ago, she's the only one I've ever really talked to about photography. It felt good to hear her recall projects I'd done – messy, half-formed things that even I had forgotten about – like they were something. I told her about Tom. Sort of. I gave her a sanitised version of his state. The Tom I described was someone who had arrived home a bit shaken, a bit fragile, but still himself. I told her everything had gone off without a hitch over here. I told her the treatment was finishing up and that we'd be heading home in a week. She sighed then, and said she wished we were staying a bit longer. She was travelling to Austin for an exhibition and would be out there for two weeks.

'When do you leave?' I asked, panic rising.

'Tonight, on the red-eye from San Francisco.'

'Is there any way you could get a later flight? I was hoping we could, if you were free . . .'

'I wish I could, Karl, but this is a big project for us. I wish I'd known you were here.'

'I'll drive up there today,' I said, before I could stop myself.

She hesitated. I'm choosing to believe it was the good, weak-at-the-knees kind of hesitation rather than the bad, how-quickly-can-I-vacate-this-apartment-and-change-my-name kind.

'Really?'

'Absolutely, we rented a car so I can be there in a few hours.'

'But, Karl, all I'll be doing is packing. I mean, we won't even have time to get dinner.'

'That's fine. I'll help! We can grab a drink or something and I can drop you to the airport.' So much for not coming on too strong.

'Well, that would be wonderful. But what about Tom? Didn't you say he finishes up treatment tonight?'

'Ah, he'll be fine, they've a team of doctors monitoring the whole procedure. And Baz will be there.'

'Will he be all right with that?'

'Baz? Sure, of course. We're on the home stretch here.'

She gave me her address, which I took down on the inside of my forearm, and I told her I'd be there at eight when she got home. My palm was sweating a little as I wrote. I didn't tell her I loved her, like I would have months and years ago, but I felt like saying it, and the hesitation before we said our goodbyes was almost as good. There was something familiar waking up underneath the static.

*

Knowing he'd have a puss on him as soon as he heard, I decided to hold off till the last possible minute before telling Baz that I'm leaving for the night. It's now midday and that last minute is fast approaching. Maybe I should have eased him into the notion, mentioned in passing that Clara was still in California before we left. But fuck it, he can sulk all he wants. There's no procedure for this kind of thing. I don't owe anyone an explanation for taking a day, *one day* out of I don't even know how many, to do something for myself. I've done enough postponing. I don't need a lecture. Telling Tom will be easier.

The door is open a crack when I get to his room. I can see him staring at a marked section in one of his pages. I wait a minute, watching through the gap, for him to turn over the piece of paper, but he doesn't. I knock and push the door open slowly so he can hide it. When I step into the room the box is closed over on the bed beside him. *He looks good*, I tell myself, *he looks alive again*.

'Hey, man, how's the form?'

'Good.'

'Yeah?'

'Yeah, really. No nightmares last night.'

'Really? That's good news. How many nights in a row is that now?'

'Four. And the three before that didn't even wake me.'

'I'm delighted for you, Tom. I think you've had enough sleepless nights to last you a lifetime, eh?' He nods, but says nothing.

'All set for this evening? I know the last one was tough. Really tough. I was . . . we were worried that your heart would . . . What I mean is, if you wanted to hold off a couple more days, to rest up a bit like, I could talk to Saunders about postponing?'

'He said that I shouldn't leave too long a gap between sessions, but that ultimately it was my call. If I'm doing it I think it's probably best that I do it today though.' He has his hand on the box of pages, like he's protecting it from me.

'If?'

'I mean . . . it's just . . .'

'What is it?'

'I'm not sure I can go through with the final session, Karl. There's so many things I wanted to fade, so much I tried to force out of my head. Things I didn't think I'd ever stop reliving. When I was standing out on the edge of that cliff, do you know what I was most frightened of? It wasn't the fall, or the rocks, or, you know, *death*. It was the idea of seeing those faces, hearing that gurgling and screaming, forever. That's how strong they felt, Karl. Like they could follow me anywhere.

Like they could follow me into death. The fact that there's a
mute button now, a door I can close, it feels like a miracle.'

'So what's wrong?'

'I don't know if I can let go of the last one. The day she
died. The last day he wants me to forget.'

'But, you have to. I mean, your eye, and how she . . . I
thought that was the day, more than any of the others, that
comes back to you the strongest.'

'It is. An hour hasn't passed since I woke up in the hospital
when I haven't thought of it, of her. The metal ripping through
her chest like it was . . . the way she fell . . . the shell hitting
before I could reach her . . .' He chokes up, sitting on his
hands to try and steady himself, his chest heaving with breaths
held and released.

'So why would you want to hold on to that? No one
should have to see somebody they love die that way. It's not
natural.'

'We're removing the bridges in my brain, Karl. Turning
memories into islands I can see but never reach again. Is that
natural?'

'I don't think any of this is natural, man, but it is necessary.'

'I know, and I'm glad, believe me. But this—'

'Why punish yourself, Tom? Let it go. If anyone deserves a
bit of peace it's you.'

'You know what the funny thing is, Karl? It was easing off.
There were whole days in those weeks, sometimes two or three
in a row, when no one died. We could have strolled by the
river hand in hand like teenagers and it would have been OK.
I always thought she had some sort of protective force field

around her. Isn't that the stupidest thing you've ever heard? But she could make you believe it, the way she carried herself. She went to work every day, every day, during the worst of it. The morning after they brought the kids from the football game in. The summer of '93 when it felt like the city would never stop shuddering. She never shook. Never missed a shift. Not until Hasan died anyway. She must have run across those streets a thousand times, and nothing. Scratches. But all it takes is one second. Just one step outside the door. I didn't even get to ask her.'

'Ask her what?' He puts his face into his huge, scarred hands. There's a long silence then. I want to ask again but I'm afraid of the response because I know what it will be.

'I had a ring and everything, Karl. It wasn't real of course, just an old piece of costume jewellery left behind in an empty hotel room, but still . . .'

'Jesus. Tom, I'm so sorry. I didn't know.'

'We were so bruised, so exhausted at that stage. Hollowed out. Those last months, there were days on end when neither of us even smiled. It's a little thing, I know, but she had the most knockout smile. Blinding.'

'I'm sorry I didn't get to meet her.' And it feels like we're out on the water again. On one of those aimless Irish college kayak rides. That in-between space.

'She was. You know with everything we went through, part of me thought I'd lose her when it was all over; like maybe we'd have to go our separate ways so that she could start a new life. One without any reminders of how brutal and sense- less it all was. I knew she loved me, I knew that, but I worried that it wouldn't be enough, you know? That no matter where we went or for how long, she might never be able to look at me without thinking of her brother, her father, those kids. Or worse, that somewhere along the way she had seen through to the part of me that hadn't come back for her, or for the hospital – the part that just wanted to *see* it all, the part she suspected was there right from the beginning; and how could she let herself build a life with someone who had that impulse inside them? Of course I wanted the siege to end, but in my heart I was terrified of what would happen when it did. Does that make any sense?'

'I think so.'

'No matter how tight she clung to me when the shells dropped, no matter how many times she told me she loved me, how often she trusted me with her mother, her patients, I couldn't get that splinter out of my mind. Until those last few weeks. That last morning, really. I didn't ask her like I should have. I still hadn't quite worked up the nerve. But she talked about the future as if we were already married: concretely, in a way that she never had before, a way that wasn't just a distraction from the blasts or a daydream to stave off the hunger. A way that said we could be more than what we were allowed to be there. It lit her up inside, Karl, you could see it. I knew then that we'd end up walking out of the city together. And that feeling, it meant everything to me. I would have stayed with her in that glow for days, forever. But instead we got an hour. One hour. If I had been just a few metres closer to her, Karl. If I'd stepped out ahead. I've spent so long regretting that.'

'You've got your whole life left, man. I know that seems too fucking painful to even think about right now, but it won't always be this way. Trust me.'

'But it won't be the same.'

'No, but nothing ever is.'

He gently touches the pads of his fingers to the patch over his eye, like he's reminding himself of what the material feels like from the other side. 'Remembering that moment, that hour – I just, I don't think I can let go of it.' He looks up at me like a lost child, waiting for an answer that will make everything all right. So I give him one.

'You have to, Tom. You have to leave that day here – in that lab, in that chair. All of it. You have to walk away from it. It's the only way you'll be able to start again. I wish it didn't have to be this way.'

'I can't do it, Karl. I can't—'

'Well you're going to have to!'

He nods, and looks down at his feet again.

'Listen,' I continue, softer now, 'everything is gonna be fine this evening. I promise. I believe Saunders when he says he just wants to help. He's a good man. And Baz will be right there on the other side of the glass, keeping an eye on things in case he tries to give you a boob job or anything.' Nothing, not even a pity smile.

'What about you?'

'I have to head up to San Francisco for a few hours. I'll probably stay there tonight and come back early in the morning. Something I have to take care of. I'll be back before you know it. Cool?' More nodding. 'Great. You get some rest, OK, and I'll call later on tonight to check in.'

'OK,' is all I get out of him as he lies down flat on the bare bed and closes his eyes. I rise and leave, closing the door over as softly as I can.

When I look up, Baz is standing there, lighting one cigarette with the hot stub of another, with a face on him like a bulldog licking shite off a nettle.

Chapter 16

'You can't be fucking serious, Karl. Not now.'

'Good afternoon to you too, sunshine. What's eating you today?'

'Tell me I didn't just hear you say to him you were leaving.' I take his arm and lead us both out of earshot.

'Spying on me now, is it?'

'Ah piss off with that, I was on my way to see him and I caught the tail end from outside the door. There shouldn't be anything to spy on anyway.'

'I'm not "leaving". I'm going to San Francisco for the night because—'

'I know exactly why you're going to San Francisco.'

'No, you don't. How?'

'Because I'm not a fucking idiot, Karl, no matter how much you want to paint me as one. You don't think it crossed my mind when you said we were off to a clinic four hours down the road from where your ex-girlfriend lives? You thought that six months was long enough for me to have forgotten about the twenty letters that came through the post box in the house where I *live*? Pink envelopes with a San Francisco return address on them. Are you fucking serious?'

'I didn't think . . . I don't—'

'And like a fool I thought, I *hoped*, that you'd copped on after he arrived home. When we all saw what a state he was in . . .' He trails off, trying to get the words out, and spits on the ground next to us.

'For Christ's sake, Baz –' laughing, though I know I shouldn't '– you think this has all been some elaborate scheme I concocted? Flying halfway around the world to spend one evening with Clara?'

'I don't care what it is, or for how long. That lad in there is circling the drain. We're supposed to be shadowing him, propping him up till he gets his head fixed and you're telling me you won't be there because you're off chasing ghosts.'

'Ghosts? I'm only asking for one fucking night with her. Jesus, I'd probably be married to the girl if it wasn't for this kind of shit.'

'Hang on. "This kind of shit"?'

'I didn't mean that.'

'I can't believe this.'

'What I *mean* is—'

'No, no, I know exactly what you mean. That's it. That's why it's different for you, why you think of yourself as the exception to your own fucking rule. Jesus, all this time I thought it was just the guilt. Like we all have. Like we *should* have. But it's more than that. You actually *blame* him. You blame all of us.'

'Don't reach for epiphanies, Baz,' I say, tapping my head, 'you'll only fucking hurt yourself.'

I'm on my arse in the dust now, left eye throbbing from where his big middle knuckle connected. I position myself into a crouch and lunge at him, but he side steps the tackle and hurls me back onto the ground like a rag doll.

'There's the animal we all know and love,' I sneer at him. 'I knew you couldn't domesticate him for long.' I wish he'd put the boot in at this, but he doesn't. He just looks down at me, wounded, and backs away like I've picked up a broken bottle.

'If Gabriel could see you right now,' he says, quiet.

'Don't fucking mention my brother to me, you self-righteous cunt. What the hell could *you* possibly know about it?'

'Oh yeah, sure, what could I know about it? I'm just the dope you keep around for company. How could I possibly figure out anything?'

'That's not what I said.'

'It's not about what you said. I know what you've been thinking, in the back of your mind, since he died. That if Gabriel hadn't been so bleedin' selfish you'd have been able to leg it out of Dublin without anyone batting an eye. Or if I had more go about me you wouldn't have turned into such a fucking waster? Or if Tom would just cool it with the suicide attempts you could have a lovely beach holiday with your bird and everything could be happily ever after. Un-fucking-believable. You're nothing but a coward, man, and worse, you're using our problems as your excuse.'

'Fuck you, Baz.'

'Remember what you said to me out in the desert, hmmm?

When I asked you, *begged* you, to let me stay out there? "He. Needs. Us." Both of us. Now what do I have to do to force that back into your thick fucking skull?'

'I organised this trip for him, Baz, remember? I convinced you to come. I made a hundred calls to the hotel and the clinic trying to get him on the phone. I talked to his mother, his doctor. I brought him to Gabriel's grave. I did everything I could while you were too shit scared to deal with any of it so don't talk to me about what he needs.'

'Yeah, fine, maybe I took too long to get my head around it all, and I'm sorry for that, but at least I can say I'm here, now, for the right reasons. At least I don't blame him for taking time away from my bloody rom-com reunion.'

'Why are you being like this, man? I've been here, start to finish. Can I not do this one thing for myself?'

'No. Not till it's actually finished.'

'There's nothing I can do for him here that you can't do.'

'Keep telling yourself that, Karly. Maybe you'll believe it by the time you get to her.' And that's it. He turns away from me and walks off toward the zebra herd. I call after him, but he doesn't look back.

*

3:45. Two hours out from the Golden Gate and I should be giddy. I should be practising what I'm going say; how I'm gonna play it cool, build up to asking her about her life, subtly suss out whether or not she's been seeing anyone. If her future plans are set in stone.

It should feel like the revival of something in me. Agency or passion or, I don't know, *something*. Instead my mind keeps drifting away from her. Gabriel's voice in the desert. Tom's eyes pleading with me to tell him what he so desperately wanted to hear. That look on Baz's face before he turned away from me. How disgusted he was. Like I'd betrayed him in some careless, irreparable way.

When did everything get so fucking serious? Yes, it started that way, for Gabriel and me anyway, and yes, the last lengthy stretch hasn't exactly been a barrel of laughs for anyone, but there were years in between when we were all happy. I know we were. Christ, I've done everything I can to keep it alive in my head. We were a unit and the unit worked; at least it did for a while. We went on ten quid benders that are more memorable to me than a thousand self-medicating nights out since. We fought to keep each other safe. We were loyal to each other and loved each other with a fierceness that no one has the energy for any more. That's more than most can say. So when did it all change? When did that drift begin? When Tom first heard foreign gunfire as a siren's call? When Gabriel climbed into himself and couldn't find a way back out? When Baz let all that anger and frustration take the reins? When I stopped moving toward anything, and started blaming everyone else for it. Would the lads we were at seventeen, the ones that sat slurping stolen whiskey under the stars, would they recognise us now? Deadened, demented, decomposed. If I saw my seventeen-year-old self on the street today I'd duck down an alleyway to hide. I'd be embarrassed to show that kid how many of our promises I've broken these past years.

Not that I was anything special back then, but at least I had balls. I didn't have to lie to my friends, to myself, about what I wanted. I made actual decisions about how my life was gonna go, and I believed in them so ardently. I knew myself and the lads would be thick as thieves forever. I knew Gabriel would be in my corner no matter what happened. I knew I was going make a go of it in California with Clara. She'd paint, I'd take pictures. We'd work in beachside bars to cover the rent and get drunk on cheap tequila and go skinny-dipping in the Pacific. When I was eighteen and nineteen and twenty, I never doubted this future, not for a second. Forget how impossible, how contradictory it all was. It never occurred to me that the trajectories of the people I loved weren't inextricably bound to mine forever. That each of them wouldn't make it the focus of their own young adult years to follow my impossibly greedy blueprint for happiness. That I couldn't just dip in and out of their lives when it suited my own.

Maybe it's too easy to dismiss them as fuckups, borne of ignorance or cowardice, these things I've done and failed to do since Tom left. There's always a vein of self-administered absolution running through those excuses. When the truth is I never cared enough; about their lives, their futures, their *survival* – in every sense of that word. If I had, if they were more to me than just supporting players in my own story, then there'd be no mystery to the shell shock, the court summons, the sodden cries for help – any of it. Because I would have been there already, I would have wanted to know. That's what it would have meant to truly care about these men.

At yet another Point of Interest roadside pull off I take out a cigarette, light it, and sink to the ground behind the car's dusty bumper. I sit there, staring out over the barrier for a few

minutes, until the beep of the shitty digital watch I bought at
a petrol station snaps me out of it. Tom's last treatment is due
to start in two hours.

*

Fucking rush hour traffic. I didn't even think they had that
out here. It's 6:24. The period before the shot is administered
has never taken longer than twenty minutes. I wait outside
the gates, slamming my palm into the car horn over and over,
throwing coins at the security cameras until all I have left
is three useless, ash-stained pennies. I launch the heel of my
boot into the sparrow centrepiece but apparently it can't be
resuscitated by brute force alone.

'Theo!' I bellow into the camera lens, and wait. Nothing.
I haven't climbed anything more challenging than a flight of
stairs in years. The first two attempts leave me cursing in
the dust. On the third, I manage to wedge my toe into a gap
in the metalwork and drag myself into a standing position.
From here I grab the flat base on either side of the tall centre
spike and swing my right leg till the ankle hangs over the
other side. I remember a story Eugene told myself and Gabriel
the night we got caught climbing over the barbed railings of
the Ringsend power station. About some fella who ripped his
ballsack open trying to sneak into the Stillorgan reservoir.
Impaled on the gate for an hour before the fire brigade came.
Said the only good that came from it was that, from then on,
the lad was able to predict bad weather by the ache in his
balls. 'A cautionary tale' is what Eugene called it before leaving
us on the bench in the Garda station for another hour while

273

he reminisced with the sergeant, who, of course, was an old friend of his from the Cretaceous Period. For years afterwards whenever he caught me adjusting myself in the sitting room he'd look up from his paper and say 'storm coming, Karl? You'd better run out and get the washing off the line'. Then he'd burst himself laughing. This is what I'm thinking about as I carefully swing my back leg over the top and hang drop onto the ground on the other side. The sting of impact shoots from the soles of my feet up through my shins. My watch says 6:27.

Zebras clear a path as I sprint through the field. It might look impressive if I didn't have to stop every fifty metres to hack up a wad of tar-blackened phlegm. I can see Unit 5 straight ahead of me. The door is opening and a man is coming out. It's Theo. By the time I reach him I'm so out of breath I feel like vomiting. I can feel the beads of sweat trailing past my temples.

'Theo . . . ! Lemmein . . . gotta . . . Tom . . . gimmeyourcard!'

'It's all right, Mr Sullivan, just take deep breaths through your nose. In and out. In and out.'

'There's no time for that, Theo. I need to stop the fucking treatment. I need that card.'

'I'm afraid it wouldn't be of much use to you, Mr Sullivan.'

'"Karl", Theo. Christ, at this point I think we can drop the formalities. *Why* wouldn't it be of much use to me?'

'Because Mr Dempsey's final treatment was cancelled.'

'Seriously? By who?'

'By Mr Dempsey himself.'

'What? Tom pulled the plug? Is he all right?'

'As far as I know, he's fine. In fact, if you'll just look to your right . . .' Theo trails off as his outstretched arm gestures toward the fence on the far side of the property. There, leaned languidly against the wooden beams, sporting twin expressions of utter bemusement, are Tom and Baz.

Sarajevo, September 24, 1997

It's been strange, the mood here. Like a lost heartbeat returning long after the time of death has been called and the paddles put away. It seems so unlikely as it's happening, almost surreal, but then things stabilise and the old rhythm returns as if it had never left. I didn't think I'd ever come back. But it's important, finally seeing the city as something more than a war zone. The resilience of people. The dogged refusal to be victimised any longer. Men and women strolling to work through exposed intersections. Reading newspapers in the windows of tramcars. The morning hum of activity on Baščaršija as the wooden shutters rattle open. The vendors haggling behind their stalls at the Markale. The smell of strong coffee wafting through the streets. It'll never be the way it was of course, they all tell me, no one could expect that. But it has survived. It's still recognisable. That's not nothing.

A few days ago, maybe an hour after I arrived in the city, I found myself back at the Holiday Inn. Standing there, staring up at the hotel's battered exteriors, it occurred to me that in the months, the years, I lived in Sarajevo, this was the longest I'd ever stood stationary outside the hotel. The longest time spent examining the place that was, for a while at least, my home. I had called Saunders from a payphone at the airport, his voice coming through clear despite the ten thousand kilometres of distance between us. I told him my itinerary, or as much of it as I had figured out, and where I was headed first. Saunders said it was up to me; said that if I felt ready to sleep in one of those rooms again, he wasn't going to instruct me otherwise. 'Remember what we talked about though, Tom,' he cautioned before we said our goodbyes for another week. 'You can't force any of this.'

And I knew that I wouldn't. Not this time anyway. When I reached the reception desk, manned by people I didn't recognise, I couldn't bring myself to ask for a room. The thought of climbing those same stairs and walking those same hallways and staring out at those same views – I just couldn't do it. So instead, as if I had never set foot in the building before, I asked in my rusty Bosnian if perhaps they could direct me to the bar. I sat down on a newly upholstered stool and tried to decide, as I waited for the bartender to turn toward me, if I wanted his to be a familiar face.

The bar was better stocked I suppose, but otherwise it seemed unchanged. All except for one modest addition. Hanging there, from the corner of the mirror in a small, scratched-up wooden frame, was a picture of Goran – his brown eyes and slightly crooked smile facing out toward me as they had so many times before.

'Over three years now since he is gone. It is hard to believe.' I nodded, and examined the barman's face as he stared at Goran's. He was older, early forties maybe, and just familiar enough to make me think that maybe our paths had crossed in those final foggy weeks of my time here. For all the thousands of moments filed away from those years, that final stretch is a blur. He poured me a large drink and held up his palm when I reached for my wallet.

'*Hvala*,' I said.

'I am glad to see you better,' he said, and returned to the end of the bar to cut a bag of limes into wedges.

It was nice then, just to sit and have a drink and know that the conversations happening around me would carry on, uninterrupted by blasts or tears or over-the-wire alerts of fresh carnage that needed to be covered. When I rose to leave, the barman, whoever he is or was to me, nodded and so I did the same, and left.

*

I've been thinking a lot about the tapes we used to play. Blaring bass heavy songs to try and drown out the shelling. Saving up the last bit of charge in the Walkman batteries so we could listen to a slow one together before falling asleep on a rare quiet night. U2 are coming here in a week's time. There are hundreds of colourful PopMart tour posters plastered over bullet-blasted walls across the city. It's been the only thing on everyone's lips since I arrived. The band suggested a charity gig, some sort of fundraiser, but people said no. Just add a Sarajevo leg to the regular tour, they said, and do it like you do all the others. It'd be nice to be here for that, to see people enjoy themselves again.

But I can't stay. The grand opening is on Saturday. The man who twice fell asleep smoking and set his own pillow on fire is now a licenced publican. We thought about requesting a copy of the CCTV footage at the bank that day just to see his post-loan approval catatonia first hand, but they probably have a rule against that. Karl and I are the 'official guests of honour', according to himself. I argued that it should be Karl alone, after the miracle he pulled off with Locko's brother, but the two of them wouldn't hear of it. Our duties include security, nicotine gum dispensing, and, most importantly, making a series of short, glowing speeches about his innate entrepreneurial acumen. 'The Illustrated Man' is the name he settled on, which I think meant a lot to Karl.

He's been working pretty steadily since the *National Geographic* issue came out, building his portfolio whenever we take a trip together, sometimes for the foundation, sometimes for magazine spreads. Honestly, I don't think I would ever have accepted Mac's offer if Karl hadn't come on board too. 'NGOs like ours always need a decent shutterbug,' Mac said, 'if he's interested and he doesn't mind the travel then we have a job for him.' They've been good to me, all of them, everyone, this past year. Patient, especially in those early months. But Karl has never left my side. It's only recently that I've realised how much I've needed that.

I've been visiting your grave every evening, just before sunset when the place is a little less crowded. I only bring one flower each time, the same as the earrings you wore, so as not to crowd the others left at the base of your headstone. A lot of people miss you here. Parents bring their children every day. They leave little cards and notes written with coloured markers. They won't forget you, I'm certain of that. I wonder if the things they tell me are true, if there's any chance you can hear me when I talk, or see me from where you are. If there's any part of you still alive out there. It's not something

I've ever believed, you know that, but I want to now so badly. I haven't forgotten either, I never could. Not you, not the way it felt to be with you. There's no change in me that could ever touch that. I can walk past the library or through the market or into the hotel, and those memories don't sting the way they did. They don't overwhelm, and I'm grateful. Of course I'm grateful. It means everything. It means survival. But the things that haven't dimmed mean more. You'll always mean more.

The day I arrived in the city there was a bunch of wilted yellow lilies leaning against your headstone. Affixed to their bound stems was a small white card inscribed with the words *'Sve je preteško bez tebe, moja najdraža kćeri'* – It's all too hard without you, my dearest daughter. I've been to the house every day since, but she hasn't returned. None of the neighbours have an address for her. Neither does the library director or the staff of the English department at the university. All I have is the sliver of paper she handed to me that day in the basement of the library, her careful handwriting almost faded.

I'll keep trying though, I promise you that. I'll keep sending letters and making phone calls and checking in with strangers until I find her.

Until I'm certain she has someone beside her to share the load, like I have had.

Chapter 17

So that was how my daring jail break attempt played out in the end. With me collapsing in a sweaty heap on the grass, linked hands pressed tight against the back of my head as I tried not to vomit. As soon as I could speak full sentences again, I apologised to both Tom and (far more grudgingly) Baz with Theo and a sizeable audience of zebras there to witness the full force of my mumbled contrition.

'It's OK, Karl, really, I understand,' Tom said, helping me to my feet. 'You came back.'

'I mean, you'd have saved yourself a lot of trouble, and embarrassment, if you'd had the cop on not to leave in the first place but—'

'You know, Baz, the gracious fucking thing to do while I'm standing here, cap in hand, is to accept the apology.'

'All right, all right, I'm sorry too.'

'Yeah?'

'No, obviously not. I didn't do anything wrong, you fucking eejit.'

'I take it back, I'm not sorry at all.'

'Too late, I've already accepted your apology and I forgive you.'

'You're a prick.'

'C'mon now, bring it in, both of you. It's been a long few weeks. It's time for a hug.'

'I will stab you if you try to hug us, Baz. Honest to God I will.'

'Too late, buddy, just let it happen.'

*

'It just felt like that morning, that memory, was the key somehow, you know?' Tom said later that night as we sat with Saunders around a fire pit at the back of the compound. 'The lens I'd look back through to see the rest. All my good memories of her. And if I clouded it, or pushed it away from me, then all the others would lose their sheen too, and I'd be left with some muted version of her, a dumb show of this person I loved.' We nodded, eyes fixed on his mouth as he stared into the embers. 'I don't know if that makes sense, or if there's any logic let alone any science to it, but that's how it felt, how it feels, to me. That's the only way I can explain why I couldn't go through with it.'

'Well I'm glad you didn't,' I said, Baz nodding in enthusiastic agreement. 'You did the right thing.'

'I hope so. It felt like the only thing I could do, but I don't know if that makes it right.'

'It's the first real choice you've made since you arrived,' said Saunders, rubbing his hands slowly together over the last hot breaths of the fire. 'And it didn't come from resignation, or panic, or mania. You chose to engage. You chose to remember. That's significant.'

'But does it make sense?'

'It does to you, Tom.'

'So I'm deluding myself?

'Far from it. We're not dealing in objective realities here. Only with what's inside your head. Your memories – the form they take, their emotional impact – are what matter, and the ones that sustain you are every bit as important to me as the ones that have broken you down.'

'But what if this ends up undoing all the work we've done?' Tom started, but already Saunders was shaking his head.

'The treatment has been a success, Tom, you'll see that more and more in the weeks and months ahead, but it was never designed to be a panacea. Our goal here is and always was to bring you back from the brink, to get you to a point where you can be an active participant in your own recovery.'

'And you think I can?'

'The fact that you've mined a moment from the most traumatic day of your life, and used it to trace a route through the joys you felt throughout that awful time, the fact that you fought to hold on to it, to remember it the way it was, should tell you the answer to that question.' He stood then, breathing in deeply the cool night air as he rose, and let out a huge sigh of satisfaction. 'We're at the beginning of a new stage, gentlemen. You have a long road ahead of you, Tom. But you'll be walking it clear-eyed, and you won't be alone. That much is now abundantly clear.'

*

There were a few more days of decompression after that night. Tests to be administered, relaxation techniques to be detailed, worksheets to be printed out, head holes to be patched up; a dozen little loose ends that had not occurred to me as I scaled that fucking gate, the after effects of which stayed in my muscles and joints for the better part of a week. But then it was time to go.

Saunders and Theo shook our hands warmly and sent us on our way, laden with binders of notes and contact details should we feel the need to check in before we got back to Dublin.

'I still consider you my patient, Tom. If you need anything, day or night, you have my number. Mr Sullivan, Mr Connolly, he's in your hands now. Take care of him.'

We packed up what little we had brought with us and drove away. Away from the cedar wood silo and its spiral staircase, past the mile of unlit tiki torches and grazing zebra herds, through the ornate double gates, and out into the softly falling dusk. We crawled through the darkness in silence, listening to the low whoosh of the ocean as it broke against the shore. When a half hour or so had passed this way, we pulled off the road to smoke and piss and delay the return for just a little bit longer. At the entrance to a cliff path, which wound down some twenty feet to a bank of flattened brush that looked out over the water, Tom spotted one of those heavy, animal-proof rubbish bins and decided to jettison the box that held his Sarajevo pages then and there.

'It's the last thing I have to do,' he said, moving to unclasp the rusted latch that held the box closed. 'I've turned this thing into a casket. It's not healthy. I'm done staring at it, working myself up about what's buried inside.' He carefully lifted out the stack of rumpled pages and rolled them into a tube before removing Theo's spare hairband (ocean blue, of course) from his newly built ponytail. When he was satisfied with how tautly it fit, he slipped the tube into the deep innards of his coat's breast pocket, and moved to dump the box.

'Hang on a sec,' Baz, cigarette dangling from his bottom lip, yelped as he shook himself off all over his shoes. 'You can't just toss it into some random skip full of fucking dirty nappies and tampons and syringes and god knows what else.'

'Jesus, Baz,' I said, 'there wouldn't want to be much more than that in there. Where is it you think we've pulled in to?'

'I'm just saying, we should give it a proper send-off. Something befitting the end of the adventure, y'know?'

'You think so?' Tom asked, lowering the box from the edge of the bin's dark entry shoot. I shrugged, struggling to think of a precedent for this kind of carry-on.

'What did you have in mind, Baz? Push it out to sea and shoot flaming arrows at the thing?'

'Bingo.'

'I was joking. Where the fuck would we get a bow and arrow out here? Leaving aside the fact that I've seen you play darts. The thousand monkeys with the thousand typewriters would finish before we did.'

'I think he probably means just burning it, Karl.'

'You say that, but I genuinely wouldn't be surprised—'

'Of course I mean just burning it, you smart bollocks. C'mon, you lads don't think that'd be a more majestic finish to things? It's traditional, like. You have to set things on fire at the end.'

'I'm writing down that last quote to use on your headstone, Baz. Tom, thoughts?'

'Very hard to argue with that sentiment,' Tom said, failing to stifle a smirk. 'Far be it from us to mess with tradition I suppose.'

From his back pocket Tom produced the remnants of a booklet of matches, and a small notebook. He tore out ten empty pages, moulding each into vaguely canoe-like shapes, and lined them up on the floor of the open box. When every inch of that floor was covered, he took a flimsy match from the packet and ran its green head slowly against the streaked striking pad. It seemed to me that the match took an extra beat to ignite, but when it finally did, the flame hissed to life and held steady: a tiny, barely flickering bulb of fire creeping downward toward Tom's calloused fingers, their nails bitten down to the quick. He lit the bottom right hand corner of a tapered page, and carefully placed it on top of the crinkled pile of paper vessels. Unfortunately, though wholly unsurprisingly given the team in charge of this project, the wind coming in off the ocean chose that moment to kick into overdrive and blow the fire out before the flames had a chance to spread. The six remaining matches met a similar fate and our only lighter, when it was eventually found at the bottom of Baz's pocket where I fucking said it was the whole time, was all out of juice. On top of this, while we were searching underneath the car seats for a spare, a pointed gust sent three or four of the barely singed canoes out into the inky dark.

'Well,' I said, shouting now to compete with the gale, 'this is the most majestic fucking thing I've ever been a part of anyway.'

'I think I know what to do,' said Tom, his lank hair whirling high over his bandaged forehead. With a wink, he took off in a sprint down the path, whooping like a madman as his piston legs propelled him toward the cliff edge where his origami was being tornado-sucked into the night sky.

'Tom, no!' I screamed uselessly after him.

Instead of jumping though, in a move I haven't witnessed since his football days, Tom drew back his right leg and hoofed the box, with what remained of its contents, high and hard into the black waves below.

'Well,' he said when he re-emerged from the cliff path, still grinning, 'how was that?'

'That,' said Baz, 'was fucking majestic!'

'Better than fire?'

'Much better. Cleanest strike I've seen in years. Karl thought you were gonna jump, by the way.'

'I fucking did not.'

'Yes, you did, I heard you howling.'

'That was the wind.'

'Course it was.'

'So you knew he was winding up for a long kick-out then, eh?'

'Absolutely.'

'Bullshit.'

'Hand to God. It's all in the approach, you see, Karl. That's why you would have never made the senior team: no vision on the pitch.'

'Fuck off.'

'He could be right, Karl. Intuition is what usually sorts the greats from the journeymen.'

'Well the pair of you will have plenty of time to discuss it on the walk back to Los Angeles. This is rattlesnake country though, so make sure you have your vision and intuition turned on. I'd hate for you both to get bitten in the arse and die roaring.'

We had it back then, the three of us, in those dawdling moments. The easy way of just being together, that had always been ours, once upon a time. And we knew that it wasn't much more than an echo, conjured up collectively for the first time in years, and not a guarantee of anything permanent, not a promise of a future we didn't yet deserve; we'd have been fools to think otherwise. There was too much still waiting for us; too much shitty, painful, probably impossible work still to do. But it was something. It was enough.

Acknowledgements

Míle buíochas libh go:

Kirby Kim, my brilliant agent, for your advice, advocacy, and friendship.

My wonderful editors across the pond, Sophie Buchan and Jennifer Kerslake, for their invaluable edits and tireless support.

Everyone at Janklow & Nesbit, Weidenfeld & Nicolson, Ig Publishing, Cullen Stanley International, The Center for Fiction, Literary Hub, and *Guernica*.

Jasminko Halilovic, whose War Childhood mission is an inspiration.

Caroline Walsh, whose kindness in the earliest days of my writing career I will never forget.

James Ryan, Éilís Ní Dhuibhne, Michael Longley, and Mary Morrissy.

Maja, Jovan, and Alex.

Jon, Dwyer, Naoise, and the many friends and extended

289

family members in Dublin and New York who enrich my life every day.

My parents (Mary & Peter), and siblings (Mary, Tim, & Jack): bright, brilliant, big-hearted people and truly the most incredible family anyone could ask for.

Téa, my love, for everything.

*

Of the many books and articles vital to the writing of this novel, special mention should go to: *Besieged: Life Under Fire on a Sarajevo Street* by Barbara Demick, *The Book of My Lives* by Aleksandar Hemon, *The Fixer* by Joe Sacco, *The Quick and the Dead: Under Siege in Sarajevo* by Janine di Giovanni, *War Childhood* by Jasminko Halilovic, *War Hospital* by Sheri Fink, and Michael Specter's 2014 *New Yorker* profile of Doctor Daniela Schiller and her work, 'Partial Recall: Can neuroscience help us rewrite our most traumatic memories?'

blog and newsletter

For literary discussion, author insight,
book news, exclusive content,
recipes and giveaways, visit the
Weidenfeld & Nicolson blog and
sign up for the newsletter at:

www.wnblog.co.uk

For breaking news, reviews and exclusive competitions
Follow us @wnbooks
Find us facebook.com/WeidenfeldandNicolson